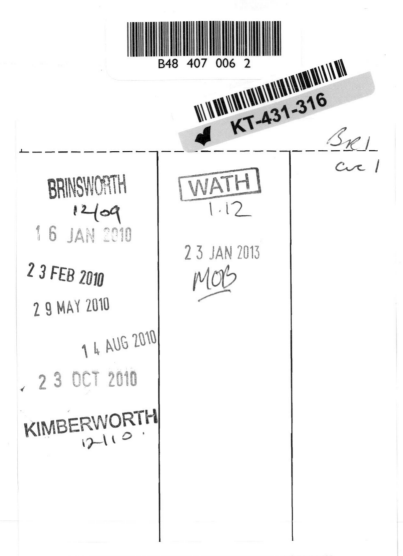

Midsummer Madness

Midsummer Madness

Stella Whitelaw

ROBERT HALE · LONDON

© Stella Whitelaw 2009
First published in Great Britain 2009

ISBN 978-0-7090-8914-8

Robert Hale Limited
Clerkenwell House
Clerkenwell Green
London EC1R 0HT

www.halebooks.com

2 4 6 8 10 9 7 5 3 1

Typeset in 10½/14pt Palatino
by Derek Doyle & Associates, Shaw Heath
Printed in Great Britain by the MPG Books Group, Bodmin and King's Lynn

To

Martin Patrick, Director, the cast and team of the Oxted Players'
production of *Twelfth Night* in 2005 at the restored Barn Theatre,
Oxted. Guess who was the prompt?

And guess who read the entire part of Olivia at the last dress
rehearsal, to resounding applause?

My sincere thanks
to

Paul Longhurst
Martin Patrick
Robert Stevens
directors

Andrew Killian
lecturer on Shakespeare

Gill Jackson and Lee Bowers
editors

William Shakespeare
playwright

MALVOLIO: Go to, thou art made, if thou desirest to be so.
OLIVIA: Am I made?
MALVOLIO: If not, let me see thee a servant still.
OLIVIA: Why, this is very midsummer madness.

Twelfth Night, III. iv. 50–53.
William Shakespeare

CHAPTER ONE

'Line, Prompt. Line!'

I leaned forward from the prompt stool huddling into the banana-striped Mexican poncho around my shoulders. The icy draughts in the Victorian theatre in a tiny street off the Strand end of Waterloo Bridge were homing into my corner with spiteful, scissor-sized fingers. Why didn't the cast just learn their lines? I thought irritably. That's what they were paid for.

My feet were still frozen, despite the thermal socks over bootleg jeans – standard prompt wear. The prompt corner was off-stage left, by the footlights.

'Wake up in the corner there!'

I peered at my copy of *Twelfth Night*, trying to recall where we were in the play.

'A blank, my lord,' I said clearly, best Emma Thompson voice, *Sense and Sensibility* posture. Under my breath, I continued: 'She never told her love, but let concealment, like a worm in the bud, feed on her damask cheek.'

The words of hidden love filtered through my mind in a never-ending stream of glittering goldfish. I savoured them. I knew all about hidden love. In fact, I am the world's number one concealment expert.

I stared dreamily up into the tangle of ropes and wires in the flies. *Twelfth Night* was my favourite play – when I wasn't so cold.

Our leading lady, Elinor Dawn (she was born Elinor Entwistle, try saying that when you're tired) was divine as Viola, making the dual roles of a lady of Messaline and a page boy at the court of Duke Orsino look easy. She was a good actress but Father Time was

11

not on her side. Elinor was knocking the late forties even though she peeled back the years with Botox and Restylane injections to help relax her wrinkles and lines. She was a lunchtime Botox junkie. Hardly time for a fat-free shrimp and rocket sandwich.

'I can't help the wrinkles,' she'd say, coming back from the Harley Street clinic with a stiff mouth after a lunchtime appointment. 'My face is expressive.'

West Enders was a newly formed company, brimming with talent, surviving on an Arts Grant. I thought myself lucky to be part of the production team even in my humble role. My enthusiasm was taken for granted and I was asked to help out with everything. *Sophie, do this. Sophie, do that.* And Sophie did, like a frantic hamster on a treadmill. I make a lot of lists which spectacularly self-destruct.

The second lead was the tall and icy Jessica Bond. She was a graduate from a top stage school, playing the role of Olivia. She took everything seriously, had an iron grip on humour. I'd never once seen her laugh so she was right for Olivia, a rather cold and self-contained character initially. I wondered how she was going to cope with Olivia's sudden wild infatuation for Viola, the socially inferior page boy. She'd be feeling her way.

Claud Rudolph played the pompous servant Malvolio, and Byron Tantrick was in his playboy element as the gracious Duke Orsino. Poor Claud had selective deafness which made him difficult to prompt. Byron was hopelessly forgetful and needed every word I could give him. I thought of charging them both by the minute, like a lawyer. I'd make a mint.

I looked over at the others. Elinor was biting her nails, neck muscles taut, which didn't help her chin contour. She was wearing her uniform black trousers, black silk shirt, black ribbed M&S cardigan. I was disturbed by the look on her face, a haunted look, and wondered why she was worried. She had more talent in her big toe than the whole of Fran Powell's skinny size eight body. Fran Powell was a hungry understudy in more ways than one. She wore cleverly knotted scarves to conceal the hollows in her collarbones. Her false eyelashes looked like a pair of spiders perched on her eyelids.

'Line. PROMPT.'

The strong voice vibrated round the auditorium. I had been daydreaming and had no idea where we were. I flipped a few pages hoping the prompt good fairy would help me out but she was taking a sickie.

'Do we have a prompt, or am I expected to perform this duty as well as direct the show?'

Joe Harrison leaped up on to the stage and walked over to the wings, carrying a hand mike. Talk died away. No sirens, no outriders. Everyone waited apprehensively. He caught sight of me in all my thermal glory and I knew from his expression that he had found his prey.

'So you are Madam Prompt? How nice to meet you. Would it be too much trouble to ask you to contribute a minimum of attention to this afternoon's rehearsal? Is the time convenient or have you something more important to do? Like looking for another job?'

He hadn't recognized me and I breathed a sigh of relief. This was Joe Harrison. I had managed to keep out of his way the previous day when he arrived from New York, jet lagged and overstretched, and hoped he would stay that way. It was my own fault for losing concentration. A good prompt needs all her power of concentration.

My voice was trapped inside my own head. It was the shock of seeing him again, hearing those gravelly tones, dodging the piercing eyes. He hadn't changed much.

'I apologize,' I said, pushing my mop of hair out of sight. It was considerably longer now and back to its natural outrageous red. 'But it isn't the end of the world. The theatre won't close. It's a routine rehearsal. The punters can hardly demand their money back. They aren't asking for all the blue Smarties.'

The cast were stunned. Sophie rarely answered back.

'The first thing my company has to learn is that every rehearsal is a performance,' said Joe Harrison, coldly. 'You give your utmost at all times even if the only person in the auditorium is a deaf cleaner.'

'Understood, sir,' I nodded. 'Even a deaf cleaner.'

'And do you have to be wrapped up like a bundle of putrid Mexican washing? You look about as glamorous as a reject pile in a charity shop.'

'Raise the temperature in the prompt corner and I'll wear a gold Lurex bikini,' I offered. The draught had settled round my neck like a hoar frost.

A short grunt was my only reply. Joe Harrison turned on his heel and jumped down into the auditorium, an athletic movement. He was a powerful man. The cast used the moment to snatch a glance at their scripts. I knew that Joe Harrison could heave scenery like any scene-shifter. I'd seen him do it, long ago. He had stamina that drove him on when everyone else was falling apart and calling for a drink or a doctor or both.

'Back to work, if Madam Prompt can find the place,' he bawled. Some of the cast tittered, the two-faced traitors. I'd been saving their skins all day.

'Let's take your line, Orsino, down left centre. Can you remember that? "What do you know, Cesario?" Quiet, please. If you want to chat, go outside, and pick up your cards on the way.'

I shrank back into my corner and turned the dimmer light on to the page. I had never wanted to see Joe Harrison again and yet here he was, causing chaos, upsetting cast, alienating stage crew. He might be big in New York but that didn't give him the right to scare everyone to death.

Time and time again my low clear voice had to feed a forgotten or fluffed line. I was an expert at pitching my voice so that the cast could hear but not the audience.

Once I had longed desperately to be an actress. I walked away with all the best parts in school productions. Sophie Gresham, thespian star of the Fifth Form. (School report: *Sophie has a real talent for acting. It should be encouraged.*)

I was lucky enough to win one of the coveted places at RADA, the Royal Academy of Dramatic Art, but that was when the torment started. I suffered from severe stage-fright and I mean severe. I was physically sick, every time I had to go on stage. It wasn't fair. They had a bowl in the wings called Sophie's bowl. Even if I was the maid and only had four identical lines, it was a nightmare. In the end I hung up my sooty black eyelashes and retreated to working backstage, relieved to disappear into part of an unseen team.

'Cut! Stop! Cease! Or whatever one has to say to bring this

charade to an end. Is this a one-woman show?' Joe Harrison paced the aisle with an air of incredulity. 'Shakespeare didn't write this play as a monologue for the prompt. Doesn't anyone know their lines? This is bungling, slip-shod work. I suggest ten minutes. Find a script and remind yourself of what this play is all about.'

He switched off his laptop, slapped the seat in front of him with his clipboard, practically cracking it – the clipboard, that is – and strode off. Straight to the nearest Caffé Nero, I hoped.

The cast grabbed their books. Their nerves were shredded. They collapsed into corners, thumbing worn pages. Some headed for the coffee machine, believing that caffeine was the answer to actor's block.

The Royale Theatre needed a Lottery grant spent on it. It was old and draughty despite all the velvet drapes and gold cherubs. I came out of my corner, rubbing a stiff neck, and ran tepid water over my hands to bring back the circulation. I might die standing up, I thought. My headstone: *she never missed a line.*

'Don't think I'm going to discover you,' said a voice in my direction. 'There's no need to pitch that prose at me. This is not an audition.'

I was momentarily confused. He still didn't know me. He towered six feet tall, no shrinkage with the passing decade. Spikes of floppy dark hair were falling over his granite-bright eyes. But there were lines of fatigue on his face. Fame brings stress despite three layers of packaging called money, money, money.

'Are you picking on me again?' I said in my most Natasha Richardson voice, definitely Natasha, sucking in my cheek-bones.

'No voice beautiful, please. It doesn't work. I have starlets from here to New York trying to impress me, dressed or undressed. So don't waste your time or mine.'

A calm temperament does not go easily with red hair. He'd walked out on me all those years ago without even a scribbled thank-you note on the back of an envelope.

'I have no intention of trying to impress you, Mr Harrison. If you would prefer me to prompt in a flat, boring monotone, then I will oblige. But you, of all people, with your reputation for the feel of words, should know that the emotion in a line is as important as a reminder of the actual words. I try to put myself in the character of the part. As for impressing you, a two-ton steamroller wouldn't make any impression.'

It was a great speech. I was proud of it. Perhaps I could get a job as a speech writer (freelance) now that I'd blown this job. Pity. Being a prompt required considerable skill.

'Heaven preserve us,' Joe Harrison muttered, rubbing his chin. 'I've a prompt with attitude. I don't deserve this.'

He walked away, not even looking at me properly. He didn't remember me at all and that's how I wanted it to stay. I might shed a tear or ten, late at night, but not now.

'For goodness sake, Sophie, be careful. You're treading on dangerous ground.' It was Bill Naughton, the stage manager, strolling over to my side. 'We don't want the great Joe Harrison flying back to New York on the next Virgin Atlantic, do we?'

Bill Naughton was younger than me. He was having a hard time from our guest director. Even his thatch of fair hair looked dejected.

'Does he need a plane?' I asked. 'Surely this guy can walk on water?'

I heard a short chuckle. Joe Harrison, again. Could he hear everything anyone said? 'I don't need a commercial airline, for sure,' he called out. 'I hire a private jet, use my pilot's licence, fly myself over. No queueing at the check-in desk.'

I decided to make myself scarce. The last thing I wanted was a conversation. I fled to the scenery dock, shielding my tea from spills. The flats and boat trucks were a good place to hide. I'd been hiding all my life and I needed to hide now, tuck my head under my arm like a bird. Was there a prompt bird? I knew there was a secretary bird.

One of the attractions of working for West Enders was the series of guest directors. The great and the famous flocked to our stage. Joe Harrison was the latest. He had crossed the Atlantic from Britain to the USA a decade ago and proceeded to make his name on Broadway with his stunning stage designs as well as production skills. But his reputation preceded him like a bad weather forecast. Watch out for squalls.

His rehearsals were dreaded by most of the company. We had a hot-line to the Samaritans. Nervous breakdowns were epidemic.

I leaned against a solid piece of court scenery, cupping my hands round the warm polystyrene beaker. Scenery was all front and no back. I couldn't remember all the shows Joe Harrison had directed but he demanded perfection from everyone. His rehearsals were fast and furious, reducing the cast to the point of mental and physical exhaustion.

Once Joe Harrison had been a struggling actor, lean and hungry, out of work and with nowhere to stay. I'd landed my first job as an ASM (assistant stage manager) with an out-of-town repertory company and was flat sharing with another actress. It was optimistically called a flat. It had two small, cramped bedrooms and a shared kitchen area the size of a wardrobe.

Joe had applied for work with the same company but was turned down for being too opinionated, too tall and too inexperienced. He was a late starter, having drifted around commercial art school for a couple of years, daubing paint on scenery and getting under everyone's skin.

We were in the cheap café next to the theatre when he came in and joined our crowded table of actors and crew in the steamy, smoky atmosphere. He was wet and cold, wearing unsuitably thin summer clothes that clung to his lanky body. He'd been moving and making scenery all day to earn the fare back to London. The weather was locked into winter and the day was dark and gloomy, the sulphur street lights already on, eerie and disconnected, casting shadows like slate across the pavement.

'Hi, come and sit down with us,' I said, brightly. I was barely nineteen and not gifted with tact. 'So, did you get the job?'

Usually I found it hard to talk to strange men but he looked so wet and forlorn, long hair flattened to his head like strokes of paint. His eyes were dulled with despair as if he was lost.

'No. They didn't like me. Everything about me is wrong. They didn't like my ideas.' But his voice was rich, resonant. It stirred some kind of lunacy in me. Being the one with a job and a salary gave me a small cushion of confidence.

'Perhaps they were looking for an actor, not someone with ideas.'

'The theatre lives on ideas.'

'Mostly other people's,' I said flippantly. I didn't know what I meant.

He was looking at my plate of tangled spaghetti topped with tomato sauce and grated Parmesan cheese. I was an early-stage vegetarian. The cheese was melting and glistening like a gold-spun volcano. It was an 'eat all you can for two pounds' meal. A special offer which no one could resist. So here I was, eating all I could, stacking it within for imminent Stalingrad siege.

He said nothing but his eyes were hungry.

'Would you like some lunch?' I said.

CHAPTER TWO

'So why are you in this mad, mad world?' Joe asked, not really looking at me, eyes still blanked with recent rejection. He was focused on my spaghetti.

'I've been stage-struck since the age of six, dressing up in my mother's dresses and hats, tottering about in her shoes, you know,' I said, sipping my coffee. At least he wasn't invading my caffeine. I knew I was rambling. I rambled when I was nervous. 'I made up plays and copied television, acted them all out. Adverts were the best. Cate Blanchett, Meryl Streep, Glenn Close, Goldie Hawn, Emma Thompson . . . I can do them all.'

'Like Minnie Mouse, wearing your mother's shoes,' he said vaguely, sucking up pasta like he hadn't eaten for a week. It seemed he hadn't.

'That's right. I learned Shakespeare by the yard, spouting Ophelia in the bath, Juliet from the roof of the garden shed.'

'So why aren't you out there acting? I saw you rushing round the stage with props and moving bits of scenery.'

'Sheer terror. Stage fright finished off my acting ambition,' I said, reliving the nightmare. 'I am physically sick when I go on stage. I can't control my legs or my voice. Everything shakes. Imagine a maid coming on with a tray of drinks that rattle. My voice disappears down my throat. I'm a walking disaster. So I changed direction eventually and went backstage. It's my natural home and I'm happy enough there. My acting career was over before it even started but I still love everything about the theatre. What about you? You're an actor?'

19

'I think I'm an actor but management doesn't seem to agree,' he said bitterly.

'But you keep trying. That's good. You'll get a job somewhere.'

'I'm consumed by what I don't know. Sometimes I want to act and then I want to produce, direct. Then I want to design sets. It's like some monster eating into my flesh, making me something different every day. I don't know what direction to take or if I'm doing the right thing.'

He obviously knew the direction to my plate, chasing the last of the sauce. I moved my coffee out of his reach.

'Tell me about your monsters,' I said with a Goldie Hawn smile. It seemed a safer subject. I had monsters too.

We talked until the owner of the café turned us out for not buying anything. His coffee was lukewarm now anyway. My hair was pulled back into a severe knot in those ASM days and tucked under a floppy black beret. No frivolity in the wings, please. He couldn't see what a mess I'd made of it, trying to dye it ebony with a home-kit supermarket dye. I was into the white make-up Gothic look.

Joe pulled up his jacket collar and heaved a shabby rucksack off the floor. 'All my worldly goods.'

Snow was beginning to drift from the leaden skies. I didn't know what to do. I could hardly leave him to trudge through the snow to goodness knows where. He'd be found frozen in a doorway and carted off to a mortuary with a toe-tag.

'I've nowhere to go and barely enough fare money.' It was a statement not a hint. He looked right over my head, he was that tall.

'There's only a sofa,' I said. 'And the springs are broken.'

'Sounds like the Hilton to me,' he said. 'I'll be gone before you're even awake. St Peter is watching, you know, the Pearly Gates doorman. He'll put you down in his Good Book.'

I fancied being in someone's good books. Joe was really down and out. It was nothing really, only the loan of a sofa with broken springs and a spare blanket. It was a clean blanket.

'Sophie? I thought I'd find you hiding among the scenery.' It was Elinor, hovering like a black widow spider ready to pounce and eat

Joe Harrison. 'I'm absolutely terrified of this horrible man. It's a nightmare. Any moment he's going to start counting my wrinkles.'

'We all have wrinkles,' I said, coming out from behind the scenery. 'I've at least fourteen, sixteen after a good night out. Ignore him.'

'I freeze in my boots every time he opens his mouth. But at least you'll be in your corner, giving me confidence. That's such a comfort.'

'You'll be all right, Elinor. You're a wonderful actress and your name was in lights when he was wearing Pampers.'

'That's what I'm worried about,' she said with a stifled laugh.

I took her hand. It was thin and veined with too much dieting. She never ate real food. Half a stick of celery for lunch. The acting profession is merciless even if stage lighting can be kind.

'Now listen to me, Elinor. Go back to your dressing room and take a few minutes to really relax. Be indifferent to him and confident in yourself. Don't let him wear you out. It's only words, after all. You know that you know them all and you'll be perfect on the night.'

'He might replace me. Fran is working on it. She's so young.'

'But she can't act. She's a talking clothes hanger, a wire one, the kind the cleaners give you. She'd do absolutely anything for a moment of fame.'

'Oh Sophie, I'm scared.'

'You have a gift. Say it to yourself.'

I drifted back from the scenery dock to the side studio where it looked as if Joe Harrison had wasted no time in making his mark. Drawings and samples of material were thrown over the long trestle table by the window, heaps of iridescent colour.

I had no right to be there but I was past caring. His designs interested me. There were several paintings of medieval costumes, some like stained glass. I loved one in particular, a velvet cloak in all shades of gold. I'd like to hang it on my sitting room wall. My current studio flat was several upgrades from that single room of long ago, but still rooftop. I was destined to live with the birds.

I also collected pictures, mostly from charity shops or market stalls. I wondered if this odious man would donate one of his paintings to a humble prompt?

There was a hard cough behind me and a shadow fell over the table. I froze.

'Do you mind,' said Joe, removing the painting from my hands. 'It isn't even dry yet. And stop following me about. I'm not auditioning you today or any day.'

'I wasn't following you and I didn't know where you were. The studio seemed empty. You weren't shouting so how could I possibly know you were around?' Nice one, Sophie. 'Are these your paintings? They're really very good.'

He held one at a distance as if he'd never seen it before. He'd seemed unaware of me. He went to the window and held the painting to the sky.

'Well, I suppose it's mine. They are the work of another person, someone I used to know. A young man who wanted to paint day and night and bring his paintings to life on the stage. Then he discovered there was more money and fame in directing shows. So he left having fun behind. This was a disaster for him.'

'Why was it a disaster?'

'The painter went to the wall.'

What I was hearing was different from the aggressive man, demolishing everyone on stage. There was a small scar on his top lip. That was new. Maybe some irate leading lady had knifed him?

The light from the window was playing on his face, throwing his craggy features into relief like a Florentine statue. For some reason the mask had dropped. He was vulnerable and tired. No sofa on offer this time. He was probably staying at Claridges with twenty-four hour room service and a mini-bar.

'This painting is beautiful,' I said, finding my own voice. 'Not a wall painting. You should be proud of it.'

'Thank you for nothing. I don't need sympathy or flattery. I'm in charge here and we'll be using my designs. Anyway, who are you? Oh yes, the so-called prompt, when you are awake. You read from the book like a monkey.'

It was if he had struck me. I took a gasp of breath, hollowed with shock. What had made him become so thoughtlessly cruel?

'Monkeys can't read,' I said.

'This one can.'

He was showing me out of the studio with cold courtesy. I wrapped myself in the poncho like a registered parcel, determined not to let him know how he had shattered my composure. I could walk out but I wasn't going to. That salary was ear-marked for the Jurassic coast of Dorset. I needed every penny.

'That's all for today. Ten a.m tomorrow sharp. Look at your words. Any prompted line tomorrow and the actor at fault is selling programmes front of house or looking for work with *The Big Issue*. We've a lot of hard work to do before we have a show. At present it's a shambles.'

Joe's biting tongue had lashed at the cast till their nerves were shredded string. I'd suffered along with them, trying to find ways to help that didn't involve putting the script in front of their faces. Television newsreaders had it easy with their prompt boards. And to sell *The Big Issue* you needed a dog.

Joe was also drained. Once again he looked like the out-of-work actor who had nowhere to sleep and no money. He fed an energy into the roles which was not always matched by the cast.

'If he keeps on like this, in a week's time none of us will have the strength to crawl onstage,' said Bill, as he re-set the stage for Act I the following day. 'Who does he think he is? Did you hear the way he shouted at Elinor? It wasn't her fault. That damned fool, Byron, was in the wrong place. As usual.'

'Mr Harrison is a perfectionist,' I said. 'That makes him less than human. The most important thing to him is the play, not the players.'

'Are you sticking up for him, Sophie? Not smitten by those smouldering good looks, surely? I thought you of all people would have more sense.'

'No, not sticking up for him, just trying to be fair to the man. It's his reputation at stake. So of course he wants a brilliant show.'

'Let's forget about being fair,' said Bill, flippantly. 'How about a drink? We're all meeting at The Stage Door pub to drown our sorrows.'

'OK, but I have something to do first. Sorry, but I have to call my mother. I'll catch up with you.'

'Not again? You are the world's most dutiful daughter. You are always calling her. Why don't you go and see her instead?'

'It's too far away and when is there ever time?'

My mother had dug herself into some far-flung country hole so that no one could visit. It's something to do with my father dying at forty and her bringing me up alone. He shouldn't have died. Not my father, on a wintry night, skidding on an icy road. I hadn't asked for a widowed mother, struggling on her own. It was a wonder I had managed to get away. Never mind, she had another tender soul to care for now. I got out my mobile and made my evening call. 'Hi, it's me, Sophie. How's things?'

Joe Harrison was collecting a stack of notes and flinging them into a briefcase. He shrugged a leather jacket over his shoulders and turned for the exit. Then he looked back at me, calculating my resistance.

'Wear some warmer clothes tomorrow,' he said. 'Thermals if you must but I don't want to see that monstrous blanket thing. The court of Illyria is set in warmth and sunlight. We must generate that climate even in the wings.'

'If you say so, sir,' I murmured, very Gwyneth Paltrow, even the eyes. If heat was what he wanted, then I would generate some heat. I wanted to go home. My studio flat was a high haven with wonderful Wren church-spire views of London. It had a small flat roof where I could sunbathe among the chimneys and the pigeons, feed stale croissants to the sparrows. He couldn't touch me there. I was safe with my dreams, out of his reach.

But first came sorrow-drowning at The Stage Door. It was a crowded pub. Here, tourists, locals and traders mingled with the actors. The pub had once been an old wine cellar under a firm of exporters and the original stone arches gave groups all the privacy they sought. There were no windows, only thick basement glass where once traders had loaded wine casks from the pavement.

I was not happy with the thick fog of cigarette smoke, smokers drawing on the remains of their lives, but at least it was warm. The cast and crew of West Enders had taken over a couple of tables at the far end, coming back from the bar with trays laden with drinks, beer slopping over tankard rims.

'Come along, Sophie, help yourself,' said Bill. 'What would you like? Take your pick. You deserve a drink, sweetheart. Your throat must be out to dry.'

'Parched, p-parched,' I croaked. 'Water ... water.' It was overacting. I was somewhere in the Sahara, crawling over the sand dunes, the sun beating down on my empty water flask, my mouth caked with sand. They gave me a slow hand-clap. I took off my hat and shook out my fiery hair. It flew in all directions like flames.

'Not auditioning again, Prompt,' said Byron, taking off Joe Harrison's voice so well that I had to look over my shoulder. He wasn't there. No doubt escaped to the Ritz Bar, or wherever he was living in the luxury style to which he had become accustomed. Piloting a hired jet ... what a phoney show-off thing to say.

Bill moved a tall glass of peach-tinted liquid towards me. It was sparkling with ice, rimmed with sugar, scented with peaches ripe and ready to fall. It reminded me of the Mediterranean, sunlight and sunsets although I had never been abroad. I'd never been further than the ferry at Newhaven.

'This is peach brandy topped with soda water and ice,' Bill told me, confidentially. 'A concoction of my own invention especially for you. And guaranteed to put the sparkle back into a stressed-out prompt.'

Bill had a soft spot for me. Too squashy soft for my liking. He was trying so hard that sometimes it hurt even to listen to him. 'Lovely,' I said, my thoughts marooned on the warmer, safer shores of *Twelfth Night*. I didn't want to think about him. It was easy for me to vanish into my own thoughts.

I am always pursued by younger, shorter, fatter men. Why do short men like tall women? And why did younger men fancy me? Did I remind Bill of his mother? Did he want me to bath him, cover him in talc, read him a bedtime story?

'Sophie? Are you still with us or has that bastard Harrison destroyed your mind? Is this terminal withdrawal? I've heard of cast needing counselling, but never the prompt.' This was Claud.

I laughed, dragging myself back from sunlit shores. 'I feel fine, thanks. We need a plan to deal with Hercules Harrison, the jerk in

25

a jersey. A campaign. That man needs teaching a lesson. He can't treat us this way.'

'Sophie, you are so right,' said Elinor Dawn, clapping. Her make-up was streaked. It was unlike her not to repair her mascara before coming out in public. 'He's only a director. They're ten a penny.'

'And a guest director,' someone else said. 'He's not going to stay forever.'

'But West Enders are here forever,' I said, taking another sip of the brandy made from peaches. It burned a path to my empty stomach. I wondered if I could make a batch of this stuff with overripe peaches from the market. I'd need a really big jar. 'The Royale is our theatre and our company and we are its foundation. Joe Harrison is a passing irritant. This is a revolution. We need an escape committee.'

Everyone cheered. I was given another peach brandy with less soda water after which I did my near-famous impersonation of Glenda Jackson as Queen Elizabeth I without the eyebrow shaving. It was off with his head and no mistake. Order the straw. Oil the tumbrel.

None of the campaign plans were any good but the exercise was therapeutic. We had bonded and that gave us mutual strength. We felt dynamic. Only the openly shallow Fran was the odd one out.

'I intend to do my best at all times,' she said, sipping orange-tinted vodka, pretending that she didn't drink. 'He's brilliant. He'll soon see my potential.'

'He'll soon see your knickers, you mean.'

I walked home, swinging my bag. The moonless air was damp but I didn't fancy buses at this time of night. Nor the half-empty underground trains with drunks settling down for a Circle Line party night. I preferred to walk, knew all the short cuts down side streets, knew which were safe and well lit. Bill had a much longer journey home in the other direction and had set out at a run to pick up a late train.

I had got over the hurdle of seeing Joe. He was no longer intimidating. He had not recognized me and I could handle that. I was anonymous, nameless, lost back in time. He remembered nothing about me. It was how I wanted it.

The next morning I was almost late. It had taken time to find the final layers. I didn't care if people stared. It was like wearing a fat-suit. Joe Harrison's comments had been unfair and cruel so I had added a few extra touches. There was a stunned silence as I waddled into the theatre before the rehearsal. I heaved my new egg shape on to the stool in the prompt corner and it rocked unsteadily.

'Is that you, Sophie, inside all of that?' asked Bill, not knowing what to say.

'Of course, it is,' I said in my own voice. My brain was stifled by the heat. I would rapidly become dehydrated. My protest had lost its validity.

I took up so much room that several entrances were delayed as cast had to squeeze past my heaving bulk. Bill shook his head in despair. He thought I was heading for the big push. Joe Harrison would soon be investigating the delays and he would not be amused.

'Late, Viola, late again.' Joe's voice boomed through the theatre from his vulture perch in row D. 'Move, move. Don't lose pace. If anyone is in the wings who shouldn't be there, push them out of the way.'

'Sorry, Joe,' said Elinor. She hadn't slept well, taken a handful of sleeping pills in the early hours and was carrying a woolly hangover. 'Arctic mountain in the wings. It needs digging out. There's a snow shovel somewhere out the back.' She was attempting funny. It didn't go down well, more like a lead balloon.

Joe was up onstage in three strides but he stopped in his tracks when he saw me. I emerged one foot at a time, wondering what kind of verbal avalanche was about to descend upon my head. He walked round me slowly, nodding, taking in the multitude of layers I had managed to get on. I was wearing more clothes than the entire cast put together.

'So the Abominable Snowman has joined the company,' he said. 'It's amazing. I wonder if we could use this in publicity. Different angle.'

'You did say wear warmer clothes,' I said, sweat running down every crevice and crack. I was starting to itch like I was being attacked by theatre mites.

'So I did and I approve of such a diligent application of my words. Back to work everyone and remember the mountainous hazard of wool, fleece and Damart underwear in the prompt corner. Give yourself extra time.'

No reprieve. I waddled back to my seat. He'd not been in the least annoyed. Instead, the wretched man had been amused. I was growing hotter by the minute. Sweat was running down my neck, inside the padded ski suit and Wonderbra.

I managed to shed a couple of layers, eased off the fur boots, scarf and woolly hat. My jeans were sticking to my skin. Somehow the joke had rebounded. I was the one melting like strawberry jelly on a Sunday School outing. The icy draught had gone walkabout to spite me.

Joe passed through backstage, spine held stiffly as if he was in pain. I wondered when he had injured himself.

'Try that again and you're out,' he growled.

'Only following orders, sir.'

'Your interpretation was childish.'

'So I'll catch a cold, pneumonia even. Do you want a prompt coughing and sneezing on every other line? That would ruin tempers and wreck several performances.'

'The cast won't need prompting by the time I've finished with them,' he said. 'And you'll be out of a job.' He went downstairs to Costumes in the basement, his knuckles pressed into the base of his spine.

I wiped the perspiration off my lips. I needed this job like grass needs rain. A drought would mean disaster. No stand-pipes in my street.

CHAPTER THREE

I walked stiffly to the drinks machine, flexing my shoulders. I felt as if I had run that Scottish mountain marathon where they scamper up and down hills, ticking them off on a list and collecting heather. The coffee was undrinkable mud so I took a polystyrene beaker of tea that was too hot to hold. It was time I brought in a Thermos from home even if it meant getting up ten minutes earlier.

Fran wandered over, swinging a bottle of mineral water in her hand. It had to come from a toxic-free spa. Her life-style was pure everything. Everything had to be tested (but not on animals), classified, glorified and passed pure as undriven snow. She was wearing a fawn suede skirt the size of an A4 envelope and a skin-tight white vest top with silver logo saying I'M LEAN AND MEAN. She was right there.

'Hi Sophie,' she said. 'That outfit suits you. You look really round and warm like a tea cosy. I don't feel the cold. If you eat the right things, then your body temperature never drops.'

'Wow, I must remember that,' I said, sipping the tasteless brown brew. I wondered why she was talking to me since in her estimation, prompts were lower than stage mice in theatre status. She was understudy to the star, also played one of the ladies of the court. It meant loads of lovely sweeping gowns and she swept in front of Elinor whenever she had a chance. She had turned upstaging into an art form.

'Still overworked?'

'No, even Byron has looked at his lines and that's something. And he is beginning to remember his entrances. I don't have to keep signalling from the wings.' His memory was notorious. He ought to join a mime group.

'That's amazing. So, you won't be too exhausted this evening? Great. Super.'

'Exhausted for what?' Catch question. Had I promised to do something which I have totally forgotten? 'Harrison might call an extra rehearsal.'

'Mr Harrison,' Fran corrected with prim emphasis, flicking her blonde locks like an A-level schoolgirl. 'A brilliant director like Joe Harrison deserves every respect. It's a privilege to be working with him. We can all benefit from his immense influence and guidance. Don't you agree?'

Nice little speech. Fran had been practising this gushing role and was trying it out on every unwilling victim backstage. I was clearly not the right material.

I smiled insincerely. 'Sure,' I sang. 'He's the tops. He's the Eiffel Tower. Don't get vertigo, Fran. He's a genius in the making.'

'I do agree. A genius in the making, that's a wonderful phrase. I may use it. And I think he really likes the look of me. I've seen him watching me onstage. He may ask me to take over a couple of performances.'

'From Elinor?' I only just managed to hide my incredulity. This was news. Fran had a long way to go before she was even a tenth as good. And she couldn't project, lacked any rhythmic sense. Good prose sings. There's a melody in every line. 'What makes you think that?'

'She's making heavy weather of the part, starting to look too old, a bit jaded. You have to admit, I do have the right looks.' She did a little twirl culled from all those expensive ballet classes she boasted about.

'If you think Viola is a Barbie doll,' I murmured. I was tired of this conversation.

'Would you do me a favour, Sophie?' Now she was getting to the point. She only called me Sophie when she wanted something. 'It's a big part and I'm not one hundred per cent happy with my delivery. I'm sure Mr Harrison would appreciate it if you could give me a little coaching. He likes the way you say lines even if you are not a trained actress.'

'But being untrained, Fran, I might accidentally suggest the wrong tone, the wrong pace, promote overacting and you wouldn't want that. It could be chancy. I don't feel I have the right experience to help you.'

Her face produced puzzled. Fran nodded as if she understood a word of what I was saying. 'Just hear my lines then, please. In case I have to step in.'

I knew what she would do. She'd falter and dry up so that she could hear me say the line. She would probably have a tape recorder switched on in her pocket. Perhaps I could charge by the hour. Or I could say the lines with totally the wrong emphasis. Unspeakably bad thought. Now, Sophie, what would Bill Shakespeare think of that? He'd probably applaud my innovation, the degree of cunning. We might have a direct link . . . me and the Bard.

'I can't spare any time tonight,' I said, faking a yawn. 'I'm pole-axed. We're all worn out. Everyone, the cast and the crew.'

Fran wouldn't be worn out. Her day's work had been swanning about as a lady of the court, occasionally waving a fan, swishing a skirt. The wardrobe mistress, Hilda, had put Fran in a rehearsal skirt to swish, thinking her current-sized gear a trifle too short to do more than tweak.

'Tomorrow then? You're a brick. We'll fix a time.'

'OK, but only if there is time,' I said, brick-like.

'Wonderful. I knew you wouldn't let me down. I do so like him and want to do my best for him. It's very important for my career.'

'I'm sure your genuine admiration must make Mr Harrison feel really happy,' I said. It was beginning to make me feel ill. Or was it a substantial lack of food? Had I had time for breakfast?

Having got what she wanted, Fran didn't waste any more time on me. She shot off like toast out of a toaster towards Bill Naughton. She wanted an extra light fitted in her dressing room. So she could count her eyelashes.

I poured the rest of the tea away. Now I was a brick. Paint this, sew that, make a pile of sandwiches out of a tin of tuna and half a lettuce. Multitasking. Build a wall.

31

It was quite a quick call on my mobile that evening. I heard the news, the good, the bad and the undetermined, made a few helpful comments. Sent my love. Said good-night. Much as usual.

Time to walk home to Trinity Terrace. I wanted to walk, as I spend too much of the day sitting and that could affect my girth. Not that it was a problem yet but it might be in the future. I could become the world's largest Prompt, mentioned in *The Guinness Book of Records*. They might have to design sets to accommodate me.

I knew Joe Harrison was behind me on the pavement without even looking back. It was a sort of seventh sense. He caught up and I steeled myself for another reprimand. He was looking at me intently as if I was a social outcast. I hoped it was a smudge on my nose and certainly not paint. I hadn't been near his studio.

'Point taken,' he said, surprisingly. 'I sat in the prompt corner for five minutes and three was enough. The draught is glacial. You could sue the management for frozen assets. You can wear your Mexican poncho and anything else you need while I try to get something done about the outer doors.'

'Thank you. It's an old theatre,' I said, slightly confused by his concern. 'The draughts come with the ghosts.'

'Very commendable but not during my show. Just don't hold up any entrances. Timing is crucial. Faulty timing can ruin a line.'

'I know.'

'You know quite a lot, don't you? Not thinking of stepping into my shoes, are you? Shall I find the apron floor booby-trapped tomorrow and myself with a broken back in the pit?'

I shuddered at the thought. His back already hurt.

'My ambition is dormant,' I said. 'I've no wish to produce anything beyond a flawless performance from your cast.' I put a slight emphasis on the word 'your'.

He hid a grin. 'Nice one, Prompt. Hey, it's starting to rain. Can I give you a lift home, wherever home is? I'm getting a taxi.'

'No, thank you. I'd rather walk. I have a strong need for fresh air after being stuck in the theatre all day.' I implied I didn't want his company.

'Take your own taxi then. You'll get soaked.'

'On my salary? You're joking.'

'Then I'll have to walk with you,' he said. 'Since I'm the one prudent enough to have an umbrella.' His umbrella shot up, a huge gaudy canary-yellow canopy big enough to shelter half the cast. It had New York printed in inky black letters all round the rim.

'Is that in case you forget where you are?' I said.

'Of course. But of little use in London.'

'I don't mind getting wet,' I insisted.

'Stop arguing. We don't have to talk if you find my company objectionable,' said Joe, taking a grip of my elbow. 'I won't say a word. Start walking. I haven't got all night. There's still work to do.'

I could hardly fight him off in the street. It was chucking it down, spattering black London rain, and I was glad of the umbrella. But I didn't want to be anywhere near him, and hip-bashing under an umbrella was almost too close. The sulphur lighting was eerily yellow, gutters starting to fast-flow fast-food debris, puddles swelling underfoot on the cracked pavement. I had to do the odd skip to keep up with his long strides. Not quite dancing. It was called exercise.

True to his word, Joe didn't speak. Just the occasional muttered: 'Mind the kerb.' 'Now, which way?' 'Left or right?'

I began to regret that I had sounded so ungrateful. Somehow he would have to get back to wherever he was going. He could take a taxi if he could find one, so I needn't feel too guilty. They all disappeared when it rained.

We were turning into my street, Trinity Terrace, a forgotten crescent of tall narrow Edwardian houses, each still elegant with the faded glory of stone steps leading up to columned porches and bay windows on the first and second floors.

'You live here?' He sounded interested.

'Lots of the houses are turned into flats these days. No one can afford a whole house. A couple have been converted into small hotels. I have a studio flat in the roof. The views of London are quite spectacular but the stairs are killing. You need oxygen halfway.'

'I envy you,' he said. 'The view from my very expensive hotel room is the back wall of an air conditioning vent.'

'You should complain. You're good at complaining.'

I was sorry I'd said it the moment I spoke. Joe had been nothing but kind the last ten minutes and despite the big umbrella there were drips on his shoulders. I turned to him at the foot of the steps. He didn't look angry, more amused.

'I say these things without thinking,' I said in a hurry. 'I'm sorry. It's a sort of defence. I've built a wall.'

'So has life been that hard?' It was a casual comment, a suggestion, nothing remotely sympathetic. But then I didn't expect sympathy from Joe. He had scaled the heights. I was barely on the first rung. I didn't even know where the first rung was.

'I make very good coffee,' I offered by way of amends.

'I'm sure you do. You're very good at everything you do. It's too late now. But you can do me a favour.'

Here we go again. Sophie, do this. Sophie, do that. What was it going to be this time? Tar the shipwreck? Shampoo the red velvet curtains, the house tabs?

'People ask favours of me all the time. I'm the flavour favour of the month. One more won't make my crowded life any different.' I hid a sigh.

'I want you to run my press reception next week. We'll hold it in the theatre, invite all the newspapers, reporters and critics, get the best food and wine.' He rattled it off as if it could be put together in five minutes, give or take the odd email.

'No way. Of course, I can't do it.' I said indignantly. 'I haven't got the time. Get your secretary to do it.'

'I haven't got a secretary or anyone remotely capable. You've plenty of time. Prompting doesn't take all day.'

'Employ a professional PR man. Ask management to fund it.'

'Dammit, I want you to do it. You're sensible and efficient and for some reason that I can't fathom, you really like the theatre and the play.'

'I like the theatre and the play. That doesn't mean I have to like you.' Now this was pure Julia Roberts in *Pretty Woman*. Even she couldn't have said it better.

'Personalities don't come into it,' he said coolly. 'I want the best person available to make a good job of this press reception. Someone who is around every day. There'll be a budget for the event which you can spend how you please. And I'll make sure you get a one-off fee which will be added to your salary. It'll pay for a few taxis or whatever.'

I went for the whatever. I was always short of money. It melted in my purse like a café pat of butter. But I didn't want Joe Harrison paying me. It would add insult to insult. I didn't want to be sensible and efficient or available. I wanted to be desirable and erotic, wild enough to send a man mad and very unavailable. I was tired of my blameless existence. I wanted to be someone who wore a red feather boa and a crimson satin teddy.

CHAPTER FOUR

Joe had landed me with the job and I hardly put up a fight. It was a dirty trick and I felt licensed to kill.

I could sabotage the whole event, give a false image. It would not take much imagination, hire male strippers, serve hot dogs and lukewarm beer, give the press handouts with a sliding scale of accuracy. I could forgetfully call it a performance of *Twelfth Knight* and imply jousting at the court of Henry VIII.

Joe would be livid. But how could he blame me? I was only the prompt. Born to rectify other people's lapses of memory, not my own.

It was a satisfying daydream for a short while. We were rehearsing Act 2, scene 4. The Duke was making heavy weather of his speech, in fact he was floundering on the shore, knee deep in mud. He needed rescuing.

'If ever thou shalt love, in the sweet pangs of it remember me,' I said, loud enough for Byron to hear. He managed most of the rest of the lines, hesitantly, sweating profusely and overemphasising his stance and gestures.

'You're not supposed to be staggering, faltering,' Joe said.

'I'm a faltering lover,' said Byron defiantly. 'She's going to turn me down.'

'It gives a very echo to the seat where love is enthroned,' said Elinor with Viola's words.

'There you are,' said Byron. 'She turns me down.' He could argue anything to tea time, and carry on till supper. He looked up into the tangle of ropes and wires.

'That's not turning you down,' said Elinor. 'It's very positive. But she is assuming the role of a boy, remember? Dicey, even in those days.'

'Can we have this ethical discussion some other time?' said Joe returning to his laptop and desk lamp in the fourth row.' Back to "If ever thou shalt love".'

Byron groaned. 'I hate that speech.'

'Learn to like it,' said Joe. 'Learn to say it with feeling. Say it over and over again. Make it part of your life. That's your remit for today.'

The Press Reception was a week away. I had sent out the invitations. I wrote them by hand in copper-plate Shakespearean handwriting, sloping and twirling, on fake manuscript paper I found going cheap in a card shop. Some of the edges were curled which gave them an air of antiquity.

Joe never asked to see what I had written or whether the arrangements were in place. So far there was no food, no drink and no entertainment. It was going to be a very short party. Say, fifteen minutes at the most.

The fact was I was too tired to be bothered. Not the right attitude. I should be bubbling with enthusiasm, 'brisk and giddy-paced' as Shakespeare wrote so eloquently for the same scene. Giddy-paced was not my style or size. Far too energetic. I needed folic acid and calcium.

Bill Naughton strolled over. He had a breathing space, liked breathing down my neck. Lighting were trying to fix something in the flies above.

'How's my favourite prompt?' he asked, peering at the page. My neck warmed up. 'Found your place?'

'Want my job?' I said, vaguely Bette Davis. I'd only caught her on afternoon movies, long before my time. 'Any nearer and you can have it.'

'Just making sure you are not asleep,' he chuckled.

'Quiet in the wings.'

Joe's voice whipped over. He must have hearing sharper than a dolphin.

They can hear things miles away. And he was just as slippery. But could he do backflips?

It was a long scene. Twice I had to stretch my legs during moments of theatrical harassment. Prompt was not supposed to move. It was embarrassing but I could get stuck in one position. Then I waddled, like a duckling out of Honk!

'Are you leaving us, Prompt?' Joe asked, swinging his voice round towards my corner. 'I don't blame you. They are making a pig's dinner of this play. Maybe we could turn it into a musical and get a band to come in. Let the noise drown the words. Elinor, go and get a good night's sleep. You need it. Fran, stop flaunting the boobs. You're a lady in waiting, not a lap dancer. Byron, for the last time, learn those words. And Mr Naughton, a word about those bloody slow changes. A tortoise on the run would have moved faster.'

I shrank back into my poncho. I'd lost my brittle shell, felt soft and exposed. My script fell open at a different page. One of the mischievous theatre ghosts on the prowl. Act 2, scene 3: 'Dost thou think, because thou art virtuous, there shall be no more cakes and ale?'

Cakes and ale! Bingo. Hundreds and hundreds of deliciously scrummy cakes (keep Elinor away from them). Casks of ale? Where do I get authentic casks? What else did they eat in those days? Venison and stuffed swans? I drew a line at stuffed swans, poor things with such long necks. Did M&S sell venison? Venison sausages? Sweetmeats. What are sweetmeats? Sweets or meat? This was suddenly getting interesting. The press reception had potential.

There's nothing I like more than research on Google at the library. Shakespearean food and drink. Tell me more, oh sweet screen, thou flickering cursor.

I was on my way out when Mr Mighty Joe Harrison blocked my path. He was wrapped up in a big scarf, not liking our English wet and cold. And winter was coming. It was nipping the air with splinters of ice.

'Have you the right to look so happy?' he asked.

'I am happy,' I said. And I was. 'I love everybody but unfortunately that's not necessarily including you. That I would have to work on. Call it overtime.'

'How's the press reception?' It was the first time he'd mentioned it.

'You'll be amazed,' I said. 'It's going to be spectacular, fantastic, terrific.'

Joe looked worried. 'I don't like the sound of spectacular and fantastic. Professional, I hope?'

'Come along and find out. If there's room for you. Everyone is coming. Half of London has accepted. Stalls, Dress Circle, Upper Circle, packed.'

'Well done.' He sounded suspicious. He didn't trust me. I didn't trust me. 'Don't forget, I shall want to say something about the production.'

'I'll find you a slot,' I said. 'Before the fireworks or after the ice skating? Maybe before everyone goes out or passes out.'

'Is it going to be that kind of press reception? A medieval fountain of alcohol? No fireworks, please, unless you've invited the London Fire Brigade.'

'It's going to be wonderful,' I said dreamily, very Charlize Theron, without the flawless skin and model figure. 'Trust me.'

'I don't.'

I toured a people-packed, teeming M&S store in the break. The shelves were stacked with wonderful party food. I could eat everything. Not exactly Shakespearean but I could tweak it here and there. Casks of ale were no problem. The local brewery was willing to deliver. I found a delicatessen that would make venison sausages and honey cakes. Thirty-four plays and 154 sonnets recorded but what did Shakespeare eat? No burger bars around then but lots of street stalls selling piping hot food. Grazing is nothing new. Medieval homes didn't have cookers or microwaves and not everyone lived in a castle with a cow-sized spit.

Shakespeare lived fifty-two years, dying on his birthday, 23 April. No mean feat to die on your birthday; think of the party. He began life with a bread and dripping job, working in his father's wool and glove shop in Henley Street, Stratford. What was his mind thinking as he sold gloves to the ladies and rich merchants of the day? Daydreaming? Writing plays? He loved strolling players, followed them around. Good on you, William, the groupie. Go soak up the vibes.

But what did they eat or drink? I needed more information or this press reception was going to be dull and boring. That night I stayed up, reading the Bard. Cakes and ale, good wine, a pot of ale. Could it be served in pots? I didn't fancy roasted egg or roasted wild boar. Forget them, nothing roasted.

Beef was mentioned frequently. Then, in *Henry IV*, I hit the culinary jackpot. Cheese and garlic, pigeons, short-legged hens, a joint of mutton and pretty little kickshaws. I had no idea what a kickshaw was but I had time to find out. *Richard III* mentioned strawberries, plenty of those still around and *Romeo and Juliet* came up trumps with quinces and dates. My party menu was going to be awesome.

I was walking through Covent Garden the next day when I heard some strolling players playing music. A group of out-of-work actors, desperate for food, drink, drugs, anything. They had a lute and flute and several sorts of other medieval instruments and were playing vaguely madrigal-type music with a bit of Queen thrown in. I booked them on the spot. They had to wear Shakespearian-type gear, be on time, and I would pay them cash, I said.

They liked the sound of cash. And the music wasn't that bad. Could be catchy in a couple of centuries.

'Now I'm depending on you,' I said. 'If you let me down, then your name will be more than mud, it will be foul-smelling sludge. If you haven't the costumes, then we can fit you up out of Wardrobe.'

'Don't worry,' said Mike, the leader. 'We'll be there in green and yellow stockings and caps. We can borrow the gear. It'll be cool.'

The work was beginning to get to me. I wasn't built for this kind of hassle. I had actually lost a couple of pounds in the last week. My flat was heavily into squalor. Instead of catching up on sleep at night, I was writing and checking lists, phoning people who were never in. Could I call this expenses?

It didn't help that when I walked home that evening, I was followed by a stalker. I knew someone was a few paces behind me. Such a creepy feeling. I was sick with fear. My hand was on my mobile but how could it help me? I'd be flat on the pavement, minus bag, before my fingers even remembered where 999 was.

I'd worked in London for several years, various theatres, never been frightened before. But now I was. It was the most awful feeling, being followed, being stalked. I started crossing the street, then re-crossing, keeping a distance. They say keep a distance. Try to relax, let the tension go out of your shoulders. Strike with the palm, not a clenched fist. The fist hurts you more. I shrank into my own skin, hoping someone would rescue me first. I couldn't even aim a stamp on an envelope. Robin Hood? Wrong county. Wrong century. I quickened my steps.

'Sophie? Slow down. I'm not stalking you. Don't be afraid. I live in this street too now. I've taken on the tenancy of the first-floor flat in the same house. It may not be the most salubrious area but it suits me.'

It was Joe Harrison, puffing. He was standing behind me, laden with flight bags and cases. A carton of milk was balanced on top. I rescued it, the words sinking in. I didn't want a neighbour, especially this particular neighbour.

'The first-floor flat?' I said in a deadpan voice. My own voice. 'It's been empty for ages.'

'I know. Overpriced but I can afford it, and it's only for the run of the show. Well furnished. All white and minimalist. Do you want to see it?'

'No,' I said, following him inside like a zombie. The first floor was no climb at all. Joe was bouncing his bags and cases up the stairs. I didn't offer to help. I'd helped him once before and look what good it had done me.

He pushed open the front door of his flat. It had a hall, not straight into the living room like mine. I followed him through to the kitchen and dumped the milk. It was all stainless steel and white tiles. Not a spilt Rice Crispie in sight.

'Nice, isn't it?' he said. 'It'll suit me very well.'

I could see the living room, big bay windows and long draped ivory curtains, two three-seater sofas and thick rugs on the polished floor. Call mine an aerial rabbit hutch. Still, I did have my own birds.

'Lovely,' I said, backing out.

'Won't you stay for a cup of tea? Some sort of house-warming drink?' he shouted from the bedroom. No doubt it was also palatial and well furnished. 'I think there's some champagne in one of these bags.'

'Sorry,' I trilled merrily. 'Busy night. Big party. All my mates. Got to wash my hair first.'

The big party was watching any mates who'd been lucky enough to get bit parts on TV soaps and were hurt if you didn't spot them. Blink and you missed their line. Busy night was checking more replies. I washed my hair, that much was true. Protein for strength, it said on the bottle label in unreadable tiny print.

I sat in front of the telly towelling dry my strong hair before the drips ran down inside my collar. I was celebrating with a raspberry yogurt. Champagne wasn't that good for you. Wrinkled the skin round the eyes or something.

I was unable to hear what was going on down on the first floor so if Fran joined Joe for the celebratory glass of champagne, I wouldn't know. I couldn't spend my life counting his visitors.

My bed was a shambles. I barely had time to tidy anywhere before I left every morning. I threw over the rose-patterned duvet and gave it the odd smoothing pat. Housework done.

There hadn't been time for my usual evening call but my mother was still up, making her night-time cocoa. She answered the phone straight away.

'Is everything all right?' I asked.

'Of course, right as rain. You sound tired.'

'I am. This press reception is a lot of extra work. These things don't just happen. There's so much to think about.'

'I hope he's going to pay you.'

'Yes, he said he would. But people forget, don't they, when it's all over?'

'Then don't let him forget. Type out an invoice and present it to him in the middle of the reception when everything is going well. But keep a copy in case he loses it. Don't worry, I'm sure it'll be fine.'

I groaned. 'No guarantee of that. It could be a disaster. There's so much to arrange. My corn is hurting and that means a disaster, doesn't it?'

'No, it means your shoes are too tight or it's going to rain.'

'That, too. How's everything your end?'

'He's fine. Sound asleep. Had a busy day.'

'I miss him.'

'Do you? Come home a bit more often then. You know where we live. Come before he forgets who you are.'

My mother could be snappy. She'd had years of practise. My sense of inadequacy homed in like radar.

CHAPTER FIVE

It was the day of the press reception. The rehearsal had been a minefield, erratic fortissimo explosions. Joe eventually sent everyone home so that the stage could be cleared, swept and set up with the food and drink tables in front of scenery.

'I want everyone back by a quarter to six. Not a minute later. Glad rags and best bib,' he added. 'No punk gear.'

The brewery was setting up casks of ale on wooden trestle supports. It was also providing a mountain of tankards as they didn't have pots. No problem with the wine though, would anyone fancy elderberry or dandelion? Pretty potent, I was assured, blow your head stuff. My head already felt blown.

'And where is the music going?' Joe asked.

I had not heard from the strolling players and had no idea if they were actually going to turn up. I sent up a prayer, via Shakespeare.

'How about in the Royal Box, down right? There's plenty of room for them, a power point and no one will trip over cables and fuse the entire theatre.'

'I'll leave it to you.'

I was worried, in a red mist of panic. But food was arriving from the various shops and stores and it began to look good. I'd borrowed some huge platters from props and garlanded them with foliage stolen from a local church yard. I laid out the quinces and strawberries.

The cheese and garlic was chopped up in a big bowl for scooping up with bread. They used bread before they had plates but I wasn't providing a stew. There were heaps of short hen's legs and sliced mutton. More bread for scooping. Fresh mustard mixed in medieval pots. Millie, Elinor's dresser, helped mix the mustard till her eyes streamed. They were pretty brown eyes.

Joe was strolling around, hands behind his back, peering at the food like a health inspector.

'And what's this?' he asked, stopping in front of three long golden crusted rolls. 'Are they baguettes?'

'Beef in pastry,' I said. 'They loved beef in those days and they adored pastry. So I got a butcher to cook up a batch. It's around on menus now, but not many people know how old this recipe is. Needs slicing. Eat with your fingers.'

'Quinces?' He helped himself to a strawberry.

'They ate quinces.'

'So, but do we?'

'Does it matter? Does party food have to be boring? Be thankful I didn't roast a wild boar.'

Kickshaws I had decided were sweets, or sweetmeats, exotic delicacies said the dictionary, so I had bought a huge selection of small one-bite cakes and Belgian chocolates from M&S. A chocolate fountain was on its way for dipping. The Press would be staggering home, stomachs overloaded, searching for adjectives and the Rennies.

'Ah, sausages,' Joe said with male satisfaction.

'Venison sausages,' I said. 'I had them specially made. Very expensive and taste good. No limit to cost, you said.'

Joe Harrison stopped and looked at me. A humorous smile showed for two seconds. Or maybe I perceived it subconsciously. 'You really have been to a lot of trouble, Sophie. Thank you. It's going to be splendid. Different, but splendid.'

I shrivelled back into my shell. He hadn't told me to go home and be back by six. Perhaps I wasn't invited. Bill Naughton was still around, putting up banners and flags from the court of Orsino.

'Are you now the current favourite?' he asked, dragging over a set of heraldic emblems. He sounded peeved. Perhaps he was tired, or jealous.

'I doubt it,' I said. 'He'll have forgotten my name by the end of

45

the reception. I shall be hey-you, whats-yer-name, Madam Prompt again.'

'Where's the sandwiches and sausage rolls?'

'There aren't any. It's all genuine Shakespearean food.' What else did I have to do? My list was lost somewhere between here and Illyria.

'Didn't know food would keep that long.'

It was past five before I crept into the wings to make myself some tea. The strolling players had arrived clad in outrageous outfits in bright yellows and orange, but they were happy enough setting up their gear. It might be medieval but it was going to be amplified.

I sank down on to a stool not knowing if I was going to stay. Once it started I would be way back on the fringe, checking invites on the door, then dissolving into the night traffic and forgotten. I would go home. They'd all be having a good time (the elderberry was potent, I'd tasted it) and showing the Press that this was one helluva good show. Some of the striking costumes were on display. They would love the elaborate popinjay costume designed for Sir Andrew Aguecheek, the conceited and imbecilic friend of Sir Toby.

'Sophie,' it was Joe, again. He sounded urgent. 'Why aren't you ready? It's going to start very soon.'

'What do you mean? It is ready.'

He looked at me in disbelief. I was wearing black trainer bottoms and a shrunken Skittles Are Tops grey sweat shirt. My hair was tied back with an elastic band, the red ones that postmen drop in the street.

'Is this your idea of party gear?'

'No, work gear,' I said, numbness creeping sideways. 'This isn't my show. I didn't know if I was invited.'

Joe pulled me up off the stool and began to march me towards the basement of the theatre. His grip on my arm was tightened in case I was going to scarper. We went down the rickety stairs and along the dimly lit corridor that lead to Wardrobe and Costume storage. It was a cavern of racks of packed clothes, many in polythene bags or swathed in muslin. I'd been there many times, helping Hilda, the wardrobe mistress, to find something or change something. It was another of my Sophie do this, Sophie do that, areas. I can thread a needle.

'We're going to find you something to wear. Something feminine. Take that clobber off,' he said.

'No,' I said. 'I'm not taking anything off. I'm all right as I am.'

'Do as you are told,' he growled, flicking along the rails. 'Or I'll rip it off.'

There was a faded screen about two feet wide in the corner. It would hardly screen Kate Moss standing sideways. Joe was roaming the racks, pulling out frothy dresses and long skirts and pushing them back. He was trawling the modern section. I was wearing clean underwear but they were for paramedics' eyes only.

'What size are you?' he said.

'Dunno. I always buy One Size clothes.'

'No wonder you always look like a bundle of washing. One size is admitting defeat. Try this on.' He had an eye for harmony of colour but not this time.

I heard a grunt of approval. A red dress was flung over the top of the screen. It was a mass of shimmering fringes. It would fold away into a jiffy bag.

'It's not *Twelfth Night*,' I objected.

'I didn't say everyone has to wear Elizabethan period. Fran will be in a boob tube. Elinor will be entirely in black. Jessica will come Italian. Put that on and let's see what you look like. And be quick about it. They will be queuing at the door soon. The Press are always early for drinks.'

It was a 1920's flapper dress in geranium red silk, fringes all the way down to the knee. The neckline was scooped out but I had good shoulders to show, and my arms were equal to exposure. But this red, with my hair?

I twirled round. 'I look like a lampshade,' I cried. 'Don't turn me on.'

'Quit the Goldie Hawn. Try the shoes.'

They didn't quite fit but as they were high-heeled, cross-barred sandals, I could tighten the straps enough to keep them in place. Joe was standing behind me, grinning. He pulled off the elastic band and flung it into a bin.

'And do something with your hair. You're the first company

47

person they'll see so you must make a good impression.'

I took off the sandals and ran back upstairs to find an empty dressing room. I brushed out my mass of hair and pinned it up with anything handy. A couple of combs, some pins and a peg clip. Hit and miss but it looked fashionable in a weird and wild, abandoned way. Then I flicked on some blusher, outlined my eyes with black khol and my lips with red. Lashings of mascara. I'd probably catch some ghastly eye disease, using a borrowed mascara.

The result was surprising. No one would recognize me at fifty yards. The prompt had transformed into a butterfly. A shimmering red one, with wings.

'Good evening,' I said, standing in the foyer of the theatre as if I was the Front of House manager. 'May I see your invitation.' I wasn't having gatecrashers. 'Please go through the theatre. Food and drink on stage. Enjoy yourself.'

The strolling players were in full swing. I vaguely recognized a few tunes but they were doing their own thing. The beat was not medieval. It was rock and roll. 'I don't need an invitation,' said Fran, sweeping by. She was in a tight silver lamé dress, obviously nothing on underneath. It had tiny shoulder straps twinkling with fake jewels. She'd be frozen going home. 'I'm in the cast. I'm understudy to the lead, Elinor Dawn.'

'I know that, Fran,' I said. 'I'm checking the Press, not the cast.'

She looked at me, then gasped. I suppose it was a shock. Then her eyes narrowed. She was wearing her dead doll Barbie face so the gasp nearly split it.

'Sophie? What are you doing dressed up like that? You look a fright.'

'Mr Harrison wanted a fright on the door so that the Press didn't run the wrong way. Once past me, they'll never come out. Good for publicity.'

'Well, I don't know where you got that dress. It's seen better days.' She smoothed her lamé. 'Mine is Jens Laugesen. Very avante-garde.'

I raised an eyebrow. 'Mine is vintage 1920, I believe. One of those precious costumes only lent out to special people. Before avante-garde was invented.'

She flounced by with a huff and a puff, sashayed into the auditorium, her buttocks clearly defined. She didn't look back, already searching the freeloading critics for one who might be persuaded to write at length about her blossoming career.

There were quite a few journalists who turned up without an invitation, lost in the post etcetera. I let them in. They had a job to do. There was something for everyone to write about. I recognized several television executives. It would be good if Joe got a few sofa interviews before the opening of the show. That deep English-American accent would wow anyone at breakfast time. And he'd have plenty to say.

Elinor arrived, swathed in black chiffon. 'I wore that red in *The Boy-Friend* when I played Dulcie,' she said, nodding. 'It suits you perfectly.'

'Fabulous,' said Byron with a wink, escorting Elinor in. 'You clean up good, girl. Carbolic soap?'

'How about taking some time off,' said Joe from the doorway. 'Nearly everyone's here now. I want you to network, circulate, talk.'

I froze. 'I don't do network,' I stumbled. 'I wouldn't know what to say.'

'Talk about the play. You know more about it than anyone else here.'

He started to lead me into the theatre. It was a swinging crowd. They were knocking back the ale and the food and the noise level was decibels high.

'I could tell them that the first performance of *Twelfth Night* was in the courtyard of Wilton House for the Earl of Pembroke.'

'I thought it was *As You Like It*,' he said, his eyes narrowing, '2 February 1602, first performance.'

'The house is still owned by the descendents of the man who built it,' I went on. 'A performance of *Twelfth Night* at a feast was mentioned in an Elizabethan Diary written by John Manningham, a barrister. But your date is right.'

'It all makes copy,' said Joe, pushing me towards the drinks area. 'Have a drink, Sophie. Try the elderberry. It'll loosen you up.'

'Shakespeare died after a drinking spree with his mates. I think

Ben Johnson was one of them. He got a fever and died,' I said with determination. I was a mass of nerves now, poise fast shredding despite the gorgeous dress.

'I don't want to know about his death,' said Joe. 'He died on his birthday and that's bad enough. We want to know about his life. Go circulate and talk.'

Call the wine unusual. It tasted like water with a dash of some fragrant wildflower from a hedge. And that something was potent. It logged straight to my head. Brother, it was strong. Maybe I should eat. But the food was disappearing as if a flock of vultures had descended from the roof of Canary Wharf. I found half a strawberry and some flakes of pastry. Any minute now I'd be eating the church foliage.

It was like being on stage, all these people milling round me and talking. The female journalists wore uniform black mini dresses or black trouser suits with white silk blouses. Most of the men wore suits but had discarded the tie. Open-neck shirts were the order. Some of the older men had grey ponytails.

Fran was draped suffocatingly round a young reporter who was making notes of everything she said. Elinor had her own circle of admirers, mostly aging stage-door Johnnies but she was loving it. There was a silver-haired television mogul who seemed to be spellbound.

I looked around for Bill but he was nowhere to be seen. He was probably off down the pub for a proper pint and some chips. Receptions were not his style.

Joe made his few words dynamic and brief, plenty of sound bites. He said what was necessary and not an extra word. The Press appreciated not having to listen to loads of ethnic waffle.

I was a mass of quivering nerves by now. Stage fright, yet I wasn't on stage. Yet, I felt people were looking at me, waiting for me to say something and I didn't know my lines. I felt my muscles becoming rigid. It was an old nightmare.

The Royale Theatre began to expand, growing in size until it became huge. It was blowing me away. I was dwindling in stature, shrinking, but my blood was pumping like mad. My head was spinning. It was that red mist clouding my eyes again.

'Joe,' I said but he didn't hear me. He was talking to some blonde, svelte female journalist from one of the Sundays. She was gazing at him with calculated interest. If he relaxed too much, she'd bite his arm off.

'Did you say Wilton House?' someone asked me.

I nodded. 'In the courtyard.' It came out as a croak. I wanted to disappear but I was chained to the stage by the fringe of my dress.

'The Earl of where?'

I couldn't remember. I couldn't even remember my own name or why I was there. Not a star, not cast, nothing. Everyone was laughing and having a wonderful time. My body was folding up. Any minute I'd be a parcel.

Some place to hide. That's what I needed. I fled past my corner and down the stairs, holding on to the plastered wall. There was a sense of toppling as I lost touch with the surface.

I fell on to the last step, and sat, crying with a dazzling intensity. They were not only tears for the night, but for the years past. A time not forgotten. The memories were as clear and sharp as today.

CHAPTER SIX

Joe was leaning over me. My face was wet with tears that dripped in all directions. He gave me a handkerchief, a real linen one, not a tissue.

'Blow,' he said.

'I c-can't,' I whispered in a storm of sobbing.

'Don't be ridiculous. Why are you behaving like this? The reception is a great success. Everything is buzzing. It couldn't be better. Stop acting like a silly juvenile lead.'

I didn't want Joe around, seeing me like this. He was part of the ghostly torment. But I couldn't tell him that. It was buried under a frost of pain. I was happier on my own.

'Go away,' I sniffed. 'Go back to your adoring audience. Make another speech. Leave me alone.'

'You're talking nonsense, Sophie. Do I care about the Press? Yes, they are a necessary force. Feed them, fill them full of drink, then send them home. That's all. They know little about real life. But we need them and they need us. I care a lot more about my theatre company.'

It was a river of misunderstanding. We were talking about different things. I dragged myself back to now.

'*Twelfth Night* isn't real life,' I said, blowing my nose. 'It's all fiction and fantasy.'

'But we are real people bringing the story to life for our audiences. We're making the story seem real for them. Don't you see that, Sophie? It's nothing to cry about.'

'You can tell me when to prompt and not to prompt, and you can make me wear a red dress when in my right senses, I would never wear red with my hair. But you cannot tell me when to cry and when not to cry.'

I wiped mascara and black liner on to his pristine handkerchief. Try getting that out without using Vanish. It was cold down in the basement, enough to freeze-dry tears. Roman ladies used to collect their tears in little glass phials. They found some phials at Pompeii, only those ladies didn't have time to fill them. I wondered where exactly had I left my own clothes.

My skin was obviously turning blue because Joe got up and put his black jacket round my shoulders. It was still warm from his body and did extraordinary things to my thinking. He was wearing a black long-sleeved polo-necked jersey so was protected from the cold. Perhaps this basement ran alongside some Victorian sewer pouring effluent into the Thames. It even smelt cold.

'Collect your gear,' he said abruptly, 'and put it in a carrier bag. We're going to celebrate with some supper. I want to see you still wearing that red dress.'

It was an order. I nodded, not having the wits left to argue. A quick bite to eat, then I could go home and climb into a warm duvet. Then I remembered that Joe lived in the same house now. Anyway, I had run out of coffee so I didn't have to offer him a late, late cup.

If I had been expecting a cosy little supper for two, then I was mistaken. Nearly all the cast were putting on wraps and coats and gathering in the foyer. It was going to be feeding the five thousand, not a simple thank-you for your wonderful hard work, Sophie.

My disappointment vanished in seconds. Sometimes I was an instant party girl. The poncho didn't look bad over the red dress and it was worth seeing Fran's raised eyebrows when I gave Joe back his jacket. We piled into taxis, talking non-stop, gathering warmth from close proximity. Bill managed to squeeze himself into a twelve-inch space next to me. I could feel his thigh against mine. It was the nearest he was ever going to get, but he never quite got the message.

We went to a Greek taverna with lots of vines and bottles hanging from the ceiling and faked Roman wall paintings. Joe had

53

booked a long table. It was already set with Greek wine and masses of dips and raw veggies and other Greek bits and pieces. Illyria was somewhere Greece, wasn't it? Clever Joe. I'd forgotten I'd been drinking elderflower wine at the party, only soaked up with four flakes of pastry. I hadn't taken seriously the warning that it was potent.

Jessica, our dedicated Olivia, was sitting next to me. She looked somewhat disconcerted by the venue. Perhaps she thought we were going to be served goat.

'I'm definitely not drinking ouzo,' she said. 'That stuff is lethal. We've got to work tomorrow.'

'You've got to work,' said Claud, still in character as the conceited Malvolio. 'I get all the laughs without even trying. But those wrinkled yellow stockings are ghastly. Talk about Norah Batty. I ought to be paid danger money. I could be arrested.'

'The wine looks like straight Greek table wine. Nothing to worry about,' I said, reassuring Jessica. A nice-looking Greek waiter was pouring it out all along the table. I gave him a smile. 'It'll taste lovely.'

More waiters were bring out grilled lamb dishes and kebabs, artichokes and asparagus salad and stuffed aubergines. A cheesy sort of tart arrived topped with anchovies that looked mouth-watering.

'Not a goat in sight,' I said, prattling on to no one in particular. 'Did you know that Shakespeare invented the word anchovy? He invented loads of words, zany, vast, useless, grovel. If he couldn't find the word he wanted, he made up one.'

'So how do you know that the word anchovy didn't exist before him?' Bryan asked. He was in a good humour because he'd had his photo taken with Elinor for *The Sun*. He thought that meant he was still appealing to younger readers. They were, in fact, going to take the mickey out of his velvet smoking jacket and Garrick Club tie. It was one of those 'worst dressed men' stunts, I'd heard.

'There wasn't an English word for little salty fish, only the Spanish anchova. It's in *Henry IV*, something to do with Falstaff's pocket—' My voice trailed off. I felt like Renee Zellweger in a Bridget Jones extremely sozzled flap.

'What a brainbox,' said Fran, sucking on a carrot stick. 'No wonder Sophie never gives prompts on time. Her nose is always in some book, reading useless facts.'

'But I don't think that's useless,' said Elinor, calming waters. 'I think it's fascinating. Thank you, Sophie, for telling us. Now who wants some of this delicious salad?'

Elinor was looking like a cat who'd found the double cream opened. I think she had met someone new.

Joe was watching me. I could sense his eyes aimed in my direction. I kept my head down when it was not in a wine glass. The good-looking young waiter had my measure and kept filling it. I began to like him very much.

At some point in the supper, Joe stood up, glass in hand, tapping it with a spoon. It rang clearly like a bell.

'I know you don't want another speech from me, one is quite enough. But I can't let the occasion pass without thanking the young woman who made our press reception such an outstanding success. The food might have been a little strange and the music not entirely original medieval but it all worked, and that's what matters. Please stand and raise your glasses to Sophie, our hard-working prompt.' Joe grinned in my direction. I suddenly realized that he meant me.

Everyone stood up including me. Bill tugged at my arm. 'Not you, you daft twit. Sit down. We're toasting you.'

'To Sophie, our hard-working prompt,' said the cast, slurping more drink. 'Our g-gorgeous prompt.'

'Sometimes our prompt,' Fran added with her usual brand of acid. 'When she's awake.'

'Thank you,' I said, nodding generally. 'You are all very kind. My dear friends. Well, most of them, anyway.'

Ice creams, sorbets and fresh figs were arriving now but I couldn't eat a single mouthful more. It had been a lovely supper and a mile of taste buds away from my pedestrian beans on toast and chopped cheese and apple in front of late-night telly. I wanted to tell Joe how much I had enjoyed it, but Fran was superglued to him and ready to pounce if I so much as looked.

'That was a lovely meal, wasn't it?' I said to Jessica. She had relaxed and was telling me about her early days in rep. But she had no sense of humour and her stories were relentlessly banal. Maybe one day she would make a joke and her porcelain skin would crack.

Claud, on the other hand, had launched into his repertoire of jokes. He'd once been a standup comic when he could stand up. He'd worked all the clubs.

Everyone was leaving, a little unsteadily. I didn't think I could stand up, let alone walk. Perhaps I would wait until everyone had gone and then I could crawl out.

'Come on, Sophie, we may as well share a taxi,' said Joe. 'Stir yourself.'

Fran sidled up to him, flashing her smoky eyes. 'How about coming back to my place for a brandy?' she said. 'A nice way to round off the evening.'

Round off the evening? Was that what horizontal wrestling was called these days? Joe was shaking his head. He was always so polite.

'Sorry, Fran. Early start tomorrow. I've the technical in the morning.'

Bill groaned and clutched his chest. 'The technical. I'd forgotten all about it. Jesus, it'll be a bloody disaster.'

'No, it won't,' I said comfortingly. I had no idea what I was talking about. 'Not a disaster. Perhaps a bit of a shambles. You mark my words, mister.'

Joe was pushing my head through the poncho and pulling me to my feet. 'Where's your bag, lady?'

'What bag lady?'

'Your clothes. Remember them?'

Elinor put the carrier bag into my hand. 'Are you looking for this, my dear?' She was amused at my disarray.

Taxis appeared like magic on the street or had Joe ordered them? We all piled in, dropping people off at different places. This time I was squashed between Joe and Elinor. They kept me more or less upright. I very much wanted to go to sleep, a real sleep, like a ten-day coma with a handsome TV doctor hovering at my bedside.

Street lights flashed by like it was Christmas, only it wasn't Christmas. Not yet. I wondered where I was being taken. Perhaps back to the theatre. Did I have to do the clearing up? Yes, was that it? Do this, Sophie. Do that. Find a j-cloth.

The taxi stopped in a street that I vaguely recognized and Joe hauled me out on to the pavement, paying off the driver. 'Thank you. Goodnight.'

'I'll go and clear up now,' I said, wavering, happy to go and sweep.

'Clear up what?'

'The theatre,' I said. 'I'll have to clear up the stage after the party before the . . . before the. . . .' Now this was worrying. I was not sure of what it was before.

'Yeah, yeah, you can clear up the theatre tomorrow, Sophie, but first let's get you into bed.' He was unlocking the front door and propelling me into the hallway, both at the same time.

I sort of remembered the place, which was nice. And Joe smelt nice. He smelt very nice, after-shave and shower gel, and plain macho masculine. I sniffed the aromas and wallowed in the sensual pleasure.

'Up we go,' he said, pushing me towards the stairs.

'Up we go,' I said, leaning on him. He was one tall guy. I had forgotten how tall he was. 'Up we go.'

Except that I wasn't going up. I was more like sitting down. The word up didn't have a recognizable meaning. I looked at him for clues.

'Ye Gods, I can't carry you up three flights of stairs, Sophie,' he said. 'I'm not Superman. How much do you weigh? You've got to help.'

'I'll help,' I said happily, holding on to him. 'Up we go.'

I'm not sure how we got there but Superman must have been giving me a hand. Then Joe was looking in the carrier bag for my keys and unlocking the door to my flat. He seemed to know what he was doing even if I didn't. It was always thus. He was always the one who knew what he was doing.

'Home,' said Joe. 'Into bed now.'

'Up we go,' I said.

'No more up we go, it's down we go now, into bed. Where is your bed?'

'I don't know. I don't know where my bed is. It's probably been taken away,' I smiled knowingly. 'Yes, it's been taken away.'

He was pulling off the poncho and the sandals. Then he carefully slid the red dress over my head and hung it on a chair. He guided me towards my bed and wrapped the duvet round me like I was a parcel. That's right, I was now actually a parcel. Send me somewhere sunbaked and sandy.

'This is your bed,' he said. 'It's for sleeping in. Goodnight, Sophie.' He hesitated for a second, on the verge of going, as if he might kiss me, but he didn't. I think he sighed and stood back, a shadowy figure now as he turned off the bedside lamp.

I was not surprised. After all, it wasn't Christmas yet, despite the bright lights outside. Christmas was a long way off, at least I thought it was.

'I think I'm going to sleep now,' I said, even more happily. 'Night, night, my Superman.'

CHAPTER SEVEN

Hangovers are not my normal scene. But it was there the next morning, staring me in the mirror. I put my face in cold water hoping to freeze out the dull ache in my head. It was many years since I had felt this bad.

I looked at the wavering idiot in the mirror. 'And just who are you this morning?' I asked.

The reflection didn't have the strength to reply. It staggered back to bed.

About midday I surfaced again and managed to struggle into yesterday's clothes. My face was streaked with stale make-up. Breeding ground for early wrinkles. Always clean face, moisturise, tone etc, they say. How long since I last toned? It was a foreign word.

I drank some water, tottered downstairs and let myself out. The fresh air hit me like a wet sponge. It would have to be the bus this morning. I couldn't walk more than five yards without serious help.

I normally enjoy stalking London from a bus top. Watching the streets and houses pass by and curtained windows appearing above shops. Glimpses into other people's homes. Everything looks different from the top of a bus. Trees brushed their golden leaves against the framework like gloved hands, clouds were like bruises. By the time I reached the theatre, I felt almost normal.

'You look dreadful,' said one of the stage hands as I walked backstage. He was either Alf, Bert or Fred. He was carrying some of the court tapestry hangings.

'I am dreadful,' I agreed. 'But I'm working on it.'

Bill Naughton and the stage hands were running around like demented squirrels who have forgotten where they buried their nuts. The lighting wizard was dancing over his switchboard in the projection box. He knew his remote controls, memories, pre-set keys and thyristor dimmers. The lighting for the cyclorama was crucial, especially in the shipwreck scene. Joe Harrison was roaring instructions into his mike from the stalls. This much had to be done. If the technical was not right, then it didn't matter what words the actors said. That much I knew from my days as the lowest ASM of ASMs in rep.

That was my non-scary route to being a prompt. ASMs often had to prompt if no one else was around. And I was also call-boy, in charge of props, frequently all jobs at the same time. It had been a ruptured learning curve but one that I took on board with humility. I wasn't going to be a star. No name in lights. No first nights. So I trained myself to anticipate every need. It was an unrecognized art.

And I'd taken on other part-time jobs, waiting at tables, bar work, Christmas sales assistant. Once I'd prompted two shows at the same time, which meant a lot of running between theatres and timing as precise as Greenwich.

I sank back into a chair in the back stalls. They paid a lot of money for this seat but the view wasn't that good. Did management know that? I rarely spoke to management, believed in keeping my head down and out of sight. They were faceless people, banking the money, signing cheques, making decisions.

Joe Harrison did not look as if he had been up half the night, wining and dining his cast and helping the idiot prompt to bed. He was fresh and dynamic, on top of his world, trousers pressed, open-necked white shirt and dark navy fleece. It was sickening. He was talking to Lights on the intercom.

'Let's get the balance of the lighting right, footlights and battens,' said Joe.

Hilda had been working on his costume designs for days. She was trundling back and forth with armfuls of velvet and brocade and seafaring hessian. I slide out of my seat and took a devious route to wardrobe.

'Do you want any help?' I said.

'Oh, would you Sophie? Thank you,' said Hilda, brow furrowed. 'I can't sew and show. He wants to see everything at once. You know.'

'I know,' I said. 'What's next?'

'This is Olivia's costume for Act I.'

I climbed the stairs with my arms overflowing with stiff black material. It was intricately pleated with tiny looped buttons. Olivia was in mourning for her brother. I felt swamped with her grief, just carrying the dress. Some of it was the hangover.

'Sophie? What the hell are you doing here?'

'It's so terribly sad,' I said to the empty theatre. 'She's lost her brother, a man she adored. For seven summers she will keep afresh a brother's dead love.'

'For heaven's sake, Sophie. Leave it, will you? You're not prompting now. This is a technical.'

'Here is Olivia's costume,' I said, holding it up. 'Made to your design. Does it suit the role? What do you think? Is she mourning enough?'

'Black is black,' he barked. 'It'll be the way Olivia wears the costume. Take it away and don't bother me again. I've got enough to do.'

'You said you wanted to see all the costumes.'

'Did I? Well, I don't remember. Bill, what's happened to the gauze? It's hooked up. Sort it out.'

'Sorry, technical fault.'

I traipsed back downstairs to Wardrobe. 'He says it's perfect,' I told Hilda. 'Exactly what he wanted.'

'Oh, good, thank goodness. He has such strange ideas. I know they'll look magnificent on stage but they are not easy to make.'

I put on a Gwyneth Paltrow attitude for my next appearance. She can be so dignified and aloof. I timed my arrival on stage with a pause in the technical proceedings. Joe was beginning to look glazed.

'Yes?' he said.

'Maria,' I announced. 'Scheming gentlewoman.'

'I know who she is,' he said wearily.

'She has a sharp and witty tongue.'

'Go away,' he shouted. 'I don't want to see you or hear you again.'

'This is her costume. Aren't you interested?'

He tore his attention away from the script to the costume I was holding up. It was a painful process. I doubted if he was taking in an inch of the serving woman's simple homespun clothing. I shook out the linen cap with downcast eyes.

'Go away and do what prompts normally do when they aren't prompting. Go shopping. Read a book. Anything except interrupt my technical.'

I vanished downstairs, gathering shreds of pride around me like another costume. There was plenty of sewing to be done and I could about see to thread a needle. Hilda made a gallon of strong black coffee which helped a lot.

'I gather it was some party after the reception,' said Hilda, trying to make a cap out of sweeping feathers for Feste, the clown.

'You didn't come?'

'No, I peeped into the Press do and then went off home. I've an elderly mother to look after and I leave her alone enough as it is. She sits in front of the television all day. Cheaper than Prozac.'

'Does she know what she's watching?'

'Heavens yes, she's a dab hand with the remote. Zaps from soap to soap, checking situations. She knows more about them all than I do. She could go on *Mastermind* easily if she could manage that walk to the black chair.'

'Good for her,' I said, sorting a box of buttons and buckles for Hilda. She needed six matching silver buckles for Sebastian's costume. Joe ought to come down here and see the miracles Hilda was performing.

There was a lot of hammering going on upstairs. The technical had finished by the sound of it and urgent repairs and alterations were in progress. We were rehearsing Act II, scene 1, the sea coast, at two o'clock. The shipwreck was a miracle in the making. Thunder and lightning and waves.

I went quietly to my corner, not that keeping quiet made any difference. The hammering and banging was horrendous. My ears went into rehab. I looked down into the stalls. Joe was fast asleep, long legs draped over the arm of the next seat, head cradled back on his shoulder, floppy hair falling over his face. He looked most uncomfortable. He'd wake up with cramp in his neck. There was nothing I could do. He wouldn't thank me if I woke him to suggest he used the couch in Elinor's dressing room.

The cast were creeping in with varying degrees of hangover. Bryan looked quite green as if he had been drinking pond water all night. Elinor was incredibly brave and jaunty but winced at every unnecessary step. Fran wore an extra inch of make-up. Only Jessica seemed unaffected. Perhaps she had been emptying her wine into the potted plant behind us.

Joe stirred, brushing his hair aside, and sat up with a jerk.

'Act II, scene 1, the sea coast. Stand by Viola and Malvolio. Enter Antonio and Sebastian. Antonio, you're an old sea captain, not the back row of *Chorus Line*. Walk like one,' he said.

Sea-legs, I noted in a margin. Walk with sea-legs. It would be fun to practise sea-legs with Tony, who was playing Antonio. He was a private person. He had probably done that on purpose, to rile Joe, a touch of *Dirty Dancing*.

It was a smallish part but Tony knew his lines. I noticed he was growing a beard. Always the professional. His career was on the wane although once he had been a matinée idol, loads of lead parts in low budget Ealing Studio movies. Years ago I would have queued for his autograph. Now I was prompting him.

'If you will not murder me for my love,' I said.

'I know, I know,' he said abruptly. 'It was a pause, a dramatic pause.'

'Sorry. I'll mark it.' I didn't mind.

'If you will not murder me for my love, let me be your servant,' he went on. The scene continued to the end. Viola and Malvolio followed in a street scene. It went well, flew. I could see that Joe was pleased.

'Well done, both of you. Scene 3, Olivia's House.'

The afternoon wore on as slowly as a weekend queue of

double-piled trolleys at a supermarket check-out. Singles eyed each other in case we had more than nine items in our baskets. I could feel my eyelids starting to glue. I didn't care if they knew their words. Any minute now I would prompt with a line from Christopher Robin. See if anyone noticed.

'Ten minutes, everyone,' Joe announced. 'And if you have any dramatic pauses, new or old, intentional or unintentional, please see our prompt so she can mark it in her book. You know that she needs to mark all moves, business and pauses arranged in the dialogue.'

I felt a small glimmer of satisfaction. Joe had noticed Antonio's unfairness and made it a point. Thank you, Mr Harrison. I'll carry up your post on a wet day.

My legs creaked as I tried to stretch them. The tea station was about three miles away and the biscuits would be soggy before I got there. The only sustenance available was a peppermint in my pocket which had lost half its wrapping paper and was sticky with fluff, crumbs and unmentionable debris.

Bill Naughton was there before me. He slipped his arm round the area which I jokingly called my waist.

'So how are you doing, flavour of the month?' he asked, pressing the coffee button.

'Flavour? Don't understand.'

'Haven't you seen the morning papers? Full of the press reception, highly original concept, medieval food, medieval music. Good preview of the show. Even if the chocolate fountain didn't turn up.'

'Didn't it?'

'No. Not a flake.'

'Then we won't pay for it.'

'Has he thanked you yet? You know, money?'

'No, but he made that speech at the party. It was a job to do and I did it.' Call me slob in harness.

The theatre still smelled of the party. The scent of elderflower drifted from the curtains; beef in pastry was being swept off the floor; the scent of quinces and strawberries clung to the undisturbed air. It was nearly in the past. Soon yesterday's papers would be wrapping chips.

I wondered if Joe would ever understand my passion for the play? Was he on my wavelength? Once he had been, a long time ago. Nothing that he would remember now. Hunger, starvation, homelessness were things that were purposely forgotten. I didn't blame him. I only blamed him for changing so much.

I took my tea in styrofoam and escaped to a corner where I would be undisturbed. London was outside, a crowded, noisy, fear-ridden metropolis with a history of centuries only a few feet beneath the cracked pavements. It worried me. All these Starbucks coffee outlets occupying the sites of Georgian coffee shops that had real character, real people drinking and shaping the world. Men with more than their annual million bonus on their mind and whether they could afford a journey to Middle Earth. I was nearly broke.

'Have I thanked you for last night?' It was Joe Harrison. He had a coffee in one hand, script in the other. His hair was flopping over in that old remembered way. Perhaps I ought to take a photo of his hair so that I'd remember him in thirty years. In thirty years? Where would I be when I was officially an old person?

'There was the speech,' I said. 'I don't remember a lot after the Greek taverna. That was a good idea, thank you. Loved the food, such fun. Different.'

'You drank too much on an empty stomach.'

'There's an epidemic going around.'

'Did you sleep well?'

'Like a wall.'

I had an awful feeling. Why this interest in my sleeping? How did I get from the taverna to my bed? I didn't remember the transition. Perhaps Superman had taken me in his arms and flown me home.

'How did I get home after the party?' I asked.

'A magic carpet. The Genie was navigating. But you did remember to say goodnight, very nicely, thank you.'

'Was I standing?' This was important.

Joe had a sip of his coffee. He was taking in too much caffeine. I ought to warn him. 'More or less,' he said. 'Depending on which view you took.'

He wouldn't tell me any more and I was left to guess. There was a ghost of a wink, or it could have been a strange and uncanny trick of the light.

CHAPTER EIGHT

Fran was up to something. I could smell it as clearly as a dead mouse rotting in a boat truck. And this old Royale Theatre had plenty of those. The Arts Grant had gone a long way to refurbishing the inside and outside of the old building but it had not exterminated the rat runs.

It still had an aura of plush and gilt, with cherubs and nymphs waving the masks of comedy and tragedy. And our new, rich red curtains were magnificent. Pity Joe didn't want to use them in this run. It was going to be an open stage with lighting dimmed for scene changes. No hydraulic jacks raising the floor to the roof in our theatre. We were not obsessed by theatrical machinery. The elderly stage had a slight rake, rising from the front to the back wall.

But Fran was definitely negotiating a rat run. All slinky-tailed and beady-eyed, sharpening her claws, painting them Russian red in the wings. Something was going on but I couldn't work out what it was. She had the self-satisfied look of a well-fed poodle.

'Wasn't it a lovely party?' she gushed as she stood by me ready for her entrance. I was taught that if you had an entrance you began several yards back in the wings so that your clothes had movement as well. Exits too should have the same continuation of movement. No emergency stop once offstage. She didn't work that way. Too exhausting for fragile zero frame.

I nodded. I didn't want to talk. 'The Press were great,' I murmured, not taking my eyes off the page.

'Not really, they were a bit boring, although there's a lot about me in the newspapers today. Rising star, they said. I mean the Greek party that Joe threw for us. It was my idea, you know. It began as the two of us, going out for an intimate meal, but somehow it grew. He has such a generous nature.' She looked down, coyly, as if hiding the extent of his generosity. 'I didn't mind.'

I didn't believe a word of it. Fran had been as surprised as the rest of us. And I hadn't seen today's newspapers. I ought to look at them in case I had made some monumental blunder, like forgetting to invite the editor of *Hello* magazine.

Fran made her entrance, managing to tread on my foot at the same time. Quite a skill, her maiming instinct, but I knew her real victim was Elinor. I glared at her. I wanted to do her serious harm. I would have to curb this killer impulse before Fran was found hanging from the proscenium arch, noosed in her own black fishnets.

Elinor was not having a good rehearsal. She had been in the wrong place several times and once she entered down right instead of down left which threw everyone. Joe was keeping his temper. I think he was discovering a soft spot for the struggling Elinor, which was not good news for Fran.

'I know I don't keep exactly to the scripts suggested entrances,' he said patiently. 'But every one that I have changed, I have asked you to mark in your book. And your moves, they should have been marked. They've been fixed for days.'

'I know, I know,' said Elinor. 'And I looked at them this morning, I swear I did. Just to make sure I knew them. And I do.'

'I suggest you look at them again,' said Joe. 'With your prescription glasses on,' he added.

Elinor wore fashionably narrow spectacles for close reading. Who doesn't these days? It would be me next. I'd get two for the price of one at SpecSavers. Or pick up those pound jobs which are bits of magnifying glass in plastic frames. Then I could have a pair on every shelf, in every room, beside every book. Call me Four by Four Eyes without the parking tickets.

'Prompt. Line!'

'Methinks his words do from such passion fly,' I said swiftly. Close one. They were Viola's lines.

'Surely the officers and Antonio go out the other way?' said

Elinor. She was floundering. She should not have questioned their exit, right or wrong, but kept her mouth shut and stayed within her role.

She looked around, nervously. 'Am I right?'

There was stunned silence. Joe was pacing. I didn't like that. Pacing is a bad sign. The primeval lone wolf about to attack. Footprints in the snow.

'Darling,' he said. Another bad sign. Joe never called anyone darling. This was theatrical name-playing at its cheapest level and Joe had learned everyone's name and used them.

'Darling,' he went on. 'I do stage directions. You do words and act. Stanislavsky if you can. Method if you can't. I don't mind which discipline you prefer. But everything else you leave to me. I will decide. Have I made myself clear?'

The voice was bitingly emphatic. It could be heard half way across the street. I swear buses swerved.

Elinor went white-faced, looked as if she was going to faint. If she fainted then either the rehearsal would finish or Fran would take over immediately as understudy. We were nearing the end of Act III and Viola only had a few more speeches to go.

Action is not my middle name. But on this occasion something drastic was required. I did what any self-respecting prompt would do. I fell off my stool in the prompt corner and launched head first on stage, my script flying across the floor, scattering reminder slips like feeding the ducks in St James's Park.

It was a pretty spectacular skid.

There was a united gasp that vibrated round the theatre. I struggled to sit up, gathering paper and pages in every direction.

'Somebody pushed me,' I said, catching my breath, mortified. It was a cross between Glenn Close and Meryl Streep. They both do indignation.

It is also a well-known fact that I am not a good liar. Any lie-detection machine would jump out of the nearest window in self-defence.

'Right in the back,' I said, scrabbling about on my knees, collecting Post-it notes and bits of paper that I stick in to remind myself about something. From a corner of my eye I could see that

Elinor was sipping water from the bottle she kept handy in the wings, slowly as if practising how to swallow.

I could also see that Fran was glaring at me. Oh dear, had a cunning plan gone astray at the last moment? Had she planned to take over the rehearsal?

'It was me,' said Bill, waving a carved three-legged stool triumphantly. 'I was carrying this stool and tripped. Sorry.'

Joe looked at us both, expression unfathomable. His floppy hair flopped and he pushed it back. 'As I now have a tripping Stage Manager and a flying Prompt, perhaps we should take ten. They may both be earthbound by then. I sincerely hope so,' he added. He shrugged into his jacket, closed his laptop and marched out of the theatre. He was probably going to Caffe Nero on the corner. Latte in a bucket.

'Thank you, Bill,' I said. 'That was quick thinking. Well done.'

'Quicker than tripping,' he grinned. 'We had to save Elinor from the flesh-eating harpy. How about a drink tonight at the pub after the rehearsal, if we are both still in work. My treat.'

'Sure,' I said, wondering how I could get out of it. I was a rabbit caught in his headlights. Speak first and think later. I did my Goldie Hawn smile. It always worked. He went off humming, tucking the stool under his arm. Stage Managers don't move furniture or props. A stage hand normally does that job.

I escaped into the studio for a quick peek at what Joe was designing now. On the table was a jaunty leather jerkin, being sewn with thin leather strips, some finely stitched linen underwear, long-toed velvet slippers. Rapiers and shields lay on the floor, being beaten. Horned spectacle frames sat in a communal eating bowl with a couple of pitchers. I was getting a glimpse of another century through this domesticity of items. Every item had to be historically right.

But I didn't linger. Joe forbade all visitors to his studio except Hilda and Bill, or by invitation for a consultation. Elinor's dressing room was the larger one nearest the stage. She was prostrate on the couch, leafing through her script in desperation.

'I was right, I knew I was right,' she wept, pushing her slippery glasses up off the tears. 'I'm doing what it says.' She offered me some open pages at the end of Act III. 'Look, Sophie. You read my notes. It's true, isn't it? Perfectly clear.'

Actors made their own marks in scripts as the moves are set or changes made. They are often illegible, written standing up or on the run. Elinor's writing was bold, occasionally tailing off into a scribble. I knew most of the moves in that scene and Elinor had been following her own notes. But her notes seemed different to my memory and my prompt script notes.

I squinted closely at the pages. 'Where did you leave this script last night when we went to the Greek taverna?'

'In here, in my dressing room. I didn't want to take it with me, did I? I left it by the mirror, on the counter, where I always put it.'

'And was it still there today, when you came in?'

Elinor looked dubious. 'I don't really know. I think it was. I didn't notice.'

'Because I think it's been tampered with. Look, this mark "DL" for down left looks as if it has been changed from "DR" for down right. The L is written over the R. And there are several other messy looking marks where changes might have been overwritten.'

'Joe sometimes changes his mind.'

'Sure. That's his prerogative, his job, what he is here for and what he's good at. But some of these changes don't make sense. I think someone has been tampering with your notes, messing about with your script. Trying to throw you.'

Elinor went and sat in front of the mirror, touching up her make-up, collecting her composure. She looked closely at herself, placing strands of fringe hair over her forehead. 'And I wonder who that could be,' she said, dabbing powder loosely on her nose. She was keeping her true feelings well under control.

'We can't prove it,' I said, handing back her script. 'You'd better check all your moves and entrances. Ask Joe if you can have a few minutes with him, go over the changes. He'll catch your drift.'

She nodded. 'Good idea. I'll do that. Thank you, Sophie, you're a brick. I hope you didn't hurt yourself when you fell onstage. A nasty tumble.'

'Only my pride,' I grinned. 'Slightly undignified entrance.'

'I think I owe you a drink.'

71

'Hell, I've promised to have a drink with Bill tonight at The Stage Door. You know what he's like. And I don't really want to go.'

'We'll arrive together,' said Elinor knowingly. 'That should be halfway to solving your problem. He can hardly seduce you if I'm hanging around.'

'Wanna bet? Don't go shiny-bag shopping on me instead.'

I left Elinor repairing her face, her confidence already repaired. Someone had tampered with her notes. No prizes for guessing who even though there was no way of proving it. Elinor wouldn't complain to Joe; she would say she wanted to double check. No point in creating bad feeling among the cast.

There was a minute left to get some tea from the tea machine. It was out of milk and there were none of those little cartons that defied opening. The nameless soup was undrinkable. I filled a beaker with hot water and was thankful for the promise but it was too hot to drink. Pumped straight from Earth's core.

'How are the bruises?' Joe asked as he went past the prompt corner. He didn't sound as if he cared. It was a throwaway.

'Interesting shade of blue.' I could barely remember how to do Carrie Fisher. She had been off our screens for so long. She must have got fed up with that plaited hair look and Harrison Ford never making up his mind.

'That's reassuring,' he said, leaping down into the stalls. One day he would break a leg. I didn't want to be around when it happened. 'Let's get started.'

It was a good rehearsal although there was one sulky lady in waiting, performing her duties with less than good grace. Her face was in huff medium. She knew how to do huff. Huffs do not a pretty face make.

'Are we keeping you from something, Fran?' Joe asked at last. He was remarkably patient with her. Perhaps he was good with small children.

'An audition at the National,' she said.

'I suggest you go along to it then. Don't keep them waiting. I hear they are short of programme sellers.'

Nice one. Full marks, Joe.

Fran flounced her long skirt and tossed her head. 'I'm of more value here,' she said. 'I'm the only possible Viola if Elinor is indisposed. Everyone says so. You'd be in a tight spot and need all the help you could get.'

'How kind of you,' said Joe without emotion. 'We appreciate your loyalty and devotion to the company. But Elinor is looking remarkably healthy and perky since I checked the notes in her script. Pick up the line. Line!' he shouted.

'The heavens rain odours on you,' I said. I hoped it would rain a particularly nasty odour on Fran. How about squashed frogs and farmyard sewage water? That would do for a start.

CHAPTER NINE

I need not have worried about my drink with Bill turning into something more intimate and unstoppable. The entire cast migrated like lemmings to The Stage Door, some in a state of near collapse. The atmosphere was warm and stuffy and relaxing. The pinball machines and fruit machines were playing to the latest Top Ten of tuneless, toneless one-week wonders called music coming out of the loudspeakers.

Jack Daniels, the owner of the pub, waved a cheery welcome and winked. He knew his takings were about to soar. The cast could soak it up like sponges.

Elinor was first to the bar and came back with two bottles of red Shiraz and a clutch of newly washed glasses. She put them down in front of me. The colour had returned to her face and it was obvious she was relieved the day was over. She was fighting back. She was not ready to retire or take cameo character parts on television.

'You said a drink not a drunk,' I reminded her.

'Who said it was all for you?' she said, pouring out several glasses and pushing them round the table. Fran was not there to dampen the festivities. The phantom had disappeared, wearing fake Prada and high white sequinned boots.

'She said she had a date,' said Byron, burping. 'Pardon. Left in a taxi in a hurry. To the Ritz apparently.'

'There's a great snack bar round the back called the Ritz.'

'A date with Dracula,' said Hilda, eyes brightening. She had joined us for a quickie before going home and had heard the gossip.

'Teeth sharpening this evening in the old churchyard. A lost art these days.'

'How about a rota for tomorrow's tripping?' said a voice from over my shoulder. It was Joe Harrison, his hand up for attention. I froze. But he was joking. 'Bruises should be distributed evenly among the cast. It's only fair.'

'I go for that,' I said, a short-sighted Bridget Jones emerging again, minus big knickers. I wear those low-cut short boyish things from M&S. I've a pair in black lace but I haven't worn them yet. 'What a brilliant idea. We'll have a rota. Can I put your name down? How about quarter to three tomorrow afternoon?'

'Busy then, Sophie. How about half past four?'

'Done. Let me find my notebook. And a pen. What did you say your name was?'

'Shrek. Do you know how to spell it?'

'Is the donkey coming too?'

It was obvious I didn't care what I said or who he was. But bless his homesick New York cotton socks, he took it well and pushed a chair in between me and Bill. Bill shuffled along, taking his beer with him, sending a dart of malice broadside.

Joe sat down and dived for the last glass of Elinor's wine. He was in a good mood. There was an air of excitement about him.

'I'm not staying long,' he said, after the first few therapeutic sips. 'So you can gossip about me when I've gone. But I wanted to thank you all for working so hard. I know I'm not easy to work with but I reckon it's going to be a great show. Though maybe we should chain the prompt to her corner.'

'I could fall on in the interval as a diversion,' I offered. I was totally past caring what I said to him or anyone. 'It might push up the ice-cream sales or give the Press a new angle. Prompt steals show with impromptu entrance. Get it? Impromptu?'

There was a general groan.

No one could decide whether to laugh or not, but Joe was grinning and they took their cue from him. I thought it was a passable joke. He looked so energetic and alive, bouncing with vitality from a good rehearsal. It touched my foolish heart. Those brilliant eyes. I thought about liposuction and Botox. I ought to start saving up for it. Or stop eating. Or stop drinking. Stop everything was the answer.

'Did you know that Sophie is our linchpin?' Elinor said directly to Joe, her courage returning. 'Has it dawned on you yet that this girl holds us and the whole show together, mind and body and soul?'

Now this was the Shiraz Cabernet talking, I felt sure. So I looked away and wondered how to change the subject. I suddenly remembered that I hadn't returned the red dress to wardrobe. Nor could I remember exactly where it was or who took it off. A little worrying.

'Has anyone seen the papers? Did we get any good write-ups? Did they like our medieval press reception, lute and quinces?' I was gabbling. I would be gabbling on my way to the grave. Let me out of here, you fools, I'm still breathing, you've made a ******* mistake.

'They loved it,' said Joe. 'The papers on the whole were kind, something different to write about for once. They loved the lute, especially a lute playing Queen. Some of them even mentioned the costumes.'

'You've read today's papers?'

'All of them. I've got a pile of cuttings.'

'I was going to write thankyou notes.'

'There's my girl,' he whispered but the others were listening. I went starwards, like flying beside Superman in a blue nightie. Meteors flashed by, spraying me with stardust, bathing me in moonglow.

'Just doing my job,' I choked on the words or the wine. Elinor gave me a very Florence Nightingale thump.

'Do you want to walk home?' he offered. He had forgotten everyone else round the table. Other drinks were appearing, beer and lager, vodka pops, orange juice, adding to the rings of glass stains on the table. Orange juice? That was for Hilda. She patted my arm, very maternal, her neat hair coming astray.

'You walk home with him, ducks,' she said. 'It always pays to keep in with the director.' I thought about her elderly mother, zooming like an Olympic decathete between the soaps. That would be me in forty years' time, give or take a few knee replacements.

I turned to Joe. He was looking at me as if he thought I was a strange specimen that ought to be kept in a jar. Not exactly the response I wanted but it would do for starters.

'Yes, thank you,' I said. 'When I'm ready to go home and I'm not quite ready to go yet.'

'Great,' he said. 'I can wait. My round now. What do you all want? If you don't say, you won't get.'

I remembered that cold, snowy day when he ploughed through my pasta lunch like a starving refugee. Did he remember that? Did he remember anything about that day or night? The lumpy sofa, like sleeping on cobbles? I could forgive him for forgetting the sofa. The cold, icy night, when the temperature dipped to below zero? No, I don't think he remembered any of it. But I did. Oh yes, I could recall every moment. And have, many days since.

'I need to make a call,' I said, trying to find my mobile. Where had I left it?

'Use mine,' said Hilda, passing it over.

I went outside the pub to make my usual evening phone call. My mother didn't answer straight away, dragged from watching her favourite telly. I imagined my mother, long hair, red faded to grey, escaping from a bun, like an apprentice witch. They had witches in Dorset, so the legends say.

'Hello, mum. How's everything?'

'Great, Sophie. Everything's fine. Just watching the box. Useless plot but you always want to know how it ends. Will you be down for the school play at the end of term? It's going to be very good.'

'It's a bit difficult. We'll be in the middle of a run, unless the show closes, no audience.'

'I think you have to come. This is special. I won't say why. It's supposed to be a surprise.'

'I'll make it then, Mum, somehow. Remind me nearer the time.'

I listened to her small talk, letting it filter through my head. I was missing everything, being here when I should be there. When I eventually returned to the theatre group in the pub, it was as noisy as ever. Bill was deep in conversation with Byron. Elinor was discussing costumes and wigs with Hilda. Joe seemed to have gone. So had Jessica, but then she never stayed late. I was not surprised.

Time for me to slip away. I wanted what was left of the evening for myself. The twenty-four-hour store run by the Patel family round the corner from the theatre would be open. I needed milk. I always need milk. Perhaps I should keep a goat on my flat roof. There were enough weeds up there to feed it for a week.

I knew my way blindfolded to the milk cabinet at the back of the shop and opened the refrigerated door.

'Milk,' I reminded myself, in case I forgot. I occasionally get a thirties moment.

'Skimmed or semi-skimmed?' said Joe. He was holding up two separate litre cartons. 'I thought you might be running out.'

'Thank you,' I said. 'I'm always running out. Perhaps I wash in milk in my sleep. It is possible. Cleopatra used to bath in asses's milk.'

'I'm only getting you a litre,' he said. 'So no milky baths, please. Use water like the rest of us.'

'Semi-skimmed, please.'

He paid Mr Patel for both cartons and carried them outside. He stood beside me in the eerie darkness of the side street. The pavement was inky black from rain. 'Walk or bus?' he asked.

My legs were too tired to walk and too weak to stand at a bus stop in the chilled wind waiting twenty minutes for a bus that was taking the scenic route via Richmond and Crystal Palace. He read my mind.

'How about we splash out on a taxi?'

'Start splashing,' I said.

We stood on a corner at a distance from the Royale Theatre. *Twelfth Night* was already blazed in lights high up outside the theatre. 'Opening soon' flashed on and off. It looked jazzy and full of energy. Joe looked at the lights and posters of the stars and nodded. 'No getting out of it now, Sophie. Ticket sales are going well.'

'Good,' I said. 'Nothing worse than playing to an empty house. It's demoralizing for the cast.'

A taxi cruised along with its red light showing and Joe hailed it. I climbed in. We sank back in the darkness of the leather seat even if Joe was too close for comfort. At least I wouldn't have to fight him off. Bill would have been a different matter. His hands would have been everywhere, trying to undo zips and buttons before the driver even asked 'Where to, mister?'

I didn't have to talk. We were mesmerized by the petillant of shop lights and traffic lights and the ugliness of endless street furniture which the planning department thought essential to modern living. The sodium lights jaundiced the whole panorama of rotten ideas. The post-war buildings built temporarily on WWII bomb sites were still standing, decades later, monuments to austerity.

Occasionally a genuine piece of ancient London architecture came into view, looking apologetic for being Tudor or Georgian. Not a blade of grass anywhere except on my roof. This part of London was where concrete came to die. Only it wasn't left to rest in peace. It was dug up over and over again by the utility companies in the name of progress.

I could tell by the uneven road surface when the taxi turned into our street. My backside knew the bumps. Joe paid for the taxi and said goodnight to the driver.

'Great talking to you, Sophie,' said Joe, putting his key into the front door lock. 'That's what I like about you. Such scintillating, mind-blowing, esoteric conversation. Never a dull moment in your company.'

'Sorry,' I said, searching for my key. 'I didn't want to be accused of chatting you up. No getting on the right side of the director stuff.'

'No risk of that. You're not my type.'

'Narrow escape then,' I said, accepting the milk. 'What do I owe you for the taxi?'

'How about a meal? Can you cook?'

Sometimes I can cook, the rest of the time I can't. Boiling an egg is a major culinary experiment. Dilemma. Did Joe mean now? This instant? Would he regard a bowl of cereal topped with walnuts as a meal? It was all I was planning at this time of night.

'Sure,' I said brightly. 'How about tomorrow?'

'Perfect. Goodnight, Sophie.'

His flat was on the first floor, all those spacious rooms and bay windows, furnished in white and stainless steel by some posh interior decorator. Rent not a problem. Joe unlocked the door and went inside without looking back, leaving me to climb the rest of the way to my weary eyrie by myself.

He could have seen me home like a gentleman. But then he wasn't exactly a full-blown gentleman. A gentleman would have left me a thankyou note, even one written in pencil on an old envelope would have been nice.

My studio flat might fit into one of his rooms, but he didn't have the view. And at night it was magic. Joe wasn't there to share it but I could pretend.

Happiness is a choice. I chose to be happy so went to bed happy, wishing I had a cat that would curl up in the crook of my knees. The wind was rattling the ill-fitting windows, trying to keep me awake. But it didn't have a chance.

CHAPTER TEN

If I really have to do this meal thing, then my morning was hostage to cleaning the flat and deciding what to cook. It had to be simple; after all, the shared taxi fare didn't amount to buying sirloin steak.

Pasta, I decided. You could buy packets of fresh tortellini stuffed with spinach and cheese, ready cooked, which seemed ideal. I could hardly go wrong heating it for three minutes, domestic goddess in apron. Add masses of grated parmesan, a tossed salad and a fancy ice cream for afters, and surely His High Lordship would have nothing to grumble about? I could toss a salad with the best of the sparing TV chefs. And without swearing.

The cleaning was more of a problem. I rushed around with lavender spray polish, hiding things in cupboards and putting bags of stuff inside the wardrobe. The windows needed cleaning but I wasn't going to go certifiably mad. There was nothing I could do about the carpet except move chairs to cover the worn patches.

My dining table was pretty small and stood in an alcove. Candles might disguise the utterly dismal fawn flocked wallpaper that was left over from utility days. Masses of flowers were the answer. I'd buy flowers for the table and put a plant in the fireplace in the sitting room. There was only an ancient electric bar fire and it smelt of burning dust when switched on.

I could hardly turn my studio flat into a penthouse suite in one morning. Joe would have to accept my modest lifestyle. Or get the West Enders to pay me more. A couple of thousand extra would be like winning the lottery.

If I won the lottery, I could buy the West Enders. The company and the theatre. Hire and fire. It would be brilliant. I would be brilliant.

The nearest supermarket had everything, even azaleas in a pot for £2.99. I bought two packets of pasta and read the instructions. I could manage that with a bit of forward thinking, like opening the packets with scissors instead of tearing at them with my teeth.

A tossed salad only needs more tossing. I had a bottle of extra virgin olive oil to drizzle on top. But what exactly did extra mean? Extra olives? Should I add anchovies? Anchovies for the Bard. Was he watching with approval? Sometimes I felt he was peering over my shoulder, stroking his beard.

The ice cream was Cornish Cream Vanilla with streaks of White and Dark Chocolate. I could put some grated chocolate on top when I served it. The carton went in the freezer compartment of my tiny fridge. It needed a good push to get the carton past the crushed half-opened packet of frozen peas.

By the time I got to the theatre, I was brain damaged with domesticity. Joe need not think this was going to be a permanent event. It was back to a bowl of cereal real fast.

But all thoughts of tonights meal vanished once I was inside the theatre. A row of monumental proportion was in progress. Mr Joe Harrison v Miss Elinor Dawn. It was drawn swords at dawn in Hyde Park.

'No, no, no,' she was shouting. 'I refuse. I absolutely refuse. Absolutely and adamantly refuse. And you can't make me, Joe. It's not in my contract.'

'Elinor, you are playing a boy. You can't have mountain-high hair while playing a boy. The Beatles were not around then.'

'I can stuff my hair under a cap, a beret, any kind of hat. She's a girl playing a boy. Who says she has to cut off her hair?'

'I do.' Joe was adamant.

'This is barbaric and I won't do it. You can't insist. There's nothing in my contract that says I have to cut my hair. I'm going to phone my agent.'

'I don't care who you phone. Phone Brown. Phone Obama. Your hair is going to be cut. It's essential to the part.'

'What about the last scene, Act V? The Duke says let me see thee in thy woman's weeds. I would show my hair then.'

'It doesn't say so in the script. She doesn't change her costume. It's one line right near the end. There isn't time for you to change. You're still onstage.'

'But I can't cut off my hair,' Elinor was clearly very upset. 'And you can't make me. My next part is the Greek's wife in *The Comedy of Errors*. She has to have her own long hair.'

'Wear a wig,' said Joe, tiring of the argument.

'Not when I've got hair of my own,' said Elinor, hotly. 'I'm wearing my own hair for *Comedy*. I don't care what you say.'

Fran stepped forward from the wings, low-cut jeans, bare belly, skinny top. 'I'll cut off my hair, Joe,' she said. 'Anything you say. You're the boss.'

As she already had short blonde hair this was not a sacrifice deserving special mention. A couple of snips and she would be only a few obvious physical differences away from looking like a young man. Would she go along with surgical procedures?

'That won't be necessary,' said Joe, holding his temper. 'Elinor is playing Viola. A lady in waiting can do what the hell she likes with her hair.'

'And I will,' said Fran, totally unbothered by his disinterest. 'I'll make Olivia look like the unmarried old hag she is.'

'Bitch,' said Jessica, with a cool smile.

'The hairdresser is coming here tomorrow at ten,' said Joe. 'It'll be a brilliant cut. You'll love it, Elinor. I promise it'll take years off you.'

Wrong remark, brother, I groaned. Elinor flew into a tantrum. She stamped across the stage, black trousers and shirt-tails flying, her rage reaching a new proportion. I knew why.

The part of the Greek's wife in *The Comedy of Errors* was a desperate attempt to hold on to her career. Elinor knew that time was running out for her. She wasn't ready to play Miss Marples yet.

'No, no, no,' she stormed on automatic replay. 'I won't do it. I won't be there tomorrow. You can stuff your top hairdresser.'

'Then you can stuff your part,' said Joe, going plain stubborn. 'It's the part or your hair. It's your choice. You have to look right.'

Elinor looked as if she was on the verge of a nervous breakdown.

I wondered what I could do to break the tension. Falling off my stool was not on the agenda. Elinor needed saving both from herself and from Joe. As for Joe, I was planning arsenic in the tossed salad dressing.

'Phone call for Miss Dawn,' I snapped out, very loudly, very Helen Mirren running the entire Metropolitan Police Force. I'm brilliant at improvisation. 'In your dressing room. Please take it at once, Miss Dawn. Urgent call.'

Elinor paused midstride, as if wondering where on earth her dressing room was. Then she recovered herself and remembered its location, going off stage without a further glance at Joe.

He was looking at me, hard faced and disbelieving. His mouth framed the word "liar". I shrugged my shoulders. Maybe it was a centre in India cold-calling with financial advice, as they do, frequently.

I declined to comment but went to my prompt corner, script at the ready. I refused to be drawn into an argument. In most circumstances Joe had the final word on hair, beards, make-up, costumes etcetera but Elinor's next role meant a lot to her. Maybe she could wear a wig, her own hair coiled and flattened under a stocking cap. She did have a lot of hair. We didn't need a Wig Mistress, but had plenty in store.

The scenery was almost all in place and the sets were looking good. The lighting effects for the storm at sea that opened the play were fantastic. It was so realistic that without thinking I shrank back in case I got splashed by the waves.

'I think we are going to have to move you, Sophie,' said Joe, narrowing his eyes. 'You're in the way now that we have all the scenery and the props.'

'You can't move me,' I said aghast. 'I'm always here. Offstage by the footlights. I have to be close enough to see what's happening and must have full view of the stage and the players. I can sense in a second from the slightest frozen expression or stiffening of movement—'

'You don't have to tell me,' said Joe, gathering his notes. 'I know how a good prompt works. I know it requires considerable skill and concentration. It's extrasensory perception. There's a thread between you and the actors and you are alert to any change in vibration. But that thread can be broken in a flash if someone gets in your way or barges passed with a bit of hedge.'

I glowered at him. I didn't like surprises. It would take me weeks to get used to a new place, and where would that be, I wanted to ask? Front row of the dress circle, the lighting box, dangling from the chandelier in a basket?

'You could put me in tights, gild the lily with paint and I'll be on stage as a living statue. I could stand down front on a pedestal with my back to the audience so they don't see me turning the pages.'

'Very ingenious and very stupid,' said Joe, not looking at me. 'Talk to me about it after the rehearsal. Right everyone, let's get started.'

It was a brilliant rehearsal. Everyone was on their mettle, their wits sharpened by the confrontation earlier. Elinor was almost word perfect. She was putting on a great performance, showing this upstart director what she could do, hair or no hair. I could have sat out front and painted my nails.

Even the stage crew worked well. Only a few, minor mistakes. Stool left on in wrong scene, hedge falling down, a small spotlight misplaced. Nothing that couldn't be rectified before the first night.

'Well done,' said Joe, as the last notes of the jester's song died away. 'That was good. It had pace, it had feeling. You are at last beginning to work as a team. Early night, everyone. Go home and put your feet up. No pubbing. I'll see you tomorrow for the pre-dress rehearsal.'

First night. My stomach suddenly lurched with nerves. It was almost upon us. One more rehearsal and then it would be the opening night. Another opening, another show. The crowds, the critics, the celebrities. I couldn't believe it. I loved it when we got into a run, a show night after night, when I knew all the weak spots and the pauses were second nature. But the opening night was something else. It could be magic or it could be disaster.

'Want a lift home?' Joe asked. He was dialling a nearby taxi rank on his mobile. 'It's probably raining.'

'I was going to walk,' I said stiffly to show I was upset about being moved.

'Don't you need the time? Surely lots of chopping, stirring and whisking to do? Supper's still on, I hope, isn't it? I've been looking forward to it all day.'

I'd forgotten all about the meal. Chopping, stirring and whisking barely came into it but I accepted the lift. It would take me half an hour to lay the table in a civilized manner. No tray in front of the telly. I'd only got one chipped tray.

Once back at the house, I raced upstairs to get started. I suddenly had an awful lot to do and I didn't know where to start. A case of panic.

'Half an hour?' Joe called up to me.

'Half an hour,' I shouted back. It didn't seem nearly long enough. Lay table, find candle sticks, arrange flowers, grate cheese, grate chocolate but not both at the same time. I flew around. I couldn't find the place mats as it was so long since I'd used them. None of the cutlery seemed to match. I wanted to shower and change and put on something interestingly casual.

I cut up some Christmas wrapping paper as place mats. I tipped out my supply of Vitamin C tablets into an envelope and stood the candle in the jar. The salad got a brisk tossing into an old-fashioned soup bowl. Drizzle later. Grated parmesan cheese fluffed into a heap on to a bone china saucer.

It was the quickest shower I'd ever had, thirty-three seconds flat, hair as well. I was towelling it dry when the doorbell rang. I opened the door a fraction, wrapped in a bath towel.

'Ah,' said Joe, standing there, staring at the towel. 'I didn't know it was going to be that casual.' He'd changed into jeans and a navy T-shirt. His wet hair was untidy and spiky and he was carrying a bottle of wine.

'I haven't got a bottle opener,' I said.

He dived into his pocket and produced one. 'I thought of that, too. Shall I go through and open it while you dry off?'

He was going to see the pasta packets and pathetic bits and pieces of amateur cooking in my tiny kitchen area but it was too late to head him off. He was already on his way in.

My studio flat was a large sitting room and had wonderful views of London rooftops and the spiritual elevation of Wren spires. But the sleeping, cooking and bathroom areas were the size of deep-freeze container boxes. If I turned over in bed, I bumped my head on both walls. He was hardly going to have trouble finding the kitchen.

'Love pasta,' he called back, politely. 'And stuffed with spinach, my favourite. Wow. Rocket salad. The parmesan smells good.'

His eagle eyes missed nothing. He'd probably checked the cupboards.

I pulled on clean jeans and a loose blue check shirt, rolled up the sleeves. It needed ironing but too late now to worry about anything. I pulled my damp hair back with a velvet crunchie. Touch of glitz.

'I found some glasses,' he said. They didn't match but nothing does and they were cut glass. He was pouring out red wine. 'It's got to breath for a few minutes.'

'I can't wait for it to breath,' I said, taking a gulp. My courage returned. 'Would you like to find some music while I cook supper?' My three minutes of expert, cordon bleu heating up pre-cooked pasta in boiling water were about to start. I could do it. I was all geared up. No apron.

'Sure. Is this your entire CD collection? I guess you don't have much time to listen to music.'

'I've only started collecting but there are plenty of long-playing records around. The player is under the bookcase.' I remembered, too late, what else I had stuffed under the bookcase. A load of newspapers and magazines, mostly The Stage, waiting to be read, when I had time.

I gave the tortellini four minutes, just in case, served it quickly. It smelt good. Joe nodded with approval, sprinkled a mountain of cheese on top, helped himself to salad. He was hungry.

'This is very good, Sophie. It's just what I like, very simple food, thrown together in minutes. Why waste time standing around cooking? I thought afterwards that it wasn't fair to ask you to cook supper after a heavy day at the theatre.'

'I don't eat late at night and am usually too tired to cook.'

Joe raised his glass towards mine. His hair was drying and beginning to flop around. 'To our first meal together, Sophie.'

I tried not to cough on a mouthful of pasta. It was not our first meal together. But he didn't remember that other first meal, long ago. One day I would remind him.

I wanted to find out where he was going to park the prompt. I could also try to talk him out of cutting Elinor's hair. But I did neither. I am a cowardly lion at heart. Shoot me for desertion.

Suddenly I didn't want him there, sitting at my table looking relaxed, eating my food. I didn't want him in my life again. It had taken me a long time to stand on my own feet. Love is to burn, to be on fire. Pass me the extinguisher. I was starting to think in staccato jerks.

And I forgot to make my evening call, dammit. Joe was already turning my life upside down. Where had I put the arsenic? No one is allowed to buy it these days. I could hardly spike the ice cream with bleach.

CHAPTER ELEVEN

Joe sat back from the table, stifling a yawn, rubbing his eyes, muttering about still having work to do. The ice cream was good, grated chocolate on top, though I did wonder if it also had some shreds of cheese. I hadn't washed the grater in between.

He got up and stretched his legs. 'Sorry Sophie, I'm not going to help with the washing up,' he said. 'You finish the wine. It'll help you to sleep.'

I wanted to tell him that I didn't need any help. I could sleep standing up. He would be gone soon, once the run was going well and his job done. Directors don't hang about. He could go back to New York or wherever his next production was going to be staged. Back to the penthouse suite.

So there was an end to this purgatory. He would be out of my life and I could get on with living it in my slow, rising-from-the-ashes way. Throw me a lifeline, someone, to get me through the next few weeks. That was all I asked.

He'd gone downstairs before I'd even noticed. No thank you. Perhaps he found thank you difficult to say. Some men are like that. The words stick in their throat.

I left the washing up for the morning. I wanted the scent of him to linger for a little longer. I put his wine glass to one side. This was a serious case for therapy. I curled up on the couch, half asleep, sipping wine, remembering everything, every moment, every word.

My mother was delighted to get a call in the morning. 'What a surprise,' she trilled. 'Were you doing something special last night?'

'I was having supper with the director.'

'So, is he someone special?' My mum was so nosey. It comes from living in a windswept cottage on the outskirts of nowhere. The seaside town of Swanage was down the A351, south of Bournemouth. But the schoolbus stopped at the lower end of the lane. It had home-made traffic humps.

I didn't answer. Yes, the director had once been special. 'He's going to move me, the prompt, to some totally alien spot where I won't be able to hear or see and it'll make my job a nightmare.'

'Darling, that's awful. Can he do that?'

'He can do anything. He's the director.'

'You could walk out. We'd love to have you down here. We haven't seen you for ages. This is often mentioned, especially at bedtime.'

'Hardly commuting distance for my work.'

'Get a job down here. You did it before, part-time jobs. Remember? Boots are always advertising for extra assistants. And there's the library. What about all the hotels? They need seasonal staff. There are endless work possibilities. Besides, you deserve a proper holiday. I know you love the theatre but you work such long hours. We could go for lovely walks along the cliffs.'

'Any news for me?' I could hardly say the words. They always choked me.

'Well, there's the school play but you said you're not going to be able to make that, didn't you? Any hope in sight?'

'I can't see how, unless the show folds. It could bomb but I doubt it. The rehearsal last night was terrific, everyone on top form. Pre-dress this evening.'

'Must go, darling. Someone at the door. Such a rare experience out here. Hope it's not those Jehovah's Witness people. We have such long conversations which I don't understand.'

My mother came off the phone. She chose to live her life on the coast of Dorset, not far from the sea. Living my life for me. It was where I should be, wrapped up against the wind, waddling through sea puddles in wellies.

Elinor's appointment with the hairdresser was ten o 'clock. I knew Joe would have booked some top, high-class Knightsbridge snipper, tight leather pants and a ponytail. He wasn't mean. I thought I ought to be there with last minute frantic persuasion in Joe's ear or holding Elinor's hand in sympathy.

It was a brisk walk through the milling crowds of stockbroker suits to get to the theatre on time, beating the trundling London buses. I could walk faster than a bus trundled. I was eating a banana on the run. That was breakfast. Everywhere in the semi-dark of the theatre was bleak and deserted except for the cleaners.

'Hiya Mavis, hiya Maud,' I called out.

'Hello, Miss Gresham.'

I went into Elinor's dressing room. It was empty. I toured the rest of the theatre. There was no one around. Had I missed a sudden city-wide epidemic of the plague? That Chinese bird flu? Had the Lord Chancellor closed down all the theatres without anyone telling me?

Terrorist alert. That was it. I hadn't listened to the news. Perhaps London was at a standstill. But now footsteps were arriving. Stage hands, Bill Naughton, Hilda, members of the cast dragging themselves in, but no Joe, no Elinor, no Fran. Had I poisoned him off last night? Had the ice cream reached its sell-by-date and I hadn't noticed? But I had eaten the same meal and it hadn't affected me. I hadn't used the bleach.

And no Mr Snip-Snip. This was intriguing. The plot thickened but Shakespeare didn't write it. He would have done if he had been around. He'd have called it *Not As You Would Like It*.

I had brought some black coffee and added no-fat creamer. *Ready, Steady Cook* would have made four gourmet desert dishes out of that and the banana. Plus several dozen extra ingredients whipped out from under the counter.

'Where is everybody?' I asked Bill.

'No idea. Don't ask me. Late night again perhaps. I wasn't invited.'

A nasty suspicion loitered. Perhaps Joe had not gone straight downstairs to his flat, pleading tiredness. Maybe he had gone round to Elinor's place to talk her into the boy transformation, or maybe he had a late date with the fragrant Fran. Maybe he'd taken her to that stunning new bar at the Berkeley Hotel. It was called the

Blue Bar and looked like a theatrical set. It was the perfect place for spotting stars. She would consider herself as being spotted.

'Where's he going to put me?' I asked Bill.

'I don't know. Rumour has that it's in the Royal Box disguised as a cherub. Could you manage that?'

'I don't have to be here,' I said, stomping about angrily. 'I can get a job anywhere. I was phoned by the National twice last week. They're short of prompts.' This was totally fiction, easier to say than a lie.

'Then go there or help me do these drapes and then have lunch with me. I know a terrific pub that does a great sausages and mash. Lashings of onions.'

'My favourite,' I sniffed.

Bill never gave up. He was a nice enough young man but his company bored me to tears, no, not real saturating tears, but to distraction. He was also a clumsy oaf. I can't stand clumsy men. I knew what he would be like in bed, all gropes and grunts and a penis the size of a radish, with me staring at the ceiling.

I helped with the drapes as Bill was short of hands. Where had everyone gone? Was there a company bonding day out on a Thames river steamer to which no one had remembered to invite me? Perhaps Fran had organized it, which would explain the lack of an invitation.

A few people drifted in. Hilda had to sew. She had a few of Joe's new ideas to add to costumes. Her mother was still watching soaps. Apparently she had spotted flaws in the story lines and was busy writing in to the bosses. They must love her letters.

'She's amazing,' said Hilda. 'All brain, but no body. She can barely move. Arthritis, you know. It's the devil. Very painful.'

'That'll be me when I'm a paid-up old person.'

Now this was depression setting in. I could feel smiles dying on my face. There was a mental test you could take on Google. Of course, if you took it and the result was a depressing twenty-five out of forty, what did you do next? Phone a doctor? Take Quiet Life? Life told me to go down to Dorset.

I was on my fourth black coffee when Joe arrived. He threw his leather jacket on a seat and flexed his neck. His neck always seemed to hurt. I wondered if he had fallen out of an apple tree when he was young and told nobody.

'Prompt!' he shouted. The theatre vibrated. The ghosts flinched.

'I'm here,' I said, stepping forward the required half-inch. 'But no one else is on stage and the rehearsal hasn't started, so I'm off duty, so to speak.'

'We have a crisis,' he said. 'Where are you? A small crisis, but nevertheless, we have to rise above it.'

'Sure,' I said, nodding knowingly. 'Tell me and I'll rise. What sort of phoenix do you require?'

I do say the stupidest things. Without doubt, there was a gremlin at my christening. No Good Fairy with looks and good fortune and handsome princes. My christening was the tail end of conveyer belt fairies. I got the one who was having a bad hair day.

'I've been ringing around,' said Joe, screwing his hands through his hair till he looked like a hedgehog. 'Both Elinor and Fran are down with flu. Seriously high temperatures, aches and pains, sore throats, both unable to perform. Sophie, you will have to read in Viola at the pre-dress this evening. OK?'

Who was I now? Gwyneth Paltrow, Emma Thompson, Reese Witherspoon? How about Cate Blanchett? They deserted me in droves. There was only me, Sophie Gresham, left trembling in the prompt corner. My muscles went into paralysis at the thought. At least I would have a script and I could read.

'Sure,' I said. 'I'll read and I'll prompt but don't expect any costume changes. I'm at least six inches taller than Elinor. And a bit heavier, though I'm not measuring. Since I eat pasta and she doesn't eat anything thicker than watercress.'

I was reminding him of the meal. A very good meal that he hadn't said thank you for. There was a glimmer of contrition on his face. Did he remember that he had left, gone downstairs to his luxury first-floor flat, leaving me to wash up?

'Would you mind wearing a cloak?' he asked. 'Something to swish about?'

'I'll wear a cloak, but that's all,' I said. 'Close to a clodpole.'

Neither of us understood what I meant. Shakespeare wrote something with the word clodpole but its meaning was lost in time.

Spiritualists say, of course, that spirits live on but where was he among all the misty mothers, fathers and grandparents that tap on shoulders and move watches and photographs and send loving messages? Why wasn't he tapping on my shoulder, right now? Had Shakespeare ever turned up at a public séance?

'We'll start early, two o' clock,' Joe said. Other remnants of the cast were arriving, either anxious or bewildered or both. 'Elinor is ill. Flu we think, but we'll still go ahead with the pre-dress. Prompt will read in.'

'Where's the understudy?'

'Fran's ill as well. Same sort of bug.'

'Very catching,' said Bill. He was no great fan of the luscious Fran. She had scorched him a few times with a flap of her eyelashes. 'Not up to being tested. All talk and no do. Or rather, couldn't do.'

I filled in time, helping Hilda sew on braid, then I hid in the darkened wings. Even though I was only reading, it was going to be an ordeal. Not exactly stage fright but a degree near. Joe Harrison had no idea of what he was asking me to do. He had soared high, forgetting ordinary people, in his meteoric climb. He'd probably forgotten my name. Prompt came more easily to mind. The pre-dress started.

'Curtains. Duke's Palace,' he called out. The theatre went dark. I couldn't see a thing. I could barely remember how the play began.

'If music be the food of love, play on,' said Orsino, the Duke. The phrase had lived on for 380-odd years, oft repeated. Beat that, Pinter.

Then the storm, thunder and lightning and the wreck at sea exploded on stage. It was awesome. Somebody pushed me on stage and I was pretending to be drenched with sea water, staggering from the waves.

'What country, friends, is this?' I said, shaking off sea water.

And the captain said: 'This is Illyria, lady.'

I could barely remember anything. 'Oh my poor brother,' I wept. Somehow the play went on and I remembered the words and went from scene to scene with some faltering, book in hand, but unopened. The tension was high but I was mentally soaring away with the Bard. I was there in the court, being Viola, loving the Duke, caring for Olivia. Joe had completely vanished from my mind. Who was this man? I kept strong, kept fighting the nerves. Joe who?

When the play finished, hours later, with the last note of the Jester's song, I stood somewhere, not in the right place, exhausted. I had long ago melted into a puddle of nothing. The Duke said to me: 'Your master quits you' and I went, taking his hand as he took me as his mistress.

I couldn't even remember the last lines of the play. If they needed prompting then it was too late. I had nothing more to say. I was evaporating into the air. Joe could put the prompt where he liked. How about inside an upturned boat downstage right?

There was a round of applause. Sparse but then there were only about twenty people in the audience and that included the cleaners and front of house staff and some management.

'Brilliant,' said Joe. 'Bloody brilliant.'

I didn't know who he was talking to, not me certainly. I was all done up. A sort of trashy, thrown out mess, something swept up from the Thames mudbanks. Someone put a coffee into my hand. It tasted of gravy.

'Can I go now?' I asked. I meant could I go home, go away, disappear forever, slip into a pair of old slippers.

'No, you can't. We're taking some of the scenes again. Duke, that crown looks ridiculous. I didn't design that. It's not a coronation. Look at my sketches. He's indoors, relaxing, having a glass of wine, thinking about Olivia. Sea captain, what's this with scuffed trainers?'

'Er, sorry . . . not sure. I didn't know what to wear.' Tony looked worried, as if he had been all morning at central casting.

'Go see Hilda. There are boots for you. She'll find them.'

'OK.'

'Sophie.' He demanded my attention.

'I'm the prompt. You can't give me notes.'

Joe shook his head, pushing his hair back. He held up his hands in supplication. 'I wouldn' t dream of giving you notes. I wanted to thank you for reading for us. I know it was something of an ordeal for you.'

'How do you know?'

'I could feel it. I can read the body language.'

'Quit the body bit,' I said, embarrassed.

That was new. He hadn't read my body language before, that night. In fact, he had been totally illiterate, not understand what it had meant to me.

'Don't ask me to do it again.'

'Don't worry, I won't. Both our actresses hope to be fully recovered by tomorrow and back onstage. A day in bed, lots of hot drinks, aspirins. It works wonders. Take five.'

'I'd like to take a hundred and ninety-five.'

'Then pick your cards up on the way out.'

It was like a cold slap in the face. I hadn't meant what I said. Another of my useless, zany remarks gone astray.

I collected my things, coat, bag, bottle of water, and stumbled my way to the stage door, a smile welded on with superglue. It was sort of sleep walking. Someone handed me my scarf. Another patted me on the shoulder. How could Joe be so cruel?

'You don't mean this,' said Bill, blocking my exit. 'Where are you going?'

'I've had it,' I said. 'I can't take any more. Did you hear what he said? He thanked me for reading the part, then told me to pick up my cards. Wasn't he listening? I didn't read the part. I *was* the part. I *was* Viola.'

'I know, I know. He didn't mean it. Walk around, girl. Go shopping. Do something different. The show isn't the end of the world. But we can't do without you, Sophie. Think of the others, they all need you.'

'I'll go and walk by the river,' I said. 'And think of ice fairs and ferrymen. They found dead people in the river every day in those days. They fell in when they were drunk or weak with hunger.'

'Don't fall in. Come back, please Sophie.'

'I could get work as an extra, on TV, costume dramas. They are always looking for people. There are adverts in *The Stage*.'

'Oh yes? Do you want to get up and be out before dawn, lining up with hundreds of others for your costume, waiting around for hours for awful food at the canteen? You'd hate it. Be honest, would you really like that?'

'No, I wouldn't. That's true.'

I took a walk by the Embankment, stopping to read the poems on the paving stones, watching the laden barges sailing under bridges. He had been long gone before they laid the stones. Well, I couldn't find any of his sonnets.

Why didn't they include him? He'd been around, walking to his theatre, The Globe, along this bank of the river from his lodgings. These were his footsteps.

CHAPTER TWELVE

I was walking by the Thames, thinking. My wardrobe needed a significant makeover. That jazzy red flapper dress had given me ideas beyond my means. But I wasn't going to turn into a dolly shopaholic. Twice a year was twice too often. Most shop assistants gave me the creeps, long nails and short noses and Bambi-sized clothes. I longed to be served by a normal-looking, jolly lady who said she had a daughter just like me.

Charity shops are thin on the ground in central London. Forget Oxford Street, forget Regent Street. But there was one surviving in Edgware Road, a bit trendy, fairly expensive, lots of good stuff donated from the nearby high-class blocks of flats.

I found some Ralph Lauren black jeans that fitted, several Jacques Verte shirts that were abandoned luxury cruisewear (did they get too seasick?), a floppy lilac mohair jersey that must have cost a bomb. The label alone was impressive. And a vibrant blue velvet scarf that changed colour with every movement. I had to have it. The entire lot wiped me out of ready money but I didn't care. This was the new me, not exactly colour coordinated but bright. Pulsating with energy.

It was the first time that I hadn't wanted to go back to the theatre. I was dragging my heels like a reluctant puppy who didn't want to go walkies. Normally, I can't wait. I'm drawn like a magnet but the scene offstage had unhinged me. A trip abroad might be a suitable change of plan. EuroStar was not far away at Waterloo Station. They would take plastic. The train leaves every hour. I could be in Paris in three hours. *Parlez-vous Français*? I could go and see the Mona

Lisa. We had similar smiles and maybe the same secrets.

But I was where I was and I couldn't cut and run. My new clothes would help bolster my confidence, I hoped. The old downtrodden image was gone, and my new bright appearance, when I appeared flashing designer labels, was ready to prompt. There was an unused dressing room near Wardrobe. I might even wear daytime mascara.

Surely Elinor would recover in time for the show? She was a real trooper. But Fran would be eager-beaver at the starting post to take over. It was her one and only chance of fame. She'd play Viola even if she was gargling with TCP between every scene and had cottonwool stuffed up her nose.

'What's the news?' I asked Bill as I slid in backstage, hoping not to be seen, laden with bags.

'Elinor is still prostrate, in bed, really ill apparently. Fran is running a high fever, but it may miraculously cure itself. You know Fran, any going virus for a bit of high-voltage drama.'

'Maybe she'll arrive at the last moment, dragging herself from her sickbed to save the show, etcetera. First night heroics,' I added.

'Or, if they are both too ill to perform, then Joe may have to cancel the opening night. It's happened before, many times. Shows do get postponed and people get their money back.'

'He would be devastated. *Twelfth Night* means a lot to him. He's done so much work, loves every line.'

'But Fran would love it more if the show had to be cancelled,' said Bill, shrewdly. 'Although she wants to play Viola, be an instant new star, to actually have to do it would be putting her to the test. Not a rehearsal this time. She'd have to go out there in front of a critical audience and play Viola. I don't think she can do it – she doesn't have the talent. Maybe she knows she couldn't do it.'

'Bill, that's awful but you might be right. She's so full of bounce and confidence that we are all taken in, but maybe she's not really up to it.'

'Let's see what happens. This is getting more interesting than Shakespeare. Pity he's not around. He'd have written another damned good play about it.'

Bill went off somewhere into the murky backstage pong of dust and glue-size. A knife-cutting draught came from some open door.

There was always a lot to do backstage, as I knew from my humble ASM days. At least I had moved on from then, had my own corner. If I knew where it was. I was stirring myself into a sour look mood, ready to hurl a few at him when Joe appeared.

So where was Joe going to put the prompt now? I didn't want to know. I had a feeling I was going to be annoyed, upset, desperate, or possibly all three.

I found the empty dressing room. It was veiled in cobwebs, hadn't had any polluted London air for months. I cleared a chair and draped my new clothes over the back. It didn't take me long to change. The lilac mohair was gloriously warm and the velvet scarf lay in shimmering folds round my shoulders; the black jeans clung, sex on legs. Mascara would be over the top, I decided. I didn't need it. Lashes are superfluous to prompting. They get in the way of page turning.

The cast were arriving back carrying take-away burgers and curries. The spicy smell filled the theatre. I'd forgotten food. I'd forgotten quite a lot of things and didn't know what Joe had decided to do for the rest of the day. He came in and dumped his gear in Row D.

'Because Elinor is not with us today, this doesn't mean slacking off and going home early,' said Joe. He was eating an apple. There was a bag of fruit on his desk in front of him. 'We are going to pick out the weak scenes and sharpen them up. Letter scene first, Act II, scene 3. Sir Toby, are you ready?'

Viola was not in this scene so I settled myself in the prompt corner, draping the scarf. I felt different. I began to relax, breathing evenly. No more being Viola for a while. She had time off. She could go sightseeing round Illyria.

'Much better,' he said, coming up on stage. 'Give Feste room for his song. Don't crowd him even when you are making fun of him.' He wandered over to the prompt corner and looked down his nose at me. 'Well, well, who are you? Such glamour. Have we met?'

I was not amused. My face hadn't changed, nor my red hair. It was a touch tousled and dishevelled. 'How sad, Mr Harrison, have you lost your long-distance spectacles? Or is this an early senior moment?'

'You're wearing girly clothes.'

'How would you know?'

'I recognize certain clothes, certain designers. They have a look, a label.'

'So, have I got that label look?'

He peered closely at me, squinting. 'Good heavens, it's Sophie, our delightful prompt. What a gorgeous transformation. She has joined the real world of clothes. Well done, full marks.'

He sounded so aloof and patronizing I could have hit him with my book. But I kept my cool. He was my neighbour and it would not be a good idea to antagonize him. A neighbour from hell could make life unpleasant. He might block the stairs, hide the dustbins, tamper with my mail.

And I was an essential part of the production team. I didn't want my prompt corner moved to the foyer. I'd be selling programmes next.

'Like the scarf, great colour, suits you,' he said as he turned away. 'Want a satsuma?' He put the fruit in my hand. He was smiling, not a patronizing smile now, but something more genuine, a smile that reached his eyes. Did I have time to eat it? 'There's time,' he said, reading my thoughts.

The satsuma was refreshing. Did he have another one to spare? Tomorrow I could bring in a crate. They were perfect snack material. I rolled the skin up into a smaller orange ball.

I went home alone in my new glory. Joe had gone to visit the two influenza sufferers, hopefully with offerings of flowers and grapes. The Edwardian house seemed tall and empty. I didn't even know the occupants of the basement or the ground-floor flats. Absolutely nil communication. Not even the occasional Post-it note.

The second floor had an Arab tenant and I never saw him either. He paid the rent and then disappeared to Dubai where he ran some business.

My flat felt like an old friend, a welcoming cocoon. I put crumbled stale bread out for the birds on the roof. Lots of brown London sparrows hopped around in eager anticipation, not too many greedy pigeons. Though I loved the gleam of their greeny-blue neck feathers.

The evening was mine, or what was left of it. Cuppa soup and some late night telly. None of this nauseating celebrity stuff, get me out of here, some Congo jungle or prison-like flat full of rumpled beds, dormitory style, swopping sex. I wanted to see a good film, *The Shipping News*, a documentary or something intellectual about art which I could pretend to understand.

I was practically asleep, nodding, had lost track of the plot, when the doorbell rang. Not many people managed the climb to my flat. They might need oxygen.

'Hi,' I said, without removing the chain on the door. It was ajar about two inches. It was too late at night to open the door. No room for a machete.

'It's me. Joe. Let me in.'

'Joe who? Password, please.'

'Quit joking, Sophie. I know it's late. Joe Harrison. Director. *Twelfth Night*. Take your choice.'

It was very late but I was still wearing the Ralph Laurens jeans and a jazzy cruise shirt, so I looked reasonably presentable. I let him in. Joe was absolutely shattered, worn out, passed his sell-by date. He fell on to my couch, legs over the arm, his face pale and gaunt. He needed a drink.

'What's the matter?'

'Can I talk?'

'Sure, talk. But I'll get you a drink first.'

The wine had all gone. I didn't keep a wine cellar under the stairs. No stairs. But there were odds and ends left over from Christmases long past. Those liqueurs which were brought back duty-free but no one wanted to drink, even in punch.

I made him a mug of hot chocolate laced with schnapps. That should blow his mind sideways. Joe was laid out on my couch and no one was on top of him.

'Tell me,' I said. 'I'm tired, but sober.'

'Elinor is really ill. There's no doubt. She's not faking it. High temperature, aches and pain, influenza, no voice, streaming, poor soul. The doctor says she can't go on. She can barely make it to the loo.'

'And Fran?'

'Ah, Fran, the luscious Fran, is about the same. Same symptoms. Yet I don't know about Fran.' Joe lay back on my couch, sipping the hot chocolate laced with schnapps, his eyes closed. He seemed to like the taste of it. Some of the snarl had gone out of his mouth. He had a mouth that could curl. But I knew it could kiss.

'Fran has influenza, yes?'

'I think Fran has influenza. It looks like the flu and sounds a lot like it, but there's nothing that confirms the diagnosis. She says she'll come if she possibly can, but that's not good enough for me.' He heaved himself up on his elbow. 'So, Sophie, what do you think? Could you play the part?'

Something happened to me then. I went into a sort of terrified spiral. My mind was working on a different planet. I was a prompt, not an understudy. I remembered nightmares of past shows, of forcing myself to go on stage with churning sickness. I was a victim of stage fright of the worst kind. This was a scene straight from the cauldrons of hell.

'It isn't fair,' I said, gathering a shred of courage. 'You can't ask me.'

'There's the full dress rehearsal first. You could get everything sorted out then. You know the words by heart. You really can act, no problem. You are quite perfect in the part. A natural. The way you walk, the way you talk, everything.'

'No,' I said, trembling. 'I can't do it.'

'Please, Sophie. Please help me out.'

'I won't do it.'

'What do I have to do to make you do it?' he asked. There was fear and anger on his face. He was thinking of the consequences. The show would flop. He would have to cancel. Crawl back to New York.

'You didn't help me when I needed you,' I said, all the long ago trauma hung over my head like a gathering dark cloud. 'I had to stand on my own, survive somehow, without you.'

'I don't know what you are talking about,' said Joe, heaving himself up with anger. 'Sometimes you talk complete rubbish.' But he went into the kitchen and made himself some more hot chocolate. It was getting late. I wanted to go to bed.

'You can't let the show down,' said Joe, following me into the bathroom. I was cleaning my teeth and washing my face. I certainly wasn't going to floss in front of him. 'It has to go on.'

'Go away,' I said. 'I have to go to bed.'

'This is an emergency,' he urged.

'Not till tomorrow, it's not,' I said. 'Fran will recover, you'll see. Remember, she's a budding star, waiting for her chance.'

'A budding disaster, you mean. She wants to be a star but she doesn't want the work that goes with it. Instant stardom is her aim. Not twenty-four hours of horrendously hard work and rehearsal.'

'She might surprise you.'

'I don't want those kind of surprises. I'd rather have you playing Viola.'

'Fran would knife me in the wings rather than let me go on. Do you want blood all over the set?' I said, spitting out the toothpaste. 'Now, if you'll excuse me, I'm going to bed.'

'Shall I turn off the telly, tuck you in bed, turn off the lights?'

'No, thank you. I can manage,' I said.

'Goodnight, Sophie. Dream of sunny Illyria, off the shores of the Adriatic.'

He seemed to hover, not knowing what to say.

'I'd rather dream of Skegness on a wet and foggy Sunday, thank you,' I said.

Then he had gone, as he had before, leaving the nightmare behind. It was still with me. He'd left it on my pillow, like a nasty, squashed frog.

CHAPTER THIRTEEN

I didn't sleep well. Fragments of lines from other plays swirled through my mind, lost in a mist of shifting out-of-town shabby repertory theatres. I was playing a dozen roles, in the wrong order, each in a haze of panic and mind-strapping fright. Frozen to the floorboards, superglued to the wings. No words remembered. Lines lost in a vacuum. This was my worst nightmare, an electric tangle of paralyzing panic.

I didn't want to get up. Perhaps I had flu without knowing it. I felt my forehead hopefully. It was cool. No aches and pains in any joint. I was flu-less and clueless. Could I act out having the flu? It was a possibility. Hot showers, heated wheat pack under clothes, hot water bottle strapped to my waist?

Joe Harrison would be disappointed but I was not his nanny state. In time, he wouldn't even notice. Men are programmed not to notice. I couldn't be what he wanted me to be. Words were my life but I didn't want to say them in a theatre. Call in Meryl Streep. She'd fly over for a couple of million.

Something was going to happen. I could feel a strange tingling. A Dorset awareness. It was a premonition in my bones. Even less reason to get out of bed. I pulled the duvet over my head and pretended the day had not arrived.

The phone began to ring. I ignored it. But it would not stop. My ears protested at the clamour.

'Hello,' I croaked, assuming flu mantle.

'Sophie, where are you? I'm expecting you for costume fittings. It's the dress rehearsal today, remember? Just a few alterations.'

Joe barked at me down the phone. He sounded brisk, alive, vibrating with enthusiasm, in peak mental condition. Everything I was not.

'I'm ill,' I said weakly, with a bit of a cough.

'You're a bad liar. There's nothing wrong with you. I'm sending a taxi round for you now. It'll be there in twenty minutes. Put some clothes on. Not all of them. I don't want a bloated Viola. No apparition, please.'

He rang off before I could reply. I was starting to hyperventilate. Not a good sign. I could prompt but I could not, in a million years, go on that stage.

I showered and dressed with shaking hands, trying to eat a banana but it stuck in my throat. The sky was sullen with low and ominous grey clouds like there was an imminent alien landing. One of them could play Viola. They must know every word that was ever written on this universe by every playwright, poet and author. Joe could design a costume that would accommodate extra limbs or one eye.

I told the taxi driver to get lost but Joe had paid him enough to drive me straight to the theatre. He even drove in bus lanes. The lights outside the Royale were dimmed. They didn't know what names to put up. The theatre didn't have a face. It was bare, nameless, a desert.

'I'm not doing it. I'm not doing it,' I chanted as I walked in the stage door, stiff-legged as if they were co-joined. My mantra. 'I'm not doing it.'

'Hiya, Sophie,' said a stage hand, humping a huge tapestry. 'Hear you are going to save the show. Good on you. Hallelujah.'

'I'm not doing it,' I said.

Joe was immediately by my side, tall and dark, his hand under my arm, guiding me downstairs towards Wardrobe. My legs reverted to stiff. Premature arthritis set in the joints.

'This way, Sophie. My wonderful girl. We want to try on a few costumes, just in case. A couple of minor alterations, maybe. We'll have to bind your bust.'

'I'm not having my bust bound,' I exploded. Everything was getting beyond annoying. 'My bust stays where it is.'

'Get Sophie a coffee,' Joe shouted at Hilda. 'Strong, black. She needs caffeine. Plenty of it.'

I turned to face Joe. His face was so familiar, so dear, I almost faltered. 'I'm not doing any show,' I said firmly. 'I've decided that I'll walk the dress rehearsal for you. Say the lines. But there is absolutely no way that I'm doing the opening night. Do you get me? Have I made myself absolutely clear?'

He was nodding. 'Sure, Sophie, understood. Put the pageboy costume on. I found the perfect dye for the velvet, like soft sunshine. I've tried to create a harmonious picture. Let this seam out, Hilda. What about her hair?'

'Don't you dare touch my hair,' I cried, not quite a demented harridan scream but near. 'No one, but no one, touches my hair. No opening night.'

Hilda was cowering behind a pile of material, not knowing what to make of it all. I didn't mean to alarm her. Madness was contagious.

I'd had longish red hair for years, since school days. Sometimes my mad mother snipped off a few inches, when I wasn't looking, saying they were split ends. But I always checked that her few inches were not any longer. She dare not cut more.

Since then, my hair had been either up or down, or something in between. Forget the disastrous Gothic ebony period. I liked my hair long. It kept my neck warm, hid my face.

'Find her a cap,' said Joe, beyond arguing any more.

'This was Elinor's,' said Hilda, producing a fawn velvet cap with sweeping feather.

'That'll do. Coil her hair inside it. Only for the dress rehearsal. We're starting in twenty minutes.'

'Viola starts with the shipwreck scene,' I reminded him, appalled at what he was making me do. 'The cloak and torn dress, surely?'

'Yeah, put on some seaweed,' he growled.

I still had this premonition. Something was going to happen, not necessarily to me, but to the company, to Joe, to the theatre. Could it be the plague? The Globe had been closed because of plague. Pass me a face mask.

The dress rehearsal began. It was fraught with late entrances, clothes that didn't fit, scenery that wouldn't swing or fell down, props that were forgotten. I was on autopilot. I said the words but with little meaning. It was robotic.

Joe's face was clouding over. He was fuming. It was going into terminal fusion. A terrible dress rehearsal usually meant a good first night but he couldn't see it happening. The range of lighting moods were working, at least.

'What's the matter with you, Viola? You're supposed to be madly in love with him. Where's the emotion, the hidden emotion? You know, heartbeat stuff.'

'What heartbeat stuff?' I said. The feather was tickling my nose. 'You're asking me to act? I'm reading the lines. This isn't the opening night.'

'Viola, think of the meaning of these words. You've spoken them a hundred times before, with real feeling. Yet now you're as dead as a lump of North Sea cod. What's the matter with you?'

I heard a sort of squeaking, squeaky noise. It meant nothing but I saw a few heads swivel round. There was some movement at the back of the theatre but it was too dark to see properly what was happening. Stage lights cut off the auditorium. Black as a bat.

A wheelchair came into sight. Fran was sitting in it, done up to the nines in white fur and clouds of Chanel Number Five. Her make-up was immaculate. Must have taken hours. She didn't look ill. She didn't look as if she had suffered more than a passing sneeze. Maybe she had caught the scent of fame.

'Stop this charade. Get off the stage and back where you belong in the prompt corner,' she shouted at me. 'I'm here now. I'll take over.'

She got up off the wheelchair and took the side stairs to the stage. She tottered past, throwing me a looking of distaste. 'Where's a script? I'll need a book. I've been so ill. I don't remember any words.'

'Are you sure you're well enough to go on?' Joe was lost, scrambling for some sense. It was not often that happened. He had not expected Fran to turn up at this late moment. 'Shall we break for your costume change?'

'The show must go on,' she said, dazzling him with a smile

outlined in crimson gloss. 'I would never let you down, darling. Let's start. Prompt, line.'

'Hath for your love as great a pang of heart,' I said, hardly audible. I was trying to find my corner as if I had forgotten where it was. Joe hadn't given me a new place. Perhaps he'd had second thoughts.

'Louder, prompt,' said Fran, flicking her hair. 'Sophie thinks she's an actress but no one would hear her mumblings beyond row A.'

'No talking, please,' said Joe.

Fran was certainly an actress of sorts. She could act feeling faint, struggling to get out of a chair, holding on to an arm for support, gasping for breath. It was quite a performance. I had to hand it to her. The dress rehearsal was Fran's greatest achievement. She was every inch a star making the supreme sacrifice so that the show could go on. Hand her an Oscar. A plastic one.

She dabbed away at imaginary sweat, licked her lips, called weakly for water. Millie fed her mineral water between scenes and provided a chair in the wings to rest on. If she had been physically capable, Fran would have been making circuits of the stage with a knife, with me as the main target.

'Bravo, bravo,' Bill called from the wings. There was a certain irony to his voice. 'What kind of water do you want? Thames still or sparkling from the Glens of Scotland?'

'Still,' she said with heroic fortitude. 'I'll manage with still.'

It was really cold in the prompt corner. The velvet pageboy outfit which I was still wearing, was a brief tunic and stockings, buckled shoes. I missed my boots and mohair and layers of Damart.

'Take five,' said Joe, slamming his book shut. He strode backstage to find out what gremlin was lurking in the wings. The theatre was said to be haunted but no one had ever seen or heard anything. No Victorian thespian in caked make-up taking a last curtain call. But I was sure they were there, having a laugh.

I felt a fleece being thrown roughly round my shoulders. Joe was rocking on his heels, hands thrust in his pockets, staring into the footlights. 'They've never fixed the draught,' he said. 'It's probably an iceberg at the Thames flood barriers.'

'Not high on the list of priorities.'

'Enjoy being the prompt again?' he asked, falsely hearty. 'Feel safe in your corner? Nothing too demanding for you?'

'No, not exactly feeling safe. I feel like there's a time bomb somewhere, timed to go off any minute. I didn't know she was going to turn up.' There were tears like ice in my eyes. I knew he was disappointed. I knew I had let him down.

Joe shuddered. 'No one did. Let's hope your time bomb is wrong. I can do without that kind of feminine intuition.'

He said nothing about Fran's performance and I applauded him for his loyalty to any member of his cast, good, bad or mediocre. He would support her if she was all he had. Perhaps some personal coaching was planned, the kind that included champagne and soft lights. I thought a miracle was more in line.

I put my arms into his fleece and zipped it up. He wasn't getting it back yet. He'd got his temper to keep him warm. The rehearsal was pretty much under control at the moment, but strained. He couldn't afford to upset the fragile Fran.

The dress rehearsal limped to an end. Even Feste, the jester, sang a flat-noted song. There was some penguin flapping of hands, token applause, totally without enthusiasm. They shuffled to their feet. The small invited audience were not staying behind.

'I'm not going to say anything,' said Joe, looking round for his fleece. He'd forgotten that I had it. 'Everyone is tired and you all need a good night's rest. It's going to be a great first night tomorrow. I know you can do it. The critics will all be here and this *Twelfth Night* is going to stun them.'

I didn't think stun was quite the right choice of word. The audience was going to die of disappointment, if they stayed at all after the interval.

If Fran hammed it up, as was possible with cliche gestures and expressions, then the audience might be on the verge of hysteria. It was so easy to go over the top. Guilt engulfed me in several layers of despair. It was beyond me to do anything. I could only watch and wait. A bit of praying might help.

But I could give Joe his fleece before I changed back into my own clothes and went home. I thought I was looking where I was going.

I went down the steps into the auditorium, slotting my notes back into the script, unzipping the zip, avoiding a sand bucket which had been left in the wrong place.

There was a sudden, piercing scream. It echoed through the theatre. I didn't know what it was or who it was. It just happened. Like that famous scream painting of a wide open mouth, the valuable painting that got stolen.

Fran was right behind me, writhing in agony on the floor, clutching her leg, her face contorted. She could contort.

'You fool, you blithering idiot, look what you've done,' she howled at me. 'Why didn't you look where you were going? Oh God, I think it's broken. My leg's broken.' She began to sob loudly.

There was soon a crowd gathered round her. Joe was on his knee beside her, clearing the crowd away to give her air. Millie brought a blanket. Someone phoned for an ambulance. The paramedics arrived in no time, fixed a split, had her on a stretcher, put her on a drip, said how brave she was, asked for her autograph.

It was a performance that outshone anything she did on stage. Fran knew how to act a broken leg to perfection.

I sat in row A, watching miserably. I hadn't seen her. She hadn't been behind me, I could swear. So there had been a time bomb waiting to go off. Fran was the bomb. And there hadn't been time for me to take cover.

CHAPTER FOURTEEN

Joe went with Fran in the ambulance to the chaos of the A&E Department at St Thomas's Hospital. I walked home alone, nerves jangling like wires, mildly alarmed by anyone coming towards me and crossing over almost immediately. I zig-zagged the dark streets, hoping to be only slightly mugged. It would be a lesser torment than having to go on stage.

'I am not going on,' I said with conviction.

I could run away. I could go AWOL. Lots of people did it. They simply disappeared into the night when things got too much for them and were not found for months or years. The country was populated with missing persons, all wandering about, sleeping in cardboard boxes, queueing at midnight soup vans run by City high flyers in Armani suits. I could start a poetry group on the Embankment. We could write emotive lines on stolen scraps of paper, wrapped in our lumpy sleeping bags, drinking cheap cider. *Homeless Poems*, we'd call it. They might even get published.

Or I could disappear to Dorset. No one knew about Dorset. No one would know. A job at Boots sounded quite inviting. I could stick on price labels, learn to work the till, advise customers about the range of No 7 cosmetics for their dry, normal, oily skin. I wondered if the current uniform would suit me. Navy and white was pleasant enough.

My flat was a shambles. I had never rehoused all the stuff hidden when Joe came to supper. The carrier bags were bursting from their hiding places like rampant helium balloons. Another reason to disappear.

My rent was paid until the end of the month. I could disappear, reappear casually without fanfare, get another job in a different theatre. Joe would have returned to the States. *Twelfth Night* would be on a run with the recovered Elinor in all her mature glory.

But who would give me a job? My desertion would be legendary. No management would look at my disloyal CV. A new name, that was the answer. People changed their names all the time. I knew an actress who changed her name three times but always used the same initials so that she had some idea who she was when autograph signing. That didn't make too much sense.

The newly purchased bottle of brandy in the kitchen was for medicinal purposes. This was definitely a medicinal situation. I slurped in some orange juice to take away the taste of the brandy. I was not a natural alcoholic.

It didn't take long to pack a bag with a few essentials. Thank goodness I didn't have a cat or a hamster or anything dependent. As yet I didn't know whether I was heading for Dorset or a cardboard box.

'She is drowned already, sir, with salt water,' I said to myself as I poured another tumbler of brandy. One of my favourite lines. 'Although I seem to drown her remembrance again with more.' So moving. I could have wept.

Perhaps I ought to have a shower before I disappeared. No saying when I might get a chance for another wash. Cardboard city didn't have many amenities. No tiny soap samples and stuff like that.

I turned on late TV, wrapped damply in my bathrobe. It was a riveting programme about mechanical sex aids, like a penis pumping machine and grown-up, life-size movable dolls. One of them looked remarkably like Fran. I didn't know such things existed. It was amazing. But not amazing enough to keep me awake.

Such riveting information plus the brandy soon had me nodding off. The sofa was comfortable but I knew I would wake up with a stiff neck. I forced myself to think about the day. Too late for a cardboard box tonight.

'Wake up, you idiot. You can't go to sleep in a wet bathrobe.

113

Don't scream, please. You didn't lock your front door. You should always lock your front door.'

It was Joe. He looked knackered and creased. I wondered how long he had had to wait at A&E with the fragile Fran.

'How's Fran?' I asked, as if I could care less. I hoped she was plastered up to the thigh. 'Is she all right?'

'They are keeping her in overnight, just in case. Not a broken leg. It's been X-rayed. Prognosis: a bad sprain.'

'I could have told you that. I know what a broken leg looks like. Bits of gruesome bone sticking out.'

'But she won't be able to go on tomorrow, our opening night. The doctor recommended several days complete rest.'

'Clearly a besotted male,' I said, not taking in the implications.

'Yes, he was clearly besotted,' Joe agreed. 'She was loving every moment of star treatment. Private side room. Even a menu to choose from. I didn't know hospitals served food from menus.'

'It's the new NHS. Healthy eating so you don't get sick and have to go to hospital.'

'And you need a healthy night's sleep so that you'll be fresh for tomorrow. Opening night. Your great chance, Sophie, something that you have been waiting for all your life. I'm depending on you.'

I tightened my belt hoping it would cut off my blood supply. It made me gasp and swallow hard. I had not been waiting for this all my life.

'Joe, I can't do it,' I said. 'You must know by now that I suffer from terminal stage fright. I get so sick with nerves that I can barely move, let alone say a line. In rep they used to put a bowl in the wings so that I could keep running off and be sick.'

'I can arrange for a bowl,' he said.

'It isn't funny,' I said, gritting my teeth. 'I am physically ill with the thought of going on stage in front of all those people. No one but a monster would ask me to do it.'

'I'm a monster.' He made a monster growling noise.

'You will have to postpone the opening until Elinor is better.'

'Too late now. It's going ahead. No time to cancel.'

'Then you will have to get someone else to take the part. Phone the National.' I was sinking into an abyss, losing a grip.

'There's no one available. Besides, Sophie, you know you are perfect for the part. You know every line backwards. You act with a simplicity and passion. Your Viola will be an outstanding success. A new star discovered.'

'I don't want to be discovered. I want to dig a hole and disappear down it. I'm not going to argue with you any more. Go away and leave me alone.'

'No way. I'm not leaving you. I spotted the bag packed in the hallway. So you can put any thoughts of a walkabout right out of your head. You're staying here, with me, until it's time to go to the theatre. We're both staying put. I'm keeping an eye on you. We'll go a bit early to make sure the altered costumes fit. Any scenes you'd like to go over?'

'Yes, the drowning scene. Only I won't come up for air.'

I flounced off to my bed and pulled together the flimsy communicating door. I would barricade the door if I could move any of the furniture. But the wardrobe was fitted and the oak chest of drawers so heavy I could barely open a drawer. The bedside table wouldn't stop a rabbit trying to get in.

'I hate you, I hate you,' I shouted furiously.

'Good,' said Joe from the other side of the door. 'I like a Viola with a bit of fire in her.'

The brandy put me to sleep, plus despair and murderous thoughts. I didn't care where Joe slept. I hoped the sofa was a torment to his bad back. I hoped he didn't get a wink. I hoped he had pins and needles, cramp and restless legs all at the same time.

I was woken with a mug of tea. Joe was showered, shaved, freshly clothed and he looked serious, but rested. It was a big day for him.

'In case you were worried, I slept perfectly on your floor, good for my back. And I fetched a pillow and my own duvet so I wasn't cold. I've brought up some muesli and bananas and croissants that heat in a flash in the microwave. You need a breakfast to start the day, especially today.'

I pulled the duvet up to my shoulders but took the mug with an outstretched hand. It smelt good and hot. I wondered how I was going to hold out against this determined man. I hadn't managed too well that other time.

'I have told you till I'm puce in the face that I get chronic stage fright,' I said.

'Blue in the face,' said Joe.

'I can go any colour I like,' I seethed.

'Stage fright is good for you. I'd be more worried if you said you didn't get stage fright. It's the edge of danger. It sharpens your performance.'

'Sharpens?' I scoffed. 'It cuts mine right off.'

'All the best actors get stage fright. I've heard of really famous actors walking the streets of London, reciting their lines, before curtain up, all in fear of going on stage. You are not alone in this, Sophie. Take lots of deep breaths before you go on stage and—'

'Don't patronize me,' I cried. 'I've taken enough deep breaths to launch an ocean liner.'

'I'll be there for you,' he said suddenly, as if he understood. 'I'll hold your hand. I won't leave you.'

'Wonderful,' I choked. 'So you'll follow me on stage and we'll do all the scenes hand in hand? That'll wow the critics. Totally new interpretation. Viola à la deux. The tabloids will love it. Viola and Nanny.'

Joe swung round on his heel. 'Save your voice. How about soaking in a hot bath? Got any lavender? It's very calming.'

Breakfast was a taut affair. I wasn't speaking. Joe was on his phone most of the time, pacing the small space. He escorted me in a taxi to the theatre as if I was a prisoner in custody. He didn't trust me out of his sight. It's a wonder I wasn't handcuffed.

'You're a dead ringer for Kojak,' I said nastily.

'More hair,' he said.

The theatre was in opening night overdrive. I usually loved this time. Flowers were being delivered for flamboyant displays in the foyer. The freshly printed programmes being unpacked. Everywhere being determinedly vacuumed and polished. Supplies were arriving for the bars. We were swamped with staff for front of house, for the bars and cloakrooms, ticket office staff, programme sellers. The cast became quite secondary to this influx of workers, the essential mechanics of show business. The actors and actresses were lost in the crowd.

The fire curtains were being tested. I glimpsed the sea scenery of the shipwreck. Joe had painted the backcloth of waves. They were huge and realistic, dripping with glistening spray. They'd even managed to produce the effect of moving waves on the floorboards. It was fiendishly clever.

I stared at the set and went completely cold. There was no way I could take a single step on that stage. My skin was in a cold sweat, clammy. My tongue furred up and my lungs were tightening with shallow breathing. My legs no longer belonged to me. They wouldn't obey any orders to move.

Bill saw my pallor and ambled over. 'Hiya, Sophie. How are you?'

'Don't know,' I mumbled.

'Look, if it's any consolation, Fran's fall wasn't your fault. I was in the wings, I saw it all. You didn't trip her up. Fran was going down the steps at the side of the stage and she fell on the last step. It was a pantomime fall. Comics do it all the time. Trip over their own feet.'

'Oh.'

The news was hardly a consolation. Fran was being pampered by young doctors, probably being put in a taxi at this very moment, posing for photographs, arms full of flowers and enough dates to satisfy her appetite for young men and champagne.

'It wasn't your fault,' said Bill. 'So cheer up. No sackcloth and ashes. Enjoy your moment of fame.' He thumped me on the back. Was this a good luck thump?

I tried to say my mantra but it wouldn't come out. I was already in a state of torpor, unable to remember a single word of the play.

'I can't do it,' I said drily, flapping the frantic air like a circus seal.

Joe had overheard what Bill said but didn't comment. He could see the fear on my face. I was shaking. He took me aside.

'Scary places you in a dangerous place,' he said in a low, earnest voice. 'Actors need the nerves. Nerves are necessary, they are your energy. Some actors have doubts because they are under-rehearsed. They need to practise their part to death. You need this sense of danger. It makes it exciting.'

117

'It's not bloody exciting.' I shook my head, breathing fast.

'You know your stuff. You know you can do it. Turn this sense of panic into a positive stream of energy. Use your nerves. Viola is nervous. Everything that has happened has made her nervous. She is in a strange new country, in a strange court. She's lost her brother, drowned. She doesn't know what will happen to her and has no real friends. Of course, she's bloody nervous.'

'You don't understand,' I breathed, shallow and ineffectual.

'That's it, in a nutshell,' said Bill, grinning. 'Hey, don't touch that, you fool.' He leaped on stage, shouting at some new stagehand who was halfway to touching something he shouldn't.

'Sit down, relax,' said Joe, guiding me to a seat in Row G. 'Read this play. It's good. You'll love it.'

Joe put my prompt script into my hands. I began reading automatically and some of my fear fell away as the lines soothed my spirit. *Twelfth Night* never failed to enchant me. It was a superb story and I was soon lost in the beautiful words.

The morning passed in a haze of activity, all happening outside of me. People spoke to me but I didn't remember what they said. I built a barrier of barbed wire around my space. Planted a few landmines in strategic places. Joe was not going to get anywhere near me. He would have to cancel. Cancel the show.

Elinor would be better in ten days. Fighting fit.

HURRAH.

Then I'd be back in my corner, where I belonged. That's where I wanted to be. Safe, cosy in a babywrap, in my own world.

Joe was on his mobile. He came over to me, his face ragged with a bitter smile. He handed the phone to me.

'I've just been congratulated on my wise decision to cancel the show,' he said flatly. 'The delectable and slightly injured Fran would like to talk to you.'

I took the phone. She wanted to talk to me?

'Hello, Sophie darling,' said Fran. Her voice floated, sweet as saccharin, into my ear. 'I'm so terribly sorry to hear that the show is being cancelled, but of course it's the only possible decision. You couldn't really go on, could you? No experience, no sophistication, no professional training. You need all of that to succeed on stage in front of a big audience. And you haven't got it, girl, but I have.'

'Oh. Are you feeling better?' I asked politely.

'My ankle is strapped up and I'm on very strong painkillers. Tell everyone I'll be back for opening night in a week's time. Ready to take over the lead.'

'Really?'

Joe had been listening on an earpiece. He said nothing but his face was a picture of despair. He could see his big dreams going down the drain, all his designs and sets, his imagery, the painstaking hours of rehearsal. They were all on hold. He was going to have to cancel. Put up the notices outside the theatre. Cancellation! As Fran said, it was the only possible decision.

'So lovely to talk to you,' said Fran happily. She sounded as if she was lying on a couch, munching chocolate, probably Belgian. 'Enjoy your week off. Go have a McDonalds or something. Bye to everyone.'

'Go stuff your extra strong painkillers down your throat,' I said crudely, my anger rising. 'Who said that the show was going to be cancelled? Joe never said that. And it won't. This show is going on. Watch the news, Miss Fran Powell, it's going to be a brilliant success. Make headlines. Read all about it in tomorrow's papers.'

I could hear someone saying these strident words. I think it was Glenn Close. It certainly wasn't me. Not guilty.

CHAPTER FIFTEEN

It felt like the long mile walk to the guillotine. Joe was trying to keep encouragement on his face. Some members of the cast started to clap. Their smiling faces were a blur. People moved about like mechanical ghosts.

'That's my girl,' Joe whispered. 'You can do it.'

He was guiding me downstairs to Wardrobe. Hilda went into a state of panic, knocking the screen over. She'd worked on my costumes half the night, just in case. I hoped my half-baked brain would remember to buy her some flowers.

'Here she is, Hilda. The most courageous woman in London. Look after her. I've a dozen last-minute things to do. See you later.'

I stripped behind the screen, my fingers faltering, shedding Damart.

'You won't need a vest on stage,' said Hilda, helping me into the page boy's doublet and shirt first for a last check. It fitted perfectly. She took it off and hung it on a hanger, then pulled the torn shipwreck dress over my head. I stood there like a dummy. 'It's hot under those lights. Used to be on the stage myself, you know, one of the Bluebell Girls. In the chorus line.'

I looked at Hilda with new interest. I could see a certain faded glamour, thin rather than slim, pale eyes worn out from close sewing, tinted brown hair.

'We used to make a lot of our own costumes. All spangles and sequins. That's how I got into sewing, when my legs gave up.'

'What happened to your legs?' asked my voice.

'Varicose veins. The devil they are. Painful and unsightly. And there were family problems. . . .'

I let Hilda gabble on about her ailments and looking after her mother. Despite my brave words on the phone, I didn't feel in the least bit brave. What had I said? I'd been carried away, angered by Fran's cool assumption of a cancellation. I should have kept my mouth shut. This was going to be one almighty disaster.

The costumes were beautiful. There was no doubt about it. Joe had specially dyed the velvet to the colours of saffron, granary, and fudge and sugarcane. The short cloaks were lined with shot silk, edged with old braid. Every set was going to look like a medieval painting. The harmonious colours in themselves built up the period, the atmosphere, the style. How had he got it all to look so old? Beaten it to death?

'Good thing I've got plenty of different buckled shoes,' Hilda said. 'Your feet are bigger than Elinor's. Pity, these little velvet slippers are so pretty but too small for you. She loves them.'

'She'll wear them when she comes back,' I said.

I was hardly aware of Joe returning to OK the costumes but I suppose he did. Hilda was busy. She had other last-minute alterations to do as well.

'This fitted last week,' Byron grumbled, trying to fasten a waistcoat, tugging at the edges.

'Too much booze,' said Hilda, ripping a back seam open with one of those sharp gadgets. 'Could you try not to breath for a bit?'

'You're a brick, Hilda.'

'These bloody yellow stockings,' Claud cursed. 'They look like wrinkled bananas. They won't stay up.'

'Wear yellow pants over them. Women do that with one-size tights which never fit, put their knickers on top. But don't give them to me to wash every night. You can do that yourself.'

A secondary lady in waiting came in wanting to swop her dresses for Fran's outfits, get herself modishly upgraded. Fran's costumes were much more sweeping, low cut and gorgeously decorated to reflect her status at court.

'Sorry, but you are not a size zero and never will be,' said Hilda, putting Fran's dresses back on the rail. 'But you can wear her cloak. It matches.'

121

'It's so boring having to wear black all the time,' complained Olivia, trying on her widows weeds for the hundredth time. 'I look like a nun.'

'You are a nun,' said Hilda. 'A nun in mourning for her brother. If it bothers you, wear lacy red undies.'

Wardrobe was like Clapham Junction, cast coming and going in all the time, wanting Hilda to do this, do that. Noise and commotion. It was only missing a few trains running late. Everybody acted the star when it came to their costume. I tried to help but my hands were shaking so much I could barely thread a needle.

I tried not to think. That was the only thing to do. Pretend it was not happening, hide my head under a towel. This was not happening. I stared at myself in the wall mirror and saw a ghost of a person with large frightened eyes.

Joe came down to see me. He looked harassed. His hair was standing on end, as usual, hedgehog style, from running his hands through it.

'Sound can't get the thunder and lightning to work,' he said, abruptly. 'We may have to change the weather forecast.'

I had no idea what he meant.

He took me aside, close to the basement window where sulphured London light filtered from above. 'All right if I cut your hair now?' he asked. 'Or are you going to make a fuss like Elinor?'

'What do you mean? Cut my hair?' It was like a foreign language.

'You can't have this mass of hair. Unusual colour but there's far too much of it. Viola is masquerading as a pageboy. She can't have hair flowing like Vesuvius.'

'You can't do it. You're not a hairdresser.' I couldn't think of anything else to say. I liked my hair. My long hair.

'Too late to book one. Look, have correct scissors, can cut.'

He was brandishing a slim pair of scissors. They looked very sharp. He was eyeing my hair, calculating the length to chop off. I could not believe this final indignity. I was really shaking now. One day I might take the scissors to his hair. How about a striking badger look?

'It'll grow back, Sophie,' he said. 'It's not like it's permanent surgery. You may even get to like it short. Easier to wash and dry.'

He was bustling round, finding me a chair, putting a towel over my shoulders. One thing he didn't do was place me anywhere near a mirror.

'Close your eyes and think of England,' he said. The weak joke didn't help.

His fingers brushed my neck, lifting the heavy coil of hair. I'd plaited it some time that morning, but it had come undone. He bounced the rope of red around as if guessing the weight at a fair.

'You could probably sell your hair to a wig maker. It's in great condition.'

I heard the click, click of the scissors. He had started. It was too late to do anything now. I could hardly rush away with half a head of hair. Tears squeezed out of my eyes. He was cutting off my hair.

'Don't cry,' he said cheerfully. 'You're going to look fabulous.'

I saw my hair falling on the floor, long strands of red curls, like exotic snakes writhing. A cold draught touched my neck. The scissors were cold on my forehead. He was cutting a fringe.

'I don't want a fringe,' I cried, aghast.

'Too late. You've got one.'

This was the worse day of my life. And I'd had some bad days. This man was programmed to blight my life. My fate line had his name written all over it.

'I shall look r-ridiculous,' I sobbed.

Joe stood me up, shaking the towel and turned me towards a mirror. He was smiling. But he also had a strange look on his face, something I didn't understand. 'Does this look ridiculous?' he said gently.

I stared at the woman in the mirror. I didn't know her. A bob of flaming red hair sprung like curtains either side of a scared face. Her neck was suddenly long and creamy. Her eyes were wide and startled.

'You look gorgeous,' said Joe, looking straight into my eyes in the mirror. 'Absolutely ravishing. We can really see your face for the first time.'

'Is that me?'

123

'You've been hiding behind that hedge of hair for years. This is the real you.'

'I don't believe it. You've cut off all my hair. How could you? Joe, Joe . . . it's ruined.' I wailed, fingering some of the long locks on the floor. They fell from my hands in a shower. 'What am I going to do without my hair?'

'Make-up now, Viola.' It was Elinor's dresser, that nice young woman called Millie. 'Shall I help you or do you want to do it yourself'?'

'Make-up? Surely it's not time?' Where had the day gone? It couldn't really be time. This was when I should wake up in bed and find it had been an awful, horrifying dream. But I didn't wake up. I was awake. It was a stomach-churning, out-of-body experience.

'It's time to get ready. You can't rush your make-up. Come along, you can use Elinor's dressing room. I know she won't mind.'

There was a ticking clock and it was banging away in my head. My mouth was so dry, my lips were sticking to my teeth. I barely remembered putting on the base and Millie shading and painting my eyes. She had the right touch, knew what she was doing. My eyes looked huge, petrified.

'Your hair's lovely,' she said. 'It'll look perfect with the caps Viola wears. Just right.'

I felt so sick that my face was all turned down like a morose cartoon caricature. Any minute I was going to throw up. I didn't think I would be able to make it to the stage. Somewhere on the way, I would be so ill that my knees would fold under me. That moment of bravado had been my undoing. If only Fran hadn't phoned to gloat over me. I could be sitting in front of the telly now, watching Emmerdale.

Millie was doing her best. 'Now, your first scene is the shipwreck so you wear the torn gown, the cloak and the shawl over your head. How about getting it all on now, so you don't have a rush?'

'W-where are they? Where's the d-dress and the shawl?'

'You've got the dress on. There wasn't any need to try on a shawl. A shawl fits anyone. Come along, Sophie. Wrap this round.'

She was dressing me like a child. My fingers were unable to do anything, fumbling and stiff. I looked a wreck. I was a wreck.

The shawl and cloak hid all of me. There was only this gaunt white face staring at me in the mirror. Truly, a creature from a shipwreck. I was entirely shipwrecked with nothing to cling to.

Joe appeared in the dressing room. He was nodding encouragingly, approving, but looking harassed. He took my cold hand.

'I'm going to be there, with you, the whole time,' he said. 'I will be telling you when to go on and give you the first line. I'll signal your exit and point to which exit to take but if you go the wrong way, it doesn't matter. Don't worry about exits. Millie and I will help with all your changes, making sure you have the right things on and have plenty of time for your next entrance.'

'I can't do it,' I whispered.

'Yes, you can. We are going to do it together. Once you are on stage, speaking those lines you love, you will feel wonderful. Forget there is anyone sitting out there, listening. You can't see them. Think of the play and the words that Shakespeare wrote. I bet he'll be in the wings, willing you on.'

Something like a dry laugh touched my mouth. The first of the day. 'I hope he keeps his beard off me,' I said.

'You are going to do us proud,' he said, turning me out of the dressing room. He was walking me along the crowded corridor towards the wings. I could hear the minstrels playing the opening music. The play had started. The first scene in Orsino's palace was very short. I barely heard the Duke's last words.

'Love-thoughts lie rich when canopied with bowers.'

Had he said them or had I imagined it? I was frozen with fear. I couldn't go on, my legs were like straw. The lights dimmed for the scene change. The Captain and the sailors were already in the wings, waiting, looking rugged, tense.

'It's like bungy-jumping,' said Bill, at my side. 'Only without a safety harness.'

The thunder crashed, making me jump, and lightning flashed across the stage. The floor was a mass of seething waves created with ripples of material and lights. Creaks came from the wooden ship floundering on the rocks. It was realistic and spectacular.

For a moment I was looking at the scene like someone in the

125

audience, mouth open with amazement. I was nothing to do with the play, actually. I was just watching it. Then Joe gave me a gentle push forward into the darkness.

As I went on stage the rain started. It was coming down from five sprays fixed high up in the flies, water cascading in a line across the stage and I was right under it. I was standing in a veil of rain. In seconds I was soaked, rain dripping off my nose and my face, sticking in my eyes.

I gasped with the shock of it. Thunder, lightning and now real rain. I was shipwrecked in truth. I staggered to the front of the stage, drenched, wiping my face. The stage lights went on.

'What country, friends, is this?' I said with a short, audible intake of breath.

CHAPTER SIXTEEN

I was still on stage. It had become a different world, a different universe, hazy with colours and movement. The Duke was taking my hand and gazing at me fondly.

'Here is my hand,' he said. 'You shall from this time be your master's mistress.'

I smiled back at him, tremulous with joy. Olivia hugged me with genuine warmth, her face alight.

'A sister! You are she,' she said.

The words rolled over my head, the sick panic ebbing away. These were the last few pages of the play. It was almost all over. I had nothing more to say, could stand and listen to everyone going through the last lines. The relief was washing over me in crashing waves. It was like the shipwreck in reverse.

I was still in one piece, but shredded. Literally fed through a shredder and churned out in little pieces. I had sweated buckets, wept and cried, hyperventilated, swallowed litres of water, remembered very little of what happened. It had been words, hundreds and thousands of words, spilling out of my mouth.

If I never said another word on stage again, I had had this night. I had this moment. Somehow I had got through it, played Viola, been Viola.

Then I found myself waiting in the wings and the audience was clapping, cheering. I wasn't certain of the order of the curtain calls. I was pushed and pulled in all directions by other members of the cast.

'Smile, girl' said Byron, grinning. 'Bow. We'll take the cue from you. It's all over now. Step forward, that's it, smile, another bow. Good girl.'

I smiled shakily but radiantly in all directions, any direction. I was amazed at the size of the audience. The theatre was full, not a seat left unoccupied. They were standing and clapping madly. It was an amazing sight. Any minute now the cherubs might wave and clap.

Joe came on stage now, taking his bow as the guest director. He hadn't wanted to do this but it was traditional on opening night. He turned to me and flashed a smile of such warmth and gratitude that my serrated heart nearly melted. The sun had come out, so I thought. But it was all the stage lights, dazzling.

There were flowers arriving on stage now, both for Olivia and me. I didn't know I was going to get flowers. They were gorgeous. I buried my face in their fragrance, nearly choking on the perfume. I hoped they were personal from Joe, not the management, and did I get to keep them?

We took second calls and a third. It was never ending. I was so tired, I could barely keep the smile fastened to my face.

Then the curtain came down for the last time. Joe swept me up in his arms and spun me round. My new short hair flew out like electric sparks. I was switched on and laughing.

'You did it, girl. You bloody did it.'

I hung on to him for a moment, relishing his closeness.

He sounded like Professor Higgins and I was his Eliza. I could have danced all night. Perhaps we would go out dancing.

Everyone was hugging and kissing everyone else. I got loads of hugs and kisses and genuine, heartfelt congratulations. The cast really meant it. I had saved their day, the Royale's day, Joe's day.

But at what cost? I was on the point of collapsing from exhaustion. Millie appeared with a cup of tea, properly brewed in the dressing room in a teapot, none of the awful machine stuff.

'Get this down you, before you fall down,' she said. 'You look done in.'

'Thanks,' I said tremulously. 'And thank you for helping me, Millie. You were wonderful. I couldn't have done it without you.'

'It was a pleasure,' said Millie. 'Elinor would have been proud of you.'

'And I'm so proud of her,' said Joe, giving me another big hug, nearly spilling my tea. He was obviously on a terrific high, despite the darkness of stubble on his chin. And so he should be. It was a spectacular production with sets and designs to kill for. All his work, his unique imagination, as if he had a direct line to the Bard and they had worked as a team.

I wanted to go home to the craven safety of my bed, and go to sleep, a deep, deep sleep but, of course, there was going to be a party. There's always a first night party, I'd forgotten, so everyone could wind down. It was drinks on tap at The Stage Door pub, as we were all too drained to walk far. Joe had to stay behind to talk to the media. I nipped out in case they wanted to talk to me. No comment.

I didn't remember walking to the pub. A wave of chattering people carried me along. I checked that I had my own clothes on. All present and correct.

The stage crew were late joining us as they had to get the set ready for the next performance. Bill came straight over to me, a bottle of champagne in his hand. He took advantage of the serial kissing going on.

'To our new star,' he said, waving the bottle. 'Our wonderful Viola. A star in the making.'

'Pack it in, Bill. Don't be daft,' I said wearily. 'A one-night wonder. The understudy's understudy.'

'Get a glass of bubbly down you,' he said, pouring out a flute of golden bubbles. 'You'll feel better.'

And I did. Several glasses later and I was feeling better. By the time Joe arrived, I was really a lot better, ready to face the world with a shaky smile. It was all over.

Joe did the rounds first. He had a good word for every member of the cast and crew. He didn't leave anyone out. Even Hilda had stayed for a port and lemon, the price of a taxi home in her pocket. I could guess who had slipped her that. I tried not to look at him but he was glowing with the success of the show and I was glad for him. Those dark eyes were sparkling, a sparkle I'd seen once before, a reflection of the stars.

He sat beside me the moment Bill got up to get another round for the party, like grown-up musical chairs. Bill was spending his week's pay without a moment's hesitation. He was tonight's big spender.

'So how's my star, my Viola?' Joe asked softly.

'Sozzled,' I said. 'I think this is my third glass of champagne on an empty stomach.'

'You deserve every bubble. You were wonderful, Sophie. Every line was perfect. I couldn't have given you any direction though perhaps a few hesitant smiles, here and there, as you fell in love with Orsino might have been appropriate.'

'I was hiding my feelings.'

'You hide them very well.'

'It's a habit I have.'

'Do you always hide your feelings?' he asked, peering at me. Suddenly it seemed he wasn't joking.

'Yes, always,' I said. 'It's too dangerous to let anyone know how you feel. They could hurt you.'

'I'd never hurt you,' he said.

Oh, but he had. He had. I turned my head away so he would not see the sudden tears. Oh yes, he had hurt me so much, like being pierced with burning arrows. I remembered the misery, feeling so empty and alone. I had once tried to hate him but he was a difficult man to hate.

'Can I have that in writing,' I tried a joke, very Goldie Hawn. 'I'm safe, then, from a broken heart?'

'Absolutely. I shall nurture your budding talent and when you are a big star with your name in lights on Broadway, I shall tell everyone that I discovered you in a prompt corner, wrapped up in blankets and ponchos.'

'No Broadway, no big star,' I said firmly. 'I'm a one-night wonder and that's all. I did your opening night for you. That very important night. Elinor will be back next week, I'm sure, and till then you have got your official understudy.'

The sparkle snapped out of his eyes. He was glaring at me as if I had handed him a closure notice from the Lord Chancellor. He was drinking juice. He thumped the glass down on the table, spraying orange droplets.

'Am I hearing this correctly, Sophie? I've just given you your biggest acting role, your chance of fame, a giant leap for womankind, and you're saying you won't go on again, won't go on tomorrow?'

'Don't make out you were doing me a favour,' I said hoarsely. 'You practically forced me at knife point. I never wanted to do the role, to go on stage in front of all those people. I did it for you, to save your precious skin, to keep the show on the road, to salvage your reputation.'

'I don't need you to salvage my reputation,' he said, his eyes dark and dangerous. 'My reputation can stand up for itself, something I've worked night and day for years to achieve. So don't ever think that I need you, because I don't. But the show needs you, the cast and crew need you, at least till the end of the week, till Elinor returns.'

'But I can't do it—'

'Can't, can't, can't . . . that's all you ever say, Sophie. If you'll excuse me, I'll leave you to nurse your tender ego. I've more interesting people to talk to.'

He stood up abruptly and joined a crowd at the bar, not looking back once. I sat in total shock, the champagne bubbles bursting flat. Bill nipped in and regained his seat. He'd had quite a jug full. He slid his arm along the back of my chair, brushing the bare skin on the back of my neck. No hair now.

'How's my gorgeous girl?' he said, all lovey-dovey.

'Dead tired,' I said, without thinking.

'Shall I take you home and tuck you up in bed?' he said, his eyes glazing over with the thought. 'You need someone to tuck you up all nice and cosy and cuddly and to whisper sweet dreams in your tender ears.'

I needed to be tucked up and cuddled up by Bill like I needed a lobotomy. But I did want to go home and it was very late. A taxi with Bill might be manageable if I was in charge of the situation.

Hilda. But a shared taxi home with Hilda would be ideal. I got up to find her. I searched the pub, the cloakrooms, ran out to the entrance. But someone told me she had already gone home, to put her soap-addicted mother to bed.

I stood there, hoping another taxi would come along, hugging my labelled mohair round me but I was starting to shiver. I willed one to come, to rescue me, to take me home. It was getting late, even the street lamps were darker and murky looking. It was starting to feel scary. Taxis didn't cruise around late at night these days. Too many rowdy drinkers. The drivers preferred to be safely in their marital beds, or non-marital, whatever.

Bill Naughton lurched into the entrance of the pub, grinning, swaying like a palm tree in a force eight gale.

'There's shmy girl,' he said. 'I've phoned forra cab. There shoobe one along any minute.' He tucked my hand into his arm and gave it a squeeze. 'Shoon be in bed, sweetheart.'

That's what I dreaded. I was getting myself into a tricky situation. It was like a replay, only much worse. But this time I was going to take good care of myself. I was stronger, older, considerably more sensible. Bill Naughton was going to get a surprise.

A mini-cab arrived. It was not a normal black cab. I never used mini-cabs unless they were from a firm that I knew. I climbed into the back seat and Bill followed me, all clumsy and falling about. With a little luck, he'd be dead to the world soon. He gave his address to the cab driver, not mine, thank you. I didn't like that one bit. He lived the opposite side of London.

'Hey, I've left my bag at the table. I won't be a moment,' I said, getting out the other side of the cab, hitting the roof for take-off and hurrying back into the pub.

I ran inside but there were few of our people left. They were all dead tired and drifting away. Joe had disappeared too. Without a word, he had left. Perhaps he thought I had gone with Bill.

I sat down on a chair, almost too weary to move. It was late and too far to walk. Hopefully the mini-cab driver, tired of waiting for me, would have taken Bill southwards by now.

This was a strange way to end the evening. Alone and abandoned, it seemed, left to fend for myself, as usual.

I had to sleep somewhere. I was desperate to sleep, to put an end to the day. Most London hotels were beyond my means. But there was somewhere I could sleep and no one would mind. I'd had my own key for months and the Royale's eerie midnight emptiness didn't scare me. If I saw a ghost, we'd be on nodding terms. Maybe I'd even prompt his lines.

If I could hear them.

CHAPTER SEVENTEEN

There was an old couch in Elinor's dressing room, a small crocheted blanket and a hot water bottle in the cupboard. Elinor, bless her, believed in home comforts.

It was a hard couch but the hot water bottle, held close to my mohair chest, was as effective as *Nytol Herbal*. The warmth flooded through me.

This was a day I did not want to happen again. Speaking the lines of *Twelfth Night* were a reluctant joy but the circumstances had been a nightmare.

I slid down into the deepest sleep, only remembering in the last seconds that I had not made my usual evening call to my mother. But she would soon find out why if she saw a newspaper. If she ever bought a daily newspaper, that is.

'So this is where you've been hiding. Wake up, it's morning.'

I knew the voice without opening my eyes. I was stiff and cold and the water bottle was clammy and like a rubbery fish. I let it fall to the floor.

'Oh, so it's you,' I mumbled, scrabbling at the blanket. It barely covered my knees. 'What are you doing here?'

'I looked for you last night. I saw you get into a cab with Bill Naughton.'

'Well, you saw wrong,' I said, blinking against the cheerless, airless morning light. 'Maybe you saw me get into a cab but you didn't see me get out the other side and return to the pub, did you? Everyone had gone. It was too late to find a taxi, too late to walk home, too late for any form of public transport. Then I remembered Elinor's couch.' I was so stiff, I could barely move.

'Why didn't you phone me? I'd have got you home.' He sounded angry.

'We were not exactly on speaking terms at the time.'

'You don't think much of me, do you? I wouldn't leave any member of my theatre team stranded at night, especially female and alone. Whether I was speaking to them or not,' he added.

'I didn't think of you,' I said honestly. I hadn't been thinking of him. I'd been beyond coherent thought. Getting my head down was all I wanted to do.

'Well, I was thinking of you and talking about you.'

'Oh?' I was not interested.

'With Elinor. I went to see Elinor. She said she would stay up and I was to come round any time and tell her all about. So I did.'

'Oh, that was nice,' I said again, pulling together a polite enquiry. 'How is she? How's Elinor?'

'Getting better, but slowly. She'll need a few more days to get her strength back. She's still weak and coughing a lot. She was thrilled to hear how well you did. Genuinely pleased. She sent you her love and good wishes.'

I stiffened. 'That's nice of Elinor but I don't want to talk about the show.'

'Who said anything about talking about it?' said Joe, spotting the kettle. He filled it with water and switched on. 'I always seem to be making you tea. Get up and have a wash and I'll take you out for breakfast. I know a little place that serves a real American style breakfast. Not a fry up in sight.'

'I won't be able to clean my teeth.'

'I wasn't going to check. Use a twig.'

Early morning London, even when it is cold, has a special feeling. A swathe of commuters were falling out of trains, huddled in scarves, barely awake. The night's debris was being cleared away by yellow-coated refuse truckers with grim faces. Huge decrepit and grimy delivery vans coughed their way to shops and stores, unhindered yet by the day's traffic deadlocks.

Joe walked me briskly, getting the circulation going. He held my arm as if I was being taken into custody. He'd seen too many late-night thrillers.

It was a sparkling clean café in Soho with an outrageous stars and stripes American atmosphere. Even at 8 a.m in the morning, the neat waitress was smiling brightly and pouring out glasses of water the moment we sat down at a window table. I half expected a lookalike Lincoln to be sitting at the next table.

'Good morning,' she said. 'Are you ready to order?'

'Orange juice, waffles, scrambled egg and coffee, for two,' Joe ordered without asking me. He didn't even look at a menu.

'How can she be that cheerful so early in the morning?' I groaned. I still wasn't properly awake, despite splashing water everywhere. I'd forgotten my shorn hair. It gave me a shock to see it so short and sharp in the mirror. Was this really me? I searched my face for other changes but I could only see the same terrified gaunt face. It wasn't a face I wanted to wear.

'It's an American trait. Because she likes her job, because she likes serving people and enjoys wishing people a nice day.'

'Are all Americans like this?'

'Would you like to come over and see?'

Was this Joe's strange idea of small talk first thing in the morning? Maybe I had a hangover. I didn't remember how many glasses of champagne I had drunk at The Stage Door party or perhaps there had been more bubbles than alcohol.

'Sorry, don't have a free weekend,' I said, sipping the juice which arrived in an instant. Service in most cafés is long and lugubrious, waiting time stretched into mind-numbing lethargy while waitresses gossip, do their nails, make phone calls. Thought: don't have a valid passport, don't have the money, don't want to go anywhere with you. Especially you, Joe Harrison.

'The States are worth a visit,' he was saying. 'It's a different world.' I was barely listening to what he was saying. Joe was relaxed and darkly good-looking, at home in the little café. Those glinting eyes, that fine hair, the jutting chin. I searched his skin for spots, wanting to find some imperfection, some pulsating flaw. But there was only that eyetooth that was a little out of line and that tiny scar. He had resisted going to an orthodontist to have the tooth straightened out.

'Everyone in the States wears braces, don't they?' I said. 'Like that baddie in a Bond film. Goldfinger?'

'Do they?' he said, amused. 'I hadn't noticed but obviously you are more observant than me. Yes, perhaps they do. Straight teeth are a prerequisite.'

'How did you get that little scar?' I asked.

'A chisel flew out of my hand. I was making some scenery. I've forgotten the show. A fluke. Any more questions? Is this a medical questionnaire?'

'Why does your back hurt so much?'

'You've noticed? A late-night car accident, swerving to avoid drunks in another car. Whiplash injury. Very late at night. I couldn't move for weeks.'

'Were you badly hurt?'

'A tree got hurt.'

The waffles arrived, hot and golden, with butter and syrup to spread on. They were fantastically delicious. My starved stomach went into raptures at the unexpectedly sweet offering. In an instant I was addicted to waffles.

'Enjoy!' the waitress trilled. Was she auditioning? Maybe she had recognized Joe.

'These are wonderful.' I spoke through a honeyed mouthful, unladylike but spontaneous. 'This is a terrific place. I love it here.'

'I'm glad you like it,' said Joe. 'Leave some room for the eggs. It may be the only meal you'll get today.'

I wished he hadn't said that. He'd immediately reminded me of the coming battle tonight. A battle that I was determined to win. He wasn't going to get me on that stage again. I'd cut my wrists rather than go on again. There was no way out but death.

No, that wasn't true. It was an exaggeration. I wouldn't cut my wrists. A better form of guerrilla resistance came to me in a flash. I would run away. Take a train to Bournemouth, get on the open-topped bus to Swanage, walk the high miles to my mother's remote country cottage. I would spend the days in isolation, trudging the clifftops, wind blowing through my short hair, a small sticky hand clasped in mine. No one would find me.

It was a long time since I had done that and I needed to do it again, soon. I needed to search the beach for fossils, exclaiming over each small imprint of a million years ago. I needed to paddle in the baby waves of the bay, splash and shout, swing him around in my arms. He was growing so fast and he would soon be taller than me. Maybe he was already too tall for swinging. I hadn't been there when he grew.

'Hey, come back, Sophie. You're miles away.'

There was a plate of lightly scrambled eggs in front of me, a mountain of creamy protein, glistening under the bright lights. Real food might ease the pain.

'It'll be getting cold,' Joe added. 'Dig in.'

'Have you ever hunted for fossils?' I asked.

'No, but I noticed that you have one in your flat. It's on the windowsill. Looks like the print of a snail, all curled up.'

'We found it in the Fossil Forest east of Lulworth Cove. We were out fossil hunting. It's millions of years old.'

'Amazing. It puts us into perspective as a race. Who's we?'

'I mean, I. That's what I always think. We're nothing. A speck of dust in time. A grain of sand on the beach. We don't matter.'

Joe put his hand across the table and covered my hand with his. He was looking at me with an intensity that made my nerves tingle.

'But we do matter,' he said. 'However small our contribution. It all lingers on in the great universe of time. Shakespeare didn't write those words for instant consumption and disposal. Look how they have lasted. They'll linger on for centuries whatever happens to this world, this civilization, this planet. Words continue to exist in the air. Radio waves absorb them and they vibrate forever.'

'Do you believe that?'

'Of course. The way you played Viola last night is still in the air, your voice, your emotion, your special feelings, vibrating on the ether, travelling out to other hemispheres, other planets.'

'Hope I'm going down well on Mars,' I said, trembling. His hand was still on mine, warm and firm. I wanted it to stay there forever, keeping me safe and comforted. But it was all too late. Like buses that come in threes and you see the back end of the last one pulling away from the bus stop.

'Please play Viola this evening,' he said, his voice low and deep. He was pleading with me. 'For me.'

'No,' I said in a flash. 'You're trying to seduce me again with that voice.'

'Again, Sophie?' He looked blank, pleating his forehead and took his hand away. 'What do you mean? When have I ever. . . ? I don't understand.'

'Wrong word,' I said, hurriedly. 'I meant persuade, coax, sway, make someone do something that they don't want to do.'

'The critics loved you. You've got rave reviews. Have you seen this morning's papers? I stayed up to see the first editions. It's unanimous. They all thought you were wonderful.'

'I don't care.'

'I thought you were spectacular. Doesn't that mean anything?'

I shook my head. 'No, it doesn't matter what you think. This is my life and I can't go through that ordeal again. And you can't make me. I've decided. As much as I care for the play, the theatre, all the other people in the cast, it's beyond me. OK, I've done it once. The show has opened, got rave reviews. That's all that matters. Elinor will be back on Monday, won't she?'

'What about all the people who have bought tickets for tonight?'

'Do I know them? Will it ruin their lives if for once they don't go out? They can stay at home, no late travelling, watch a bit of telly, drink a bottle of wine or two, go to bed early, make love.'

'Put like that, I'll be doing them a favour if I cancel tonight's show,' he said drily.

'You've got an understudy who's dying to go on. Use her. She'll love the limelight. The drama, saving the show, instant fame. The previews of *Phantom* were cancelled twice. It's still a great hit.'

Joe was drinking coffee, black, the pungent aroma from the forests of Columbia. His granite eyes were unfathomable. His thoughts were hidden from my gaze. He was having to make decisions. That's what directors were paid to do.

'She can't act,' he said bluntly. 'I didn't cast her as understudy. She was already in place when I came over. Casting was not in my contract. I was given a cast and my job was to direct it.'

'Which you have, brilliantly,' I said, warmly. 'And your set

139

designs are out of this world, and the amazing costumes. Sheer magic. They are all yours. The show is a success because of you, not because of some little nobody who said Viola's lines with a degree of emotion.'

'You mean the show will still be a success even without you?' he said slowly.

'Yes, of course. I'm only a small, unimportant part of the whole. Let it go ahead. A gorilla could read Viola and the show would still be wonderful.'

'I'll phone the zoo and get a gorilla,' he said, draining his coffee. 'But I'm scared. I'm really scared.' Then he added, his glance searching my face. 'I once said you read like a monkey. It was unforgivable. I apologize for my rudeness. I don't know why I said it.'

'Perhaps I'd said something that was out of place. I often say things I don't mean.'

'Never, Sophie. Not you. Never.'

CHAPTER EIGHTEEN

It was a show of a sort, the night after the opening. William Shakespeare would have called it *Eleventh Night*, or *Not Quite There*. The audience were on a high, fuelled with complimentary gin and tonics at the bar. One of Joe's last minute panic-driven ideas. The newspapers said the opening had been wonderful so the audience were prepared to be agreeable. They were also getting a degree of identity confusion. I could see them checking the programme.

Fran did her well-known shooting star impersonation. She also did some pathetic little limps in various scenes to remind the cast of her cruel disability but the audience thought it was part of the performance. Maybe Viola had knocked her knee on a rock during the shipwreck scene or something.

I sat in the prompt corner, trying to will her to put some feeling into the lines. But Fran thought she was in a *Carry On* film, flaunting boobs, buttocks, flashing lashes. A gorilla would have made a better job of it. Better facial expression.

Joe was standing beside me, dark face frozen. His body was taut. He mouthed one word at me. He was beyond speaking to me.

'Satisfied?'

I cringed, said nothing, concentrating on the lines in the script. The cast were pulling together, trying to strengthen the Viola scenes so that her weakness was less noticeable. I could have hugged them all. Bless their outrageously wrinkled orange and yellow tights. Sir Andrew Aguecheek was outstandingly foppish. Everyone loved him, especially in the fight scene. He didn't have the courage to fight a fly.

The curtain calls were rapturous but more than several decibels less enthusiastic than the opening night. My night. The audience were leaving, discussing Viola in low, puzzled voices. Newspapers do exaggerate so, they agreed. Still, the sets had been gorgeous. Loved the amazing costumes. And the shipwreck scene . . . that was fantastic, raining real rain. How did they do it?

'Where's my flowers? Where's my bouquet?' said Fran furiously, sweeping off stage, pushing everyone out of the way. 'Don't I get flowers? I'm tonight's star, for God's sake. Look what I've put into this show.'

'I'd call it nil, zero, darling,' said Bill, taking off his earphones. 'I couldn't hear a word. Learn to project, Fran. It might help if you want to get on.'

She pushed past him, past me, then swung back, her crimson mouth clamped in a tight line. 'I want a word with you, young woman.'

'Yes?' I was taken aback.

'You didn't help,' she snarled. 'I couldn't hear your prompts. What were you doing, chewing gum?'

'No, I never, but sorry,' I said.

'Don't think I don't know what you were up to. It was deliberate on your part. It was a nasty little trick, my girl, and you won't get away with it. You were set to ruin my performance.'

'I wasn't up to anything. Your lines were not secure,' I said, unwavering, clenching my nails into the palm of my hands. 'You need to look at them, Fran. I couldn't help it if you were all over the place. Sometimes you weren't even on the right page.'

'Wrong page, indeed! What a nerve, you po-faced bitch. Several times you gave me the wrong prompt, throwing me completely off track. I've a good mind to report you to the management for incompetence. Yes, I'm going to complain. You should lose your job. You'll be serving burgers at McDonalds this time next week.'

'At least they have a nicer class of customer,' I said.

This was knife throwing time. She looked as if she could kill me.

Murder in the Prompt Corner? It didn't pass as a title. No alliteration.

'How dare you!' She flounced off, eyes flashing with fury, on the verge of smouldering hysteria. 'I won't forget this. You'll be sorry you ever stepped foot in this theatre. I'll make sure you don't get a job anywhere in London.'

I retreated into my corner. I knew I had let everyone down by not going on again. That was my fault. I couldn't run with the wolves. Fran was useless. But what could I do? It wasn't as if I could take a few pills and everything would be all right. They hadn't invented stage fright pills strong enough for me. Beta-blockers stop your heart from going so fast but the fear was still there, stuck in your throat like a samurai sword.

'Cheer up, Sophie. Still in one piece?' said Bill in passing. 'Has she knifed you yet?'

'If there were stocks outside the theatre, I'd be in them by now, dodging tomatoes and rotten eggs. Fran was furious, spitting blood. She thought I had been unhelpful on purpose.'

'She needs to look at the script. She mangled the words. It was unbelievable and unreliable. I check the lines, too, you know. I have to know where we are. She shouldn't go on again. No, she's not up to it.'

'Someone has to do it. Elinor won't be fit enough until next week.'

Bill looked at me, put his hands on my shoulders, eyes deep with meaning. Oh no, not another one. 'I know someone who is perfect in every way. She brought tears to my eyes last night,' he said. 'She was wonderful. I could have cried.'

'Was she? And I thought it was rain. By the way, the rain was spectacular. I got drenched.'

'You stood in the wrong place, sweetheart. It falls in a straight line from five overhead sprays. You should stand in front of them. Then it just looks as if you are getting wet.'

'I was method acting,' I said, guessing what was coming next. He had that predatory, glazed groping look again. Oh God, men with wandering hands down the waist of your pants. 'You know, feel for real.'

'I'd like to feel for real. Want a lift home? I'll order a taxi.'

'No, thank you.'

'I can be ready to leave in ten minutes. We could snatch a bite to eat first. Would you like that?'

'No, thank you.'

'How about a pizza with lashings of cheese on top? Or sausages and mash?'

'What is there about the word "no" that you don't understand, Bill? No, thank you. I'm going home to hot chocolate and late-night telly.'

'I'd love a hot chocolate and late-night telly,' he grinned. He never gave up. 'Just my cup of tea.'

The only way to escape him was a quick visit to the backstage ladies cloakroom. It was a dingy, bleak place left over from the last century. It had lavatories with rusty pull chains and seats that looked as if they had been gnawed by werewolves. Every tile in the place was cracked and the mirrors were yellowed with age.

Sometimes I wondered how many thousands of actresses had used these lavatories. How many tears had been shed. Lost dreams flushed down the loo.

Millie had tried to cheer the place up with coloured toilet tissue and a bunch of artificial flowers bought at a local market. I chose a cubicle with pink paper. I blew my nose on a double sheet of it. I'd had enough of today's surprises.

I came out, keeping my head down, not wanting to bump into a lurking, predatory Bill. Instead I bumped into Joe.

'Sorry,' I said, head down, trying to move past.

Joe wasn't listening to me. He was talking to himself. It was the director in the throes of making a decision. He was pacing the floor, hands thrust deep in pockets, biting his lower lip.

'Fran's going to report me to the management. She says I gave her the wrong prompts,' I said but I wasn't sure if he even heard.

'Rubbish. I'll take care of that,' he said without interest, glancing over me. 'Don't worry about it. That was not a good show, was it? Tell me.'

This was not my moment to leap in and save the day again. This was my moment to go straight home, despite uncertain navigation, say hello to my wilting plants and watch some late-night telly, some predictably mind-blowingly boring reality TV. I could dig out those old copies of *Cosmopolitan* and read uplifting articles on 'How to Captivate the Man of your Dreams in Ten Sexy Moves'. Easy when you know how.

'It had its moments,' I said, trying to console.

Back in the wings, I turned out my light, tidied the corner of today's debris, tiptoed away in the direction to collect my lilac mohair and scarf.

'Not so fast.'

'Oh dear, not another reprimand?' I asked. 'I've had today's quota, thank you.'

'No, not a reprimand,' said Joe. 'You've had quite enough problems for one show. I understand that. Do you want a lift? I've ordered a taxi. No hanky-panky in the back seat.'

'What a pity. I fancied a bit of hanky-panky.'

'Then you'd better get a lift with Bill.'

'He goes the opposite way.'

'Then you're left with my offer. Take it or leave it but make up your mind fast.'

I swallowed hard. The lump in my throat felt like a foreign object, something the size of a whale. 'I'll come with you,' I muttered.

'Speak up. Learn to project. Perhaps Fran has a point.' This was below the belt stuff.

I faced up to him. 'Has she been complaining to you now?'

But he was frowning down at me, all tousled hair and tired eyes. 'And how. I got an earful. Apparently her poor performance was entirely your fault. You gave her the wrong prompts so she didn't know where she was. They completely threw her. She only managed to carry on through being in peak mental condition and her sheer personal devotion to me.'

Joe was trying not to laugh, starting to relax. His eyes were glinting and he was making a poor job of hiding his amusement.

'Is that what she said? Perhaps her peak devotion to you and sheer personal strength will motivate her to check the lines in time for tomorrow's performance,' I said, the words getting mixed up.

145

'I doubt it.'

I said goodnight to Hilda and Millie, both of whom were exhausted and were having a last cuppa together. The diva had led them a merry dance all evening. They'd been running round in circles to her demands.

'I think I'm going to cook you a meal,' Joe said, flinging his coat over one shoulder and hitching his laptop case under the other arm. 'It's my turn.'

'But what about tomorrow's show? Shouldn't you be giving Fran some private coaching?' Saying this was an awesome sacrifice on my part. I might hate the answer.

'Forget tomorrow. The only moment you can truly enjoy is now. Something will turn up. It usually does.'

I had no idea what he meant. I was not turning up. What or who could possibly show up to play Viola tomorrow? Of course, the theatre might burn down like Sheridan's Drury Lane theatre had burned down. Dear man, he'd come straight from the House of Commons and watched his theatre aflame from a nearby coffee house. 'Cannot a man take a glass of wine at his own fireside?' he'd said to his astonished friends.

Aliens might land in the West End and all the streets be cordoned off. Bird flu could sweep through the entire cast although, as yet, no serious signs of sniff or sneeze, apart from our Elinor.

I wondered if the foundations of the theatre were entirely trustworthy. The building might be perched on some perilously deep-dug and forgotten underground excavations and tunnels, buried and forgotten rivers, Neo-Gothic sewers. If it rained hard, those foundations might lose their grip and slide the lot into Victorian oblivion. But it wasn't raining that hard.

The fragile Fran might have something up her sleeve at this very moment. She might be planning to deactivate the sound system with some little pocket screwdriver, or fuse the entire theatre lighting. That would certainly be a major disaster.

'Do you think we ought to leave the theatre alone?' I hesitated in the street by the stage door. The street seemed very dark, eerily Victorian, teeming with cut throats and muggers. 'Is it safe?'

'I should imagine that after nearly a century, the theatre is used to being on its own at night. Apart from the ghosts. They are probably pretty lively, gliding around, reliving old shows and successes. What's going on in that fertile mind of yours?'

'I'm worried in case someone does something really stupid.' I didn't know what I thought.

'Such as spray paint graffiti on the walls? I hate Shakespeare. Something like that?'

'Like setting fire to the place—'

'All the more reason for you and me to get out quick. Here's the taxi. Hop in.' He held open the door for me, giving the driver our address as if we lived together and were not separated by a couple of floors. I hadn't been home for two days. I needed a shower and a change of clothes. Preferably into a warm bathrobe.

Joe slumped into a corner seat, closing his eyes in the darkness. He was going to doze the entire journey.

'Wake me up when we get there,' he said.

Catnapping was a gift. He was obviously worn out. I'd take a rain check on the meal. It was far too late to eat anyway. Heartburn was not my favourite dessert. My flat was cold and neglected. I turned on the heating and sat warming my hands in front of the mock heat. It was wonderful to be home and on my own, the politics of the theatre left far behind me. For a time, at least.

Joe had forgotten all about the offer of cooking me a meal. He said goodnight at his door, gave me a brief kiss on the cheek. But it missed and landed somewhere on my ear. A mouthful of short hair made him choke silently.

'Goodnight, Joe,' I said, patting his arm maternally. 'Sleep well.'

I made myself the promised hot chocolate, only forty calories a mug. I chose my mug with care. Each mug had its own character. The bone-china poppy mug was perfect for tonight. I sucked the froth off the spoon and switched on the telly, hoping for a decent film.

I was watching a B-movie thriller set in classic New York gangland with no clear idea of the plot or who was the baddie, when my phone rang. Someone was calling very late indeed.

'Hello,' I said, leaning on the phone. 'Who's that?'

CHAPTER NINETEEN

The trains down to Bournemouth were hourly so I planned to catch the first in the morning, at some unearthly hour when even dedicated milkmen were struggling to dig themselves out of bed.

I threw some clothes into a bag, set my alarm for 4.00 a.m. and tried to get some sleep. I joined fellow zombies on the dreaded Northern Line and reached the ticket office at Waterloo in time to buy a ticket before getting on the train. I lived in fear of being fined by some Gestapo-like guard, writing my name and address down in his little book, or throwing me off the train at some deserted station.

There was nothing to see as the train rumbled over points out of Waterloo Station on a black and sullen morning. One could not see the decay and squalor of that area of London. The darkness mercifully hid the derelict sites and swathes of graffiti.

I'd put a scribbled note under Joe's door. I hoped he'd see the folded paper and not simply tread on it.

'Sorry,' I'd written. 'Not running away, promise. Family emergency. Perhaps stage crew could prompt. Someone must be able to read. Sorry I'm always saying sorry.
Sophie.'

I tried to curl up small in my window seat to generate some body heat and conserve it within my skin. I'd known this might happen one day but not now when *Twelfth Night* was juddering along, waiting for Elinor to recover. There was no timing for these sorts of things. People died on Christmas Day. How inconsiderate was that? Something you could never forget, or minimize the shock, no matter how many glasses of punch or slices of brandy-laced puddings you'd consumed.

But my mother had not died. She was going into hospital for an operation. Something internal and female and unmentionable, she said.

'Sophie, I was going to tell you, some time, but I didn't know there'd be this cancellation. It just came up. Today. I have to take it. Sorry,' she'd said on the phone, sounding so much like me, BAFTA award for apologetic.

'Of course, you must take it,' I'd said.

'I've been waiting months. You know what these NHS lists are like. From here to the Wall of China. Then I got this call today. I've been trying to phone you but I guess you've been tied up at the theatre. At least I've got you now.'

'I'll come down straight away,' I said. 'They won't miss me. I'm not important. Anyone can prompt.'

'I'm sure you are important but you wouldn't want Mark to be fostered out by Welfare with some strange family, would you? They do that, you know, these days. Once Welfare find out he's going to be on his own. They interfere so. He'd hate it.'

'I'll catch the first train down tomorrow morning.' I looked at my watch and corrected myself. 'Today, I mean. Take care. See you soon.'

'Lovely, darling. Thank you.'

It was not an easy place to get to. My mother's cottage was on the outskirts of Swanage and perched on some forlorn cliffside. I didn't know how she was getting to the hospital, hadn't asked. No ambulance would make it to her place. They'd have to walk up a chalky path, knee-deep over gorse and sea thrift, or take the bumpy back lane, past the farm. Maybe she was well enough to make it to the hospital on her own feet, with me as escort, carrying her bag.

Bournemouth was waking up by the time I got there. I hurried down to the main square and got on an open-topped bus to

Swanage. Open-topped in this weather? They must think we are in training to dog-sleigh the Antarctic. It was far too cold to sit upstairs. I looked out of the window as we went across choppy grey water on the Sandbanks ferry, my first glimpse of the sea. Was I going to be in time to take my mother to hospital and to see Mark off to school?

My general incompetence couldn't answer any of these questions. I was doing my best, for once, but it wasn't anywhere near good enough. Somehow I was going to fail again. I caught a glimpse of Corfe Castle, the picturesque ruins that were all the Roundheads left after they rampaged in 1646.

I felt as if I had traversed through several time zones when at long last I reached my mother's cottage. It was not one of those pretty, roses over the door rural thatched picture-postcard Dorset cottages, but a farm labourer's bleak and narrow faced semi-detached, built at the turn of the century, so that the farm could keep their labour force on hand.

The house had a lost and isolated look. There was no character on its cement face, one square window downstairs, two up. It looked as if it ought to have steel cables running from each corner of the roof to keep it anchored to the ground on such a windy spot.

My mother had made an effort with the garden. She had always liked gardening but nature was determined to beat her. The wind, the salt, the chalky ground claimed her flowers and shrubs. The only plants that flourished were weeds.

I could never understand why she chose to live in such a forlorn place after my father died. He couldn't help dying, skidding on an icy road, having an argument with a very large oak tree. She would never say. She never talked about it, as if she was punishing herself.

I opened the front door, which was unlocked, and went inside. Mark was sitting at the kitchen table, eating from a bowl of cornflakes. He looked up, somewhat surprised. I hadn't seen him for a long time. The moment stretched into several minutes. He had grown so much, was far taller now. My heart lurched at the sight of him.

'Hi,' I said, with a hello wave, all cheerful. 'It's me.'

'Hi,' he said, greeting me with an independent nod. 'Gran's gone to hospital already. She had to go early. A taxi came as near as possible. I'll get myself off to school. The bus calls for me at the end of the lane.'

'Great. I'll be here now.'

'There's no need,' he said stiffly, very grown-up and off-hand, putting his bowl in the sink. 'We can manage without you. I can look after myself. You can go back to London, to your theatre.'

He turned his back on me, narrow shoulders set in disapproval.

'I don't think you are allowed to look after yourself,' I said, putting my bag down on the floor. 'Sorry, but it's the law. I think you're going to have to put up with your mother.'

'Oh, are you my mother?'

His words shocked me.

It wasn't the answer I expected. I went cold and rigid. I'd been coming down as often as I could. But show runs were unpredictable and sometimes there had been a long gap. I drowned in guilt. No excuses. I could have come on a Sunday and gone back the same day, spent a few hours with him.

Mark tidied away the milk and cornflakes packet. He was tall as I had expected, slim and wiry. Dark tousled hair, gelled spiky in today's fashion, dressed in school uniform, black trousers, navy fleece. A schoolbag was on the floor. I didn't know what to say to my own son. I went blank, like it was an impossible question rattled off at speed on *Mastermind*. Chosen subject: son.

'Gran's in ward seven. Her op is at eleven o'clock, I think,' he said. 'You could go and see her if you like. There's time.'

'Is my old bike still here?' I asked.

'It's in the shed. You could cycle into town.'

Mark was putting on his anorak. He was leaving to meet the bus that took him to school. I had to say something, try to bridge the empty conversation gap. Surely I knew how to talk to my own son?

'I'll be here when you come home,' I said. 'I'm staying now to look after both of you.'

He looked at me closely, lips pursed. 'You've cut your hair,' he said. 'Cool.'

151

*

It was a shock when your own son doesn't give you a hug or a kiss, but I suppose I didn't deserve either. My mother had stepped in during those early days, supporting me, taking care of me. I'd looked after Mark in his baby years, living with my mother, working part-time at hotels and cafés. I worked all hours, needing the money. But as soon as preparatory school loomed, my mother encouraged me to go back to London, to continue my so-called theatrical career behind the footlights.

'I can look after Mark,' she'd said. 'You go get your name in lights. Come down as often as you can.'

I'd sent as much of my earnings as I could. It was only recently, with the West Enders group, that I had enough money to rent a place of my own and still send them a decent cheque every month.

The cottage had two bedrooms upstairs, my mother's and Mark's. The bathroom was an extension built on out the back. I'd sleep in my mother's room till she came home from hospital, then it would be the sofa in the front room. At least the front room would be warmer. Both bedrooms were bracing.

This was my time for getting to know my son again. I had left it too long. Where had the time gone? No wonder he thought I was a stranger. I was a stranger.

I washed up the few things in the sink and tidied round before getting my old bike from the shed. It was in good condition. Perhaps Mum used it.

As I left, I noticed that the cottage next door was empty. My mother had never mentioned that. She must have been lonely, living up here without neighbours. It didn't help my mounting feeling of guilt.

I cycled down to Queens Road, to the hospital. The freedom of cycling was a remembered joy, skimming downhill. The sea air blew through my short hair, and for a moment I felt a surge of carefree expectation. What had Joe said: the only moment you can enjoy is now.

It was not difficult to find my mother in the hospital. She was done up in a blue paper nightie, hair in a net cap, waiting to go to theatre. She looked older than I remembered, thinner, greyer, skin like paper. Her eyes were like mine, hazel, so direct, sunlit with golden specks.

How little I knew of this woman, yet she had always been there for me. My smile almost hurt my face. I peeled back the years, remembering when I was small and bewildered, then a teenage rebel, a budding actress. She had never once criticized my wayward ambition.

'Hello, Mum,' I said.

'Sophie, sweetheart,' she said, a bit slurred from her pre-med. 'How lovely to see you. I'm so glad. I hoped you'd be here in time, to put my mind at rest.'

'You should have told me before. I would have come, anytime. Mark pretended that he didn't recognize me. Little devil. But I'm here now, to look after you both. And I'm going to take good care of you both.'

She grinned a bit lop-sidedly. 'He's at an awkward age, Sophie. It'll take time. Don't worry, you'll make friends again. You were great friends when he was little. He's a good boy.'

'Shall I stay until you come out of recovery?'

'No need, dear. I shall probably be pretty woozy. You go home and look after Mark. A phone call will do. I shall sleep well knowing that you are with him.'

I stayed with her till it was time for her to be wheeled down to theatre. She looked very small on the trolley and that frightened me. Then I kissed her and went outside, feeling lost and like a child again. My mother had shrunk. Funny, I didn't even know what my son liked to eat now. I hoped all children liked pizzas.

It was uphill going home and I was out of condition. As I huffed and puffed, I wondered what was happening with *Twelfth Night* but I wasn't going to phone. No umbilical cord. It was Joe's problem now. I had served the ball firmly into his court. Maybe Fran would suddenly find some talent and put on a good show.

I loved the view of Swanage Bay, the distant Purbeck Hills and Dulston Head, and the high white cliffs of the Jurassic coast. Mark and I could go for walks if the weather held. I turned on the radio while I pretended to do some housework. It was tuned to Radio

153

Solent, spilling out local news and music. Mark's bedroom was boy chaos, so I closed the door and didn't touch it. But I spotted that he still had Leo the lion which I had given him a long time ago. It was looking a bit bedraggled, its tawny mane chewed.

My mother's recipe book was open at chocolate muffins. It didn't look too difficult to follow so I set about making a batch. This was new territory. Perhaps they were Mark's favourite. The page looked well thumbed. I only burnt a few of them. The rest of the batch looked pretty good. I put a cloth over them.

I'd been phoning the hospital, becoming their number-one pestilent relation. Eventually they told me that Mrs Gresham had come out of theatre, and that the operation had been successful and she was back on the ward.

'Please tell her that I phoned. I'm her daughter, Sophie. Give her my love and I'll be in to see her tomorrow.'

'Right, Miss Gresham. We'll do that.'

Mark was standing in the doorway, looking a typical dishevelled schoolboy wreck, shirt hanging out, tie askew, socks rumpled. He didn't seem to know whether to come in or go out. He flung his bag on the floor.

'Gran's all right, then?' he asked.

'She's fine. She's sleeping. The operation went well and I'm going in to see her tomorrow morning.'

'Whatever. I'll come with you,' he said, off-hand. 'You can write me a sick note for school.' He sat down at the kitchen table and helped himself to a chocolate muffin. They were still hot.

The heat didn't stop him from taking a bite. The hostility slipped a fraction from his eyes as he munched. He didn't speak till he had finished eating.

'These are my favourite buns,' he said. 'Awesome.'

I didn't push things. I couldn't become an overnight mother. Mark sat himself at the kitchen table, doing his homework. He seemed to be so self-disciplined. No obligatory anti-school behaviour. While I made supper, he went up to his room and played loud metal rock music. It was a protest of sorts.

But he did come down for pizza, salad, and strawberry ice cream. He said nothing at all. He watched television while I washed up and cleared the kitchen. It was dark now and the cottage seemed more isolated than ever, but within the sound of the sea crashing on the rocks. I could hear the southerly wind, rattling the sash windows. They ought to be fixed. I didn't know how my mother could stand the loneliness, but she was that kind of person. Wasn't she? I didn't know what kind of person she was.

I went into the sitting room. Mark was sprawled on the sofa, kicking the arm, drawing in a book. I looked over his shoulder. It was an ancient castle and moat, every detail of stone and buttress correct, the wooden drawbridge in midair.

'Where's that, Mark?' I asked. 'Where did you see this old castle?'

'Dunno,' he said. 'I made it up.'

It was an amazingly detailed drawing with tiny, feathery pencil strokes of light and shade. The aging of the stones was quite remarkable work. I didn't say anything. No point in suddenly becoming the gushing mother.

I took my mug of coffee over to the armchair and sat down. Mark was immersed in the drawing.

'The painting on the wall,' I said. 'Did you do that as well?'

It was an unframed painting, daubs of bright colour that somehow merged into a raging sea. It looked very young and somehow full of energy.

'Yeah. Acrylic paint.'

'It's very good. And the paintings in the kitchen?'

'Rubbish stuff I brought home from school. But gran likes them. She put them up.'

'Would you like some coffee?' I asked, not arguing.

'I don't drink coffee,' he said, not looking up from his drawing. 'Gran says it isn't good for you.'

'Quite right.'

This was awful. I didn't know how to talk to my own son. The silence hung like a shroud. I had to learn how to be his mother all over again.

'Would you like to play a game?' I suggested.

He sent me a withering look. 'I'm too old for snakes and ladders.'

'I was thinking more of poker or gin rummy. We could play for ten pence pieces. Do you know how to play gin rummy?' I rummaged around for packs of cards.

Mark was calculating the odds already. He closed his drawing book. 'Cool,' he said.

CHAPTER TWENTY

We took spray carnation buds and a box of chocolate peppermints to the hospital the next morning. Mark said they were her favourite sweet. I wrote a note, at his dictation, for his head teacher. The boy was a born organizer. He'd appoint me as his PA soon.

He'd won £1.50 off me last night so our relationship was a rung up the ladder. It was still a slippery ladder.

My mother was looking frail, in pain, stitched up and on a drip but pleased to see us. Mark was thrown by the disinfectant smell and gory hospital atmosphere but acted cool. I was proud of him. He inspected my mother's bed chart as if he was a visiting surgeon.

This boy was only eleven, but he acted going on twenty. His genes were ahead of his shoe size. Had I done this to him? Was I at fault? Had I stripped him of a normal childhood?

'How are you feeling?' I asked, knowing it was a stupid question. She had aged. Whenever I thought of my mother, the picture in the frame was of the young widow who brought me up. I never noticed the years creeping on. They had suddenly arrived, robbing her skin, her face, her bones.

'I'm OK,' she said. 'A bit sore. Chocolate peppermints! They're my favourites. Lovely, thank you. The food here is not up to scratch. Where are all these gourmet cooks from television? I thought we would be getting cordon bleu menus.'

'When you get home, you'll have wonderful meals,' I promised, forgetting I couldn't cook.

'She does a mean pizza,' said Mark, not looking at me. He was investigating the equipment around the bed. 'And she made chocolate muffins. Some were burnt.'

It was praise of a sort. It had been a shop pizza but I added anchovies and extra feta cheese. Not exactly home cooking but a step forward. I was not at ease being talked about as if I was in another room, so I hauled him away as soon as my mother showed signs of tiring. It would be antisocial to swop germs.

That afternoon Mark went out to play football with some friends. I let him go. I was hardly his keeper. I flaked out on to the sofa, my thoughts in a turmoil. What had I done, all those years ago. Nothing more than offer a homeless actor a bed for the night. Not even a bed, a lumpy sofa.

'Sounds like five-star Hilton,' he'd said, hanging about till I'd finished my chores at the theatre. 'Take me home, lass. I'll be gone in the morning. You can't leave me here on the street, not in this weather. It would be cruelty to animals.'

I couldn't refuse him and my heart melted. I had a job and a regular salary. He was really down and out. It was nothing, only the loan of a sofa and a blanket.

It was not a long walk through the drifting snowflakes to the double-fronted Victorian villa that had seen better days, now divided into flats and bed-sits. My fingers were numb and blue and I fumbled with the key in the lock. I'd left my gloves in the café.

'Here, let me do it,' he said.

We'd climbed the stairs to the attic flat, glad to be out of the snow, but the house was no warmer and the top floor was exposed to the cold northeasterly wind that crept in all the window cracks. I'd stuffed them with paper. They'd made their maids sleep in the attic, poor girls. Up at five, to sweep the grates, to light all the fires.

I was shivering. This was life in a cold climate.

'Sorry there's no heating,' I said. 'The electric fire needs fixing and the landlord takes ages over any repairs.'

'Don't worry. I'm going to flake out in five minutes. I've had enough of today. I'll be asleep before you've made your hot water bottle.'

'I haven't got a hot water bottle.'

'You're not very well organized, are you?'

I showed him the minuscule bathroom and heard water run and the system flush while I hunted out a blanket and put a clean pillowcase on a spare pillow. My room was even more basic. A single bed against the wall, a chest of drawers, curtained space for hanging clothes and an ancient, sagging sofa angled towards a toaster-sized portable black-and-white television set.

My flatmate, Jilly, was away for the night. This was not unusual as she had a regular boyfriend. She might return at any time.

He came out of the bathroom, cleaned up, jeans folded over his arm, trainers twinned in his free hand. I averted my eyes from the bare brown legs, muscular arms, his white T-shirt almost glowing in the gloom.

I'd put on my striped M&S nightshirt. It was about as sexy as a bin liner. He couldn't see my scraggy black hair. It was tied back with a scrap of ribbon.

'Goodnight,' I said, my hand on the switch of the bedside lamp.

He folded himself sideways on to the sofa and pulled the blanket up to his ears. 'Goodnight,' he grunted.

I remembered it all so clearly, had replayed it a hundred times. I stared into the darkness, listening to his breathing. My guest did not sound at all grateful but then it had not been a good day for him. Whereas I had everything in the world to look forward to, a career, good friends, perhaps one day falling in love with the right man. I would like that.

I'd never had a man sleeping in my room before. Chalk up new but unnerving experience. I listened to the creaking of the sofa as he turned, trying to bend his long legs into a comfortable position.

It was not long before I was asleep, so I was unaware of the temperature dropping to below zero. Ice formed on the windows, outside and inside. Sometime in the small hours, he crept into my bed for human warmth and to stretch out his cramped legs. His feet were frozen.

'Sorry, I can't sleep,' he said, shivering.

I wrapped my arms round his cold body, as if he was a child. But I felt the rough hair on his chest brush against my skin and my breasts tingled. This was no child. A fine flame of awareness stirred in my body.

159

Perhaps I had been waiting for him. A man who came from nowhere. A young man whom I didn't know, so there was no commitment, no strings, no relationship involved. I wanted the experience, to feel what it was like to be a woman, to be as knowing as my friends with their flirty winks and giggles.

His mouth was on my neck, kissing my skin with sweet and gentle kisses. The fear left me. This lost and despairing young man could be the right person to teach me the secrets of womanhood. It might even be helping him, restoring that elusive male self-confidence as well as giving him the warmth of my bed.

He would be gone in the morning and no one would know. Only me and my body. I wasn't even sure of his name. I don't think he knew mine.

'Don't be afraid,' he murmured. 'I won't do anything you don't want me to do.'

It was all so new. I had never gone any further than a few kisses and furtive fumblings in the back of a car. This half-naked young man wrapping himself around me was a different matter.

'I don't know what I want,' I said, my courage almost deserting me like water down a plughole. But my body knew. It moved itself, had a mind of its own, shifted so that my breasts were against his arm. It was enough to fire him.

He cupped my roundness tentatively in case I was alarmed and pushed him out of bed, but his fingers were gently finding the nipple and with slow strokes, taking his time, he brought me alive and pulsing.

I had never felt such an exquisite sensation. I was throbbing, longing for more, desperate for a closer touch. His hand went under my passion-killing nightshirt and I gasped as his fingers trailed my bare flesh.

My whole body was coming alive but I didn't know what to do. A tingling engulfed me down to my toes. Any minute I would be out of control.

'Slowly, slowly, sweetheart,' he said gently. 'Don't be in such a hurry. We've got all night.'

His T-shirt had gone, flung off and thrown on the floor. His kisses were sending my mind into a spin, exploring the moist softness of our mouths. I was responding with an intensity I did not know I possessed.

He paused, lifting his weight off me. I saw the darkness of the night through the window. Everywhere was frosty and silent and sleeping.

'Don't stop,' I whispered.

'Are you sure?'

'Yes.'

'Really sure?'

For an answer I pulled his head down and captured his mouth in a kiss that sent his pulses racing. His hand moved down to my stomach, circling its smoothness, stroking my hips and finding the softness of my inner thighs.

I could hardly believe what was happening. I didn't know it would be like this. I was being transported to another planet that was all shooting stars and bursts of moonlight. Light was dancing on the ceiling.

'Has no one ever touched you here before,' he said softly.

'No, never.'

'Do you like it?'

'It's wonderful.' I sighed, giving myself up to this new and amazing pleasure.

Of course he had been gone in the morning before I was even awake. I should have known that would happen. He had collected his clothes and let himself out.

I stretched myself now, letting go of my long-ago dormant memories and went outside the cottage, standing in my mother's windy, weedy garden, drinking in the view and the fresh, scented air. The landscape calmed me. There was such a sense of peace even though a southeasterly gale was blowing up. Clouds were gathering like bruises. There had been warnings on the radio. I hoped Mark would get home before it got really blowy. And it was beginning to get dark. Surely he couldn't play football in the dark?

It was a long time since I had thought so deeply about that night. I didn't regret it for one instant although the following weeks had been a roller-coaster of despair and exhilaration. They had been

161

long and difficult, trying to work, trying to hide the sickness, trying to disguise my growing size.

My mother never asked the name of the father. When I told her that I was pregnant, she went very quiet. Then she took me into her arms and comforted me and brought me home. Months later, she held my newly born baby and loved him without question from that moment on.

Mark was a mirror image of his father, short of the New York glamour and, of course, as yet lacking the authority, the fame and the power. He was an unruly boy but he had the same dark rangy looks and firm jutting jaw, the same piercing eyes.

'Can we play that gin betting game after supper?' Mark called out. He was trudging along the cliff path, muddy and dishevelled from the activities on pitch, shirt flapping. He looked damp and sweaty. He needed a bath.

'Sure,' I said, relieved to see him. Mothers worry all the time but I hadn't remembered. The wind was getting quite fierce. 'But don't up the stakes.'

'I'll be making five or six quid a week at this rate,' he said confidently. 'Awesome. I need new tyres for my bike.'

'So you're planning on becoming another Bill Gates, eh? I'll be coming to you when the housekeeping runs out and we are down to bread and cheese.'

'We could go to town and have fish and chips. I'll lend you the money. Gran won't do fish and chips in case the pan catches fire.'

'Quite right, too. Chip pans are dangerous things. But we'll go to that fish restaurant on the front sometime, the one near the tourist office. They are pretty good. I used to work there, part-time, when you were a baby.'

'Did you know me when I was a baby?'

'I sure did. From the very first second of your life.'

He nodded, still off-hand. 'I guess so. That's so cool.'

I wondered if he knew another word.

CHAPTER TWENTY-ONE

My mother's progress continued steadily despite the lack of gourmet food, which really annoyed her. We went to see her every day. I realized I was going to be vacuuming around in the cottage for a long time. I was already getting first-degree cycle burn. I ought to phone management and tell them I wasn't coming back until she was better. Call it extended sick leave. They might get uppity but for once I didn't really care.

Bill Naughton took the call. I didn't want to talk to management so timed it when they wouldn't be there. Neat but cowardly.

'Hi, Sophie! Where you been? We've missed you. How are you? Are you all right? We heard it was an emergency.'

'My mother had to go into hospital. A last-minute cancellation came up for an operation she'd been waiting ages for, quite serious.' I didn't mention Mark. No one knew about him.

'Is she recovering OK? The op was OK?' Bill's vocabulary was pretty limited today. Perhaps he was stressed out.

I could hear theatre sounds in the background, which bugged me. Work was going on which I missed. I wanted to know what was happening.

'She's doing fine, smiling through a forest of drips and lines. A bit woozy, still. But how's the show? How has Fran been doing?'

'Hey, you should have been here. Fran had her Pinocchio put out of joint. Quite severely. You should have seen the tantrum. She was a danger to passing traffic. Elinor came back, bless her. A bit croaky but a walking miracle. She dragged herself from her sickbed and took over with barely a hitch. Though she did need a double Scotch in the interval.'

I felt suddenly so pathetic. Elinor had rallied and shown up. I was the fraud, the useless nonentity. She had come to Joe's rescue.

'How marvellous. I'm so glad. She's a real trouper.'

'One of the stage hands is prompting. We've got a youngster who can read. Doesn't concentrate like you, says the prompt lines like a sergeant major on drill parade, but it's OK. And Joe takes over when the boy has to change scenery.'

Joe was prompting. I felt snail-sized, ready to be stepped on. His caustic comments would deafen my ears. I ought to be put on the witness protection scheme.

'That's good,' I said with unfelt optimism. 'I'm glad all is well but I had to be with her. I've only got one mother.'

'Don't worry, we understand. We're doing fine. I miss you, of course. That lovely, frozen smile that needs warming up. I'd soon warm you up.' His voice dropped to an intimate, sexy phone call level. Thank goodness for several hundred miles of cable.

'So Mr Harrison will know how draughty the prompt corner is,' I said. 'He never got that door fixed.'

'It's been fixed now.'

'Typical. I'll be back as soon as I can.'

'Can't wait to see you, darling.'

I put the phone down. I couldn't use my mobile any more as it needed recharging and the charger was back in London. I only hoped Bill wouldn't use the redial system to get hold of this number. He could be devious. I didn't want him phoning here for off-stage late-night intimate chats.

Mark stood in the doorway, tossing a ball from hand to hand. No school today. I wasn't good at entertaining small boys. Apart from unsuitable card games.

'All right if I go down to the beach, kick a ball around?' he asked, unsure of whether he ought to ask or not. 'Some of the gang will be there.'

'In this weather?' It was dull and gloomy, scurrying clouds laden with rain. He'd get drenched.

'Gran says I ought to get more fresh air.'

'If Gran says, then we do as Gran says. OK, but take something waterproof.'

'Whatever.'

That vocabulary. Were words part of the curriculum these days?

But he had already gone, down the lane on his bike, legs stuck out sideways. I hoped his brakes were working properly. I worried about everything now.

My mother had a small but interesting collection of local books. I was reading one about the Purbeck stone and marble quarrying in Swanage, how many historic bits and pieces of old London were salvaged and brought back to Swanage as ballast in the quarry boats, columns, milestones and statues. There was an old jail house and the front of Swanage Town Hall was once the 1670 porch of the medieval Mercer's Hall in London. All the cast-iron bollards around Swanage still carried the names of London boroughs. Perhaps Mark and I would go look at them, a sort of living, walking history lesson. He wasn't very interested in history.

There was a Shakespearean play lurking somewhere in the names of the old quarries, Dancing Ledge, Seacombe and Windspit. The Swanage hills were honeycombed and scarred with ancient workings. And the clock tower on the front was from the old London Bridge, commemorating the Duke of Wellington.

I was lost in the book, my coffee cooling, when a familiar sound dragged me back to this century. Rain was spattering hard on the window panes. It was starting to hail and sleet. That big black cloud was stationery right overhead, poised to blanket Swanage in a torrential downpour. Mark was in weekend gear, sweater and jeans. Surely he'd have the sense to take cover? It would blow over eventually.

But it didn't blow over. An hour later it was still pouring. A trickle of water was running down the stony cliff path, and behind the house, a stream of rain was washing down the lane, taking loose stones and debris with it. I couldn't sit there and wait for Mark to swim home.

I put on a long, belted mackintosh of my mother's, wellington boots, tied a scarf round my head, packed Mark's waterproofs and a change of clothes into a plastic bag, threw in a packet of mints. I also put on sunglasses which seemed daft but was the only way I would be able to see in the rain.

It was too dangerous to cycle down the lane, so I splashed through the flow and puddles. I had my fingers firmly on the squeaking brake lever as I attempted to free-wheel down the steep roads that led to the sea front. A few cars passed me, drenching me with fans of spray, so considerate these warm, dry drivers on their mobiles.

I spotted Mark huddled alone under the porch of one of the seafront beach huts. The porch gave him very little shelter, and much larger drops of rain were gathering and falling on his shoulders. I parked my bike against the rails and trudged over the wet sand to him. He was comatose with cold, face pinched with misery.

'Mum,' he said in half a voice.

I put my arms round him and gave him a big hug. He didn't respond in any way. 'Here's your waterproofs. Put them on now. I've brought dry clothes as well for you to change into.'

'Ch-change where?' He was shivering.

'You can change into them at the fish and chip shop. Fancy some fish and chips for supper?'

He came marginally more alive. 'At the f-fish restaurant on the corner?'

'Yup. Where's your bike?'

'I dunno.'

I pushed his arms into the waterproof jacket, zipped it and pulled up the hood. It was like dressing a flexie doll. 'We'll find it. Come along before the weather gets any worse.'

'I've lost my ball.'

'It'll get washed up on to the rocks. We'll look for it later.'

'How do you know?'

'I used to live here, remember? Tides. Everything gets washed up eventually.'

We found his bike where he had abandoned it and pushed both bikes to the fish restaurant. I chained them to the quay railing. We went inside into a fog of steam and heat from the fryers. It was like a sauna. The smell rose up, that succulent smell of frying fish, fish freshly caught that day from the sea.

I grabbed a window seat so that we could watch the rain while we ate in the dry. Mark hurried off to the gents clutching his bag of dry clothes. Meanwhile, I ordered cod and chips for two, an orange juice for Mark and a large glass of house red, any vintage, for myself.

I wasn't too wet, considering. Gran's mackintosh had stood up to the onslaught. I was damp on the shoulders and where it flapped open. My hair was soaked but it would soon dry in this heat. I wiped the sunglasses and put them back on the top of my head.

Mark came back, half-grinning, in dry clothes and dry socks, carrying his sodden trainers. He had recovered his spirits. 'Thanks for the mints.'

He looked at my glass of red wine and was about to say something but I got in first.

'I know. Gran says drinking isn't good for you.'

'Do you drink?'

'Occasionally. Not exactly an alcoholic but I like a glass or two of red. It warms you up, cheers you up and is apparently good for the heart. Medicinal.'

'Why are you wearing shades?' he asked curiously.

'They're cool,' I said.

'Whatever.'

It was a great meal. Mark tucked into his battered cod and chips as if he had never seen a chip in his life before. Dollops of tomato sauce decorated his plate with surrealistic art. He drew in sauce. He even talked, which was a minor triumph. Not a lot, but enough to chalk it up as a civilized meal.

His conversation was mainly speculation about the dinosaur footprints found on the shore, and whether we would see Britain's only poisonous snake, the adder, on one of our cliff walks. He hoped we would. I was not so enthusiastic. Dinosaurs (footprints only) I could cope with but not snakes.

We waited till the black cloud exhausted itself and blew off to find a new area to lambaste. I hurried across the street to buy new trainers. No way could Mark walk home in that sodden pair. They were coming apart at the seams.

It was getting too dark to look for the lost ball. Mark accepted that. 'We could look tomorrow,' he said, pushing his bike uphill. He had said *we*. It was a small victory. I savoured the word.

I was getting short of clothes to change into. I'd only brought a small bag and had already worn and washed everything twice. My mother's sweaters and jerseys were too small for me. Nothing for me to borrow. I needed to shop soon.

Mark switched on the television while I made a pot of tea. He wanted to catch the result of some football match, maybe soccer or rugby union. Something that needed a ball and a field for men to run about on. I could hear the newscaster's tinny voice as I boiled a kettle and set a tray. My mother still used a teapot, milk jug and tray. Not a teabag in sight in her kitchen. She would get on very well with Elinor.

Mark stood in the kitchen doorway, eyeing me warily, as if expecting me to suddenly take off on a broomstick. He'd read all the Harry Potters. 'That theatre you work for,' he said. 'In London.'

'Yes, in London,' I agreed.

'Are you called the West Enders?'

'Yes, that's the name of the company, why?'

'And the theatre is an old Victorian theatre called the Royale?'

'Is this a quiz programme you're watching?'

'No, it's on the news. Your theatre's just collapsed down a hole. It's fallen down. Made a big hole. Pretty cool, don't you think?'

CHAPTER TWENTY-TWO

It was my awful, awful premonition, happening in slow motion. I felt as if it was all my fault, that I had willed it to happen like some twenty-first-century white witch. A couple of toads and a newt stirred in a cauldron.

They were showing dim shots of the lopsided theatre, tilting to one side, lights hanging off the front like Christmas decorations gone wrong.

No one was being allowed inside, except rescue crews, as it was still too dangerous. They were searching for any trapped survivors. Speculation was being aired of a long-ago abandoned underground tunnel that everyone had forgotten about or maybe an ancient stream that had been diverted and was now bursting its channel due to the heavy rain.

A television reporter in a belted raincoat was standing outside in the rain, under an umbrella, reading from an autocue. Behind him were police cars, fire engines and ambulances, police milling about, the public gawping at a distance at the taped-off area like a mob at a murder scene.

'It's a miracle that more people were not hurt,' he was saying, straight to camera. 'The West Enders opened only last week with an acclaimed performance of *Twelfth Night* and they have played to packed houses ever since. Here is Joe Harrison from New York, the guest director of *Twelfth Night*, designer of the set, artist supremo. Mr Harrison, how are you feeling seeing all this?'

Joe was standing in the rain, no umbrella, drenched. His face was shocked, eyes like granite. Rain dripped off his face, his dark hair flattened to his head.

'I'm gutted,' he said.

'How relieved are you that so few people were injured?'

Joe's face glazed over at the stupidity of question. 'Of course I'm immensely glad that the audience had not arrived. But my cast were there and the stage crew.'

I was stunned, seeing Joe again, seeing him so distressed. 'But who's been hurt?' I demanded of the television screen. 'Tell me, tell me, who's been injured?'

Mark came over and patted my hand. It was such a sweet gesture. I held on to his palm, feeling the soft young skin with one part of my mind, the other part shouting at the screen.

'They didn't say anyone had died, Mum. Some people injured, a few people, they said,' he said, quite sensibly.

He'd called me Mum. Second time ever. How come a moment of joy and despair could be mixed together? But it was. That was life. It deals you both cards at the same time.

'So will the show still go on?' asked the reporter, more inane questions. Did they go on a course for who could ask the most stupid questions?

Joe was obviously restraining himself from knocking the bloke's head off. 'Not at the Royale, obviously. We'll be looking for a new theatre,' he said. 'We have a magnificent cast and are sold out for weeks. It's just a hiccup.'

'Please, please say who is injured.' I asked. The screen wasn't answering. The reporter signed off and returned everyone to the studio where it was dry and warm and plenty of coffee was on hand and the newscasters were wandering about with important sheafs of paper in their hands.

I sank back, despairing. My friends might be injured.

Mark sat me down and was pouring out the tea in a motherly way. 'You could phone someone,' he said, taking charge. 'Have you got their numbers? I'll bring the phone through. The lead is quite long.'

I was drinking tea but I couldn't taste it. Joe was safe. It was a shock to find out that I really cared, my thoughts running away, worrying like crazy. Had I, all this time, cared about him? No, not perhaps on that cold and snowy night, long ago. He had been a surprise then, a sort of unexpected present. But now, it had all changed. He had come into my life again, a different person, someone I could love.

Mark was nudging me with the phone. 'Phone someone up, Mum,' he said, very grown up and bossy. Miraculously he was not one of those children glued to a computer screen or playstation. He could think for himself and for me, now. 'Shall I get your bag? Are the numbers in your bag?'

I could have hugged him to bits. I nodded before I did something he wouldn't like. Mark raced upstairs to fetch my shoulder bag, the one I'd brought down with me and barely used since.

Here he was, looking after me when I was supposed to be looking after him. He threw the bag on to the sofa and started to undo the clasp as if this was beyond my stressed-out ability. I found the scrap of paper that passed for a list of friends.

'How did the theatre fall down a hole?' Mark asked.

'Underneath London are masses and masses of tunnels,' I said. 'All dug out at different times for different reasons. There's all the underground train routes, twelve of them, streams diverted under roads and into culverts and tunnels and pipes, then the gas and electricity and phone cables. And there are some underground tunnels which they didn't use, just abandoned. It's a labyrinth down there and a wonder any building stays upright.'

'A bit like Venice.'

'Not as watery as Venice. More like a honeycomb of holes at different levels, like inside a Crunchie bar. Not very safe.'

The first to hand was Joe's mobile number. Mark was dialling it. It seemed ironic that Mark was doing it, phoning Joe's mobile. He passed it to me.

'Hello, Joe, Joe?' I said. It was Joe answering. 'We saw you on the television, all the news and had to phone.'

'Sophie, thank God. Is that you? Are you all right? Where are you? We thought you were still inside, trapped. You said it was an emergency but you didn't say where you were going. We thought you'd come back here to the theatre. They found your mohair in the debris.' His voice was shaking. 'Your lilac jersey.'

171

'My mohair? What do you mean?'

'It was downstage right of the stage that collapsed. Your prompt corner has gone. It's disappeared down a vast crater. Bit more than a nasty draught now. I've been out of my mind with worry about you. The firemen won't go near the hole or let anyone else till it's been shored up and made safe. They've been using some infra red thing that detects body heat.'

Mark was snuggled up to my hip, pressed against me, trying to listen to both sides of the conversation. I didn't blame him. This was high drama on anyone's list. 'My mother had to go into hospital for a major operation,' I said. 'It was a last-minute cancellation. I had to come down and look after her.'

'Your mother? Is she all right? We thought you were at the theatre, doing something. You know, Sophie do this, do that. I thought you were lying somewhere under the rubble.' His voice broke off, unable to say any more.

I didn't know how to explain, to put his mind at rest.

Mark took the phone from me. 'Hello,' he said clearly and calmly. 'Sophie's all right. She's not down any hole or injured. She's sitting here with me, drinking tea. But she wants to know who is injured.'

He handed the phone back to me. 'Hello?' I said, feebly. 'Joe?'

'Who was that?' he asked abruptly.

'I want to know who is injured,' I said. 'Please tell me.'

'Bill Naughton, the stage manager. He's been taken to St Thomas's Hospital. He was caught by a collapsing wall. Also a couple of stage hands, walking wounded, cuts and bruises, not critical. That's all. We were very lucky. The cast got out with a few scratches, bruises, all very shocked.'

'What about your costumes and your beautiful sets?'

'We've lost most of the sets. The costumes are still there, if we are ever allowed to go in to retrieve them. So where are you?'

'Dorset,' I said, reluctantly. 'It was a family emergency.'

'You could have told me. I've been nearly out of my mind.'

'No, I couldn't,' I said. Mark was bright-eyed with curiosity. He loved this insight into adult stupidity. He started making weird faces, hoping to cheer me up, make me laugh. Nothing was a laughing matter and I moved him away, but not too far.

'Have you got someone there?' Joe was asking. Mark was grinning from ear to ear, waving his arms about, maniac-style.

'Yes, I have someone here,' I said, trying to hold on to normality. 'But it's not what you might think, so stop asking questions. This is all personal, private and nothing to do with the theatre.'

'I want to know where you are and what you are doing,' said Joe, suddenly all New York and arrogant. 'I've been worried out of my mind, thinking you were in the collapsed part of the theatre. OK, you're safe and I'm one hundred per cent glad, but where the hell are you?'

'Swanage,' Mark yelled. He started to spell it. 'S . . . W—'

I couldn't help it. I was trying to gag him with my hand but Mark was giggling and punching and rolling about on the sofa. Talk about two juvenile idiots. I was upset about the theatre and about Bill Naughton being in hospital, but this boy by my side was the most wonderful person and I loved him more than my own life.

'I'll come up to London, as soon as I can, to help with moving the costumes. Another couple of weeks should see this through,' I said, trying to recover my status as firm mother. Mark was like a wriggling jellyfish.

'See what through?' Joe asked.

'Me, see me through,' Mark shouted again, thoroughly enjoying himself. He was in such good spirits, I couldn't tell him off. I'd never seen him acting so ridiculous and childish and downright joyous. He'd grown up before his time and suddenly he had shed all those extra years in a few minutes of wild and wonderful idiot behaviour.

'Do excuse us,' I said. 'I am trying to control a complete idiot. It's time to put him back in the dungeon and turn on the thumb screws, or I won't get a moment's peace.'

'What?' Joe was completely bemused.

'I'll phone again, soon.'

'And I'll beat her again at gin rummy,' Mark shrieked before I could throttle him. He was falling all over the place, laughing. I put the phone down.

'That was very silly,' I said. 'I was trying to have a serious conversation. People have been hurt. The theatre is a very old

173

Victorian theatre and part of it has been badly damaged. Heaven knows when we'll get any more money to repair it. I'll probably be out of a job.'

Mark sobered up a bit. 'Right. Sorry.'

'Never mind. No one has died, thank goodness, but I'll have to go and see Bill Naughton, the stage manager, the one who's in hospital, and help Hilda move the costumes into storage. They are both old friends.'

'I could come with you. I've never been to London.'

'It's not that easy,' I said, juggling plans, all useless. 'We've got Gran to think of. We can't go rushing off to London, any old time, and leave her. But I should go sometime. They need me.'

'I could stay overnight with a friend if you have to go,' said Mark, tidying the tea tray and taking it into the kitchen. He'd gone back to being a grown-up. 'You know, a sleep-over like in American movies. I could do that.'

'Well, that's a possibility,' I began, hesitantly.

'But you will come back, won't you?' he asked, a bit off-hand. 'And not stay away for years and years.'

'Of course, I'll come back. I'm never going to stay away years and years.'

'Promise?'

'I promise.' I bent towards him and caught a whiff of grape. 'Hey, I can smell wine. I think you drank some of my red wine when I went to pay the bill. What a nerve.'

He grinned. 'Didn't like it much. Shall we play poker now? Before you put me in a dungeon. You said you were going to teach me.'

'I don't know that I want to play cards with a secret drinker,' I said, getting out a pack.

CHAPTER TWENTY-THREE

It took a week for the demolition squad and builders to go in, shore the place up and announce it safe to start removing costumes and props. London seemed like a foreign city. I felt I had been away on a gap year, white-rafting the Amazon. It was so crowded and dirty, millions of busy sharp-suited ants swarming about counting bonuses. Someone was going to tread on me at any moment.

My mother was up and about but they wanted to keep her in a few days longer. It was not like a London hospital where they turf you out as soon as you could reach for your slippers.

'Of course, you must go,' she said, quite perky. 'I'm perfectly all right here. I've got my needlework and I've made some friends. Just so long as Mark is being looked after.'

Mark was staying a couple of nights with a school friend and had gone off, packed up with clothes and tucker, in high holiday mood.

'Promise?' he reminded me as he waved goodbye. 'Coming back pronto?'

'I promise,' I said.

I'd been to see Bill Naughton in St Thomas's Hospital. He was flirting with all the nurses, and being visited on a regular basis by Millie. He'd broken a leg and an arm, which made him dependent on female help for almost everything.

'Surrounded by feminine beauty,' he said, waving me to a chair. 'I must have died and gone to heaven.'

'Don't be too sure,' I said. 'That doctor looks as if he's got a forked tail. You'd better beware of him.'

'We thought you were buried under the debris. You gave us quite a fright. Especially as it was your prompt corner that went down the plug hole.'

'I'd hardly be prompting if it happened before a show,' I said. No way was I going to go on feeling guilty. 'I don't have to rehearse being the prompt.'

'And your fluffy jumper was there.'

I shook my head. 'I don' t know why you thought it was me in it. I remember that I'd left my mohair in Elinor's dressing room and went home wearing my poncho.' I didn't mention that I'd slept on Elinor's couch and then had breakfast with Joe. 'Have they found out yet what caused the collapse?'

'There's going to be an enquiry, so that'll take months, years even. You know what enquiries are like. Drag on and on.'

'I'm sorry you got hurt.'

'I'm a hero, really,' he said casually. 'I was throwing myself at the prompt corner in order to save you. I thought you were inside the fluffy jumper.'

'Thank you, Sir Galahad.'

'And I've found out something you've got to know about. Someone has got it in for you.'

'Some people always have it in for me.'

'She's been up to some pretty dirty work. You won't like it. The fragile Fran has been sharpening her nails on a grinder. Are you wearing police-issue body armour?'

I patted myself all over. 'No.'

'Well, you'd better get some.'

At least Bill's sense of humour hadn't been injured. Millie arrived with a puzzle book and a happy smile.

'We're working our way through this puzzle book,' she said. 'I'm trying to keep his brain alive.'

'A worthy cause,' I said, rising and leaving. They didn't need me. It took me ten minutes to find my way out of the multistoried labyrinth. It's a wonder I wasn't X-rayed and wheeled on a trolley to geriatrics with a plastic label on my wrist.

I stood on the pavement outside the Royale Theatre, aghast at its derelict appearance. My heart spiralled down, its edges ripping. The builders had shored up every wall and there was only one small entrance through the side stage door. It bore no resemblance to a theatre at all. Within a week the walls would be covered in boldly signed and sprawling graffiti.

'Sophie. God, am I glad to see you. You've come back, then,' said Joe, getting out of a taxi. He looked weary. There were lines on his face that I'd never seen before and the shadows said he hadn't been getting much sleep. I wanted to touch him, console him. But I didn't. 'I've missed you. How long are you here for?'

'A couple of days. My mother is still in hospital but doing very well. She's bustling round the ward, organizing everyone. She'll be allowed home soon.'

'Where's home?'

'A very small, windy cottage on the top of a dramatic cliff,' I said, ignoring what he wanted to know. 'Do you need any help?'

'Yes, all the help we can get. There's a lot of stuff to move before it deteriorates. I've found a warehouse we can rent for a few weeks while we find a new theatre. The show must go on,' he said, adding the cliché drily.

'I'm really sorry,' I said inadequately. 'It's quite awful.'

'Do you think Fran could have done this?' His voice was bitter. 'Is she up to this degree of sabotage? I know her loyalties are suspect, but this would take the skill of a bomb expert.'

'It's probably an old tunnel that's collapsed,' I said. 'There are hundreds criss-crossing under London. They excavated everywhere when they were building the underground, and sometimes abandoned ones that weren't suitable. No one knows where half of them are. Huge water pipes come from the reservoirs, and gas and electricity cables are all buried under the ground. And dozens of rivers were diverted. The Fleet was one of them and the Tyburn and the Walbrook. There's miles of water flowing down below that used to be up above.'

A smile flitted across Joe's face. 'You are so articulate, Sophie. That's what I like about you. All this information stacked in your head.'

I still felt so guilty. My thoughts had predicted this catastrophe. Had I somehow caused it to happen? Was that possible?

He took my arm. 'I'll escort you inside in case you fall down a hole and into a river. Can you swim?'

The interior was practically unrecognizable. We stepped carefully over the boards laid for us to walk on. The stage had been cordoned off, a voluminous dusty black area. My prompt corner was lost behind a boarded screen billowing with grey tarpaulin. Goodbye corner. No need to project now.

Joe took me downstairs to the basement which had been declared stable. Hilda and some stage crew, Alf and Bert, were packing costumes, boots, swords into coffin-like boxes. She threw me a weary smile. She'd been at it for hours.

'Everything has to be brushed down before packing,' she said. 'Don't want to take the dust with us.'

'I'll help,' I said, taking off my anorak. This had to be done before these priceless costumes were ruined. Joe was looking at me in a weird way, as if I might disappear in a puff of smoke, pantomime genie style.

'Will you still be here later?' he said as if scared to hear my answer. He was echoing Mark.

'I'm staying for two days,' I repeated. 'I'll be back at my flat. You'll know where to find me.'

'I have to talk to you.'

'OK. Any time.'

'You're speaking in your own voice. It sounds nice. You should use it more often.'

That threw me but I laughed. 'I'd almost forgotten how.'

Hilda gave me the low-down as we worked together. Fortunately, not many people had been around, mostly stage crew getting the set ready for the performance. A few cast had arrived but not Elinor or Fran. Jessica had been at the stage door, signing autographs, always early. Getting into her part, she'd said.

'There was this almighty groan and then a crash, like in the blitz or something, and dust flying everywhere. Everyone was coughing and choking. We didn't know what had happened. No one could see anything and we were too scared to move. We thought it was an unexploded bomb, y'know, left over from the war.'

'It might have been, quite possibly,' I said, folding Jessica's dress into mountains of tissue paper after brushing every inch. 'They don't know anything yet, do they?'

'There's an enquiry and you know how long that'll take. *Twelfth Night* will be *Fifteenth Night* by the time they decide anything. It's Joe Harrison that I'm sorry for. Poor soul. He's a lost soul without his play. Or whatever he's lost.'

Hilda still had her sense of humour despite the extra work. I should imagine Joe was making sure she got paid for the extra hours and taxis home out of his own pocket. Management were not overgenerous with expenses. Profits before people was the rule they lived by. And now they had to get their lawyers on to complicated insurance claims.

'You want to look out,' said Hilda, hours later when I was flagging. 'Fran's got it in for you. She's been spreading nasty stories about you and Mr Harrison. I mean, just because you have flats in the same building, doesn't mean that anything's going on, does it? I mean, that's just jumping to conclusions, isn't it?'

'Nothing's going on,' I said wearily. 'I wouldn' t have the energy. My flat is two floors higher. In the roof, among the pigeons.'

'She's cooking up something. I've got that feeling.'

'Probably laced with a toxic substance.'

'Want a Jaffa cake?' said Hilda, offering me the packet. 'You can't work on an empty stomach. I don't suppose you've eaten.'

My evening call to Dorset was taken by a young man tripping over things to tell me. He was practically bounding down the phone.

'So how is Superman this evening?' I asked.

'High altitude flying. Rescued a few screaming damsels in distress. Saved a couple of buildings from total destruction by aliens. The universe is next.'

'Save the universe.'

'How's your precious Royale Theatre?'

'It looks as if a bomb has hit it. Maybe it was an unexploded bomb from the Second World War. I've been dusting down and packing costumes all day.'

'You are coming home, aren't you? You said.'

'Of course. One more day here, working, and then I'm coming home. I promised, didn't I?'

'Gran will be coming out of hospital soon.'

'Good. I'll give her a quick call before they put the lights out. We'll be there to fetch her. Be nice to everyone, say polite pleases and thank yous. Miss you.'

'You bet. They've got two hamsters here. Real cool.'

He rang off. I would have to teach him some new words. He had to be rescued from word starvation.

Hilda had been listening to my half of the stilted conversation. She looked at me enquiringly, trying to make out the age of whom I was phoning. I didn't enlighten her. I wasn't ready to share Mark with anyone.

I walked back to my flat, almost legless, but not a unit consumed. I was exhausted. Who says the theatre is glamour? It's bloody hard work. Forget your name in lights. I climbed the stairs to my flat on autopilot, almost beyond the designated floors. Inside was a damp, chilly reception and a pile of junk mail someone had kindly brought up. No heating or fresh air for days. Go pile on the thermals.

There was some warmth from the electric fire. It said a mellow, dusty hello. I fell down in front of it, like a humble disciple of Buddha. My bones were dissolving with exhaustion.

I curled up on the rug like a dog, only I didn't have a dog. If I lived in Dorset, we could have a dog, and a cat. I'd like a cat, a knee-hugging cat, all purrs and claws, like a breathing hot water bottle. Mark would like a cat and a dog, a hamster, anything that moved.

There was a knock on my door. I knew that knock. It was Joe so I opened the door without checking.

Joe was holding a big bag of groceries. 'Long ago I promised you a meal,' he said. 'So here it is. Can I come in?'

'Any bringer of gourmet food can come in,' I said. 'This is a food desert, Mother Hubbard land, the empty cupboard. The most I can offer is two packets of out-of-date crisps.'

'Crisps and caviar? How does that strike you?'

'The caviar sounds good.'

Joe tipped out his carrier bag like some contestant on *Ready, Steady Cook*. There was scampi, rice, peppers, caviar and a bar of dark chocolate.

'So what are you going to do with that?' I asked.

'Watch me. I am trained,' he said, taking off his jacket and going into the kitchen.

Now, I did have a bottle of red Merlot hidden away for emergencies and this was definitely an emergency. Joe had shed his coat and was rolling up his sleeves. But he was tired. I opened the caviar so it could breath, put out a dish of crisps.

He was cooking rice with peppers in the microwave, scampi in a pan of olive oil. I opened the wine and poured it into two of my best cut glass.

'Do you know that Fran has sent a letter to the Press saying that you and I are having an affair which is apparently jeopardizing the success of *Twelfth Night*,' he said, stirring. 'How having an affair could create a hole that size, I fail to see.'

'A dynamic affair perhaps? She's an idiot. Nobody cares about affairs these days,' I said, wishing it were true. I'd like an affair with Joe. Never mind the stairs. I'd crawl up or down them, to be with him, whichever way I had to go.

'You don't mind the gossip?' He looked at me wonderingly. 'People talking about us.'

'I don't care about people talking. Who's interested? It's only gossip for the tabloids. Twenty miles out of London and nobody reads it. I don't mind what letters she writes. I'd be more concerned if she tried to get me the sack.'

There was a split second of softness between us but then it had gone.

'That, too.' Joe was heating dishes. I rushed about laying the table with my best as if royalty were coming. 'She's written a complaint to the management.'

That stunned me. I wanted my job. I loved it and I needed it. I had to keep young Mark in trainers and bicycle tyres. And there was no reason for a complaint. I had done nothing wrong. Quite the reverse, I had supported her poor performance all along the line, to the limit. She ought to be grateful I'd not thrown the book down and gone off in a huff.

Joe was dishing out scampi and rice on to plates. It smelt gorgeous because the scampi was fresh and he had thrown in some herbs. My basil. We sat down at the dining table and faced each other.

'Eat,' he said. 'Before we both fall down with exhaustion.'

We ate and talked. It was a lovely meal, wrapped in being together. I don't know what he planned to cook with the bar of dark chocolate, but we ate it straight from the silver paper, on the sofa, watching late-night television. Don't ask me what the programme was. Some flickering classic film resurrected from the archives.

Joe was slumped against me, almost asleep. Somehow I edged my way out from under his weight and put a cushion under his dark head. I took off his handmade shoes and stroked his black silk socks. Then I covered him up to his shoulders with the duvet from my bed.

So this was an affair? Joe on the sofa, as before, me curled up in my teddy bear pyjamas in bed, freezing. Fran didn't know what she was talking about. She needed to wake up to the real world, and what the hell was my mohair doing in the rubble? I couldn't remember moving it from Elinor's dressing room.

It hadn't got there on its own woolly legs.

CHAPTER TWENTY-FOUR

Fran Powell pulled a surprise rabbit out of the hat. She appeared on the outback version of the television programme *I'm a Celebrity, Get Me Out of Here!* Her minuscule outfits were too weird for words. Scraps of torn itzy-glitzy material held together with Sellotape and Blu-tak. She was taking this jungle thing a bit too far. I didn't know how such an air-head managed to get herself on to the show or knew she could have time off from *Twelfth Night* in advance. More little trip-ups?

It was all very suspect but no one could be bothered to work it out. Mark and I saw one hysterical episode where she was in a pit of snakes and rats and worms, in a tiny sequinned bikini, screaming her head off. Mark's eyebrows went skywards. She never earned food for her team, always too selfish. She got voted off pretty soon, mainly because no one could stand the sight of her.

'So she's an actress?' Mark asked like it was an alien race.

'Sort of aspiring actress. Understudy for Viola. And lady in waiting, but she didn't have any lines.'

'What's aspiring mean?'

'Shortage of breath.'

But I heard Fran reappeared instantly at the management office of West Enders demanding that her role of understudy be upped to one matinée and one evening performance a week, on the strength of her new television celebrity status.

'People will come to see the play because it's me,' she said confidently.

'That's absolutely outrageous,' said Elinor, on the phone. 'I've never heard of such an arrangement. Sometimes it happens when a lead is new and untried and has eight performances a week. An understudy might take over matinées, to give the lead a break. But I'm fine now, and as soon as we move to a new theatre, I'll be right on the ball. And I shall tell her so.'

A new theatre was in sight. A pretty dreadful play about a man living in a sewer had folded after two weeks of dwindling stench-retching audiences, and the management were only too pleased to house Joe Harrison's flamboyant production of *Twelfth Night*. Special terms and all that. The theatre was plain, functional. I'd have a draught-proof concrete corner. Plenty of room in the wings.

Joe phoned me. I don't know where he got the number from, somebody doing some clever redialling. My number was circulating like a round robin.

'We'll need you back soon,' he said. 'There's going to be a very tight rehearsal schedule before we can reopen. Is your mother getting better?'

'She's home now and doing well,' I said. 'I'll come back to London whenever you need me.'

I didn't want to leave Mark. We were becoming good friends, good pals, often walking the cliff paths together (no adders in sight), cheering on at football matches, had the occasional fish and chip supper when Gran had gone to bed early. The wild sea thrift and gorse on the cliff top hide dozens of plants and flowers on our walks. I tried to remember their names from Botany, but Mark was more interested in their shape and colours. He would examine a petal as if it was under a microscope.

'This looks like it should be growing under the sea,' he said, absorbed.

'Perhaps it was, once, millions of years ago.'

'I don't approve of this fried junk food,' said my mother every day, her tongue no worse for the bits removed from her body. 'All these E-additives. They are not good for you. Radicals or something.'

'I don't think chips have E-additives,' I said. 'These were oven-cooked.'

Mark kept a straight face. We had talked about food, junk

consumed in moderation. We had talked about almost everything under the sun. I no longer need to hot walk him like a frisky racehorse. But he never asked me about his father. And I wondered why. What had my mother told him? One day I would find out.

I knew this time together was coming to an end and I couldn't bear it. London no longer held that special magic for me. The hurrying, unyielding crowds made me cringe. I wanted to be saturated in sunlight reflected from the white cliffs. Joe would go back to the States. I started to think about staying in Dorset, finding some job which would keep me nearer to my son while he was growing up. I'd already wasted too much time pursuing my so-called theatrical career.

Then a letter arrived from London from the management of West Enders. They were still using the old Royale Theatre stationery and envelopes.

Dear Miss Gresham.

Following numerous complaints about your inability to prompt efficiently during recent performances of *Twelfth Night*, we regret that we have to give you a month's notice.

Due to circumstances beyond our control, the show has been without a theatre for some weeks, therefore we suggest that you consider yourself not employed by us from now onwards.

Yours truly etc.

I was stunned. Unshed tears grated like sand in my eyes. I could not believe that the management would act on the tittle-tattle of a posturing, one-dimensional, mediocre actress like Fran Powell, whose entire talent lay in being able to paint her toe nails without smudging them.

Numerous complaints? One complaint surely? Unless Fran had blackmailed half the cast into backing her up. It was disastrous money-wise. I needed a steady income to support Mark and my Mum. The London flat would have to go for a start.

Bill Naughton was out of hospital now, hobbling around on crutches, superintending the rebuilding of the set in the new theatre. He sat on Orsino's ducal throne, which had been rescued from the rubble, directing the work.

'So when are you coming back?' he bawled down the phone, over the sound of hammering and drilling. 'Rehearsals start next week. Opening night is Wednesday week. You'll be here?'

He couldn't hear my reply. 'What? Can't hear you. You've got a sack, the rack, a bad back?'

'I've been sacked, dismissed, given notice,' I repeated. 'I'm not coming back. Lots of the cast complained about my prompting, apparently, not only Fran. I've got a letter, giving me a month's notice in reverse.'

'Bloody nonsense, I don't believe it,' he snarled. 'This smells worse than the play they've just taken off. I'll find out about it. Does Joe Harrison know?'

'Don't know. I haven't told him. He's got enough to worry about. He'll soon find someone else. Prompts are ten a penny. We are not exactly a dying breed.'

'But you're worth a solid gold antique sovereign to him and he knows that. He won't let you go. Mark my words.'

I cheered up momentarily, though I wasn't sure about the choice of antique. 'Thanks, Bill. At least I know you didn't complain about me. I must go now. I've promised to help a local school with their musical version of *The Lion, the Witch and the Wardrobe*.' I nearly said my son's school, but stopped myself in time.

'My only complaint is that you never let me get anywhere near you,' he growled. The phone was sizzling with rampaging hormones.

I spent the afternoon at Mark's school, trying to sort out a state of chaos, noisy children milling about everywhere, a harassed drama teacher realizing she had taken on more than she could masticate.

Miss Ferguson pounced on me as if I was Andrew Lloyd Webber in drag. 'Could you hear these children's words? They don't seem to understand they are being animals or how to act like animals. And then the Ice Queen? She's saying her lines as if she's umpiring a netball match. I'll take the chorus through their songs.'

It was quite fun once you got their attention. The children tended to think drama classes were an extension of playtime and it would be all right on the night without having to learn words or know where they came on.

But once I got them acting like squirrels and moles and beavers, they had a whale of a time and the Ice Queen began chipping her words with an ice axe. She was going to make a terrific queen. Mark had a small chorus part but he wasn't rehearsing with me. He was with Miss Ferguson.

Mark and I cycled home together. I was tired, but happily tired. For a whole afternoon I had not thought about the letter and the problems it brought.

'Miss Ferguson said you were bloody good,' said Mark, cycling ahead of me.

'Don't say bloody, say very,' I gasped, going uphill slowly. No gears.

'Very bloody good,' he grinned back. 'She said you could be a drama coach.'

I must talk to him about his language. I didn't know where he got it from.

It was easier to walk up the last stretch of the lane. My mother was watching television with a tray of tea at her side. She was taking her convalescence seriously. No lifting for six weeks, they said. She could manage to lift a teapot.

'Some one called Harrison Ford phoned for you,' she said, not looking away from the screen. It was one of her favourite soaps, new life-threatening situation every five minutes. She lived every moment. Perhaps this was how I got my love of the theatre. I was living my mother's ambition for her.

'You mean Joe Harrison?' Harrison Ford, I could wish. I would walk water for that craggy man.

'He sounded like Harrison Ford. A very nice man. He said he'd call back.'

'Did you say where I was?'

'I said you were helping out with a school play.'

Helping out. It was Sophie do this, Sophie do that, all over again.

187

I was on the hamster run. A school play was a way to strangle parents with their own umbilical chords. They had to attend, with cameras and videos.

'I've spoken to this man, Joe Harrison,' said Mark, spreading bread and making mashed tuna sandwiches. Lots of Omega 3. 'Is he your boss?'

'He's the director. He's famous in New York and came over to guest our production. When did you talk to him?' This was alarming. I knew nothing about this call. My fragile deception was beginning to unravel. It frightened me.

'Dunno. You were out somewhere. Yeah, that was it, you were bringing Gran home in a taxi from the hospital. He wanted to know who I was.'

My heart thudded to a stop. What had Mark said? I didn't dare think. 'And what did you say?' I asked, nonchalantly washing and shredding three kinds of lettuce with studied indifference.

'I told him I was the lodger, occasional handyman, TV repair man, general fixer.'

'What a nerve,' I said with a wave of relief and laughter, chopping tomatoes. 'What fixer? You couldn't fix a leaking duck in a bath.'

'I fixed your watch when it needed a new cell battery. Remember?'

'So you did. And brilliantly, at that. It's still working.'

It was all I could manage at a stagger for supper, tuna sandwiches and salad. The school rehearsal had drained all my energy. No wonder teachers have nervous breakdowns. Those children needed chains and padlocks and that was only to take the register.

During the evening, Joe phoned again. This was getting a habit. I took the call in the kitchen, propping myself against a worktop for stability. He was furious.

'Have you seen this damned letter?' he demanded. 'Half the cast signed it apparently. They said you were no good, that you let them down, that you gave them the wrong prompts.'

I could barely speak. Tears came into my eyes and I wiped them away with a tea cloth. What had I said, had I done, to make them hate me enough to get rid of me?

'I don't know why,' I wept quietly. 'I don't understand any of this. I've always done my best for everyone. They could lean on me. Sometimes I've propped someone up for a whole show, when it was a bad night.'

'I've told them that if you go, I'll go. Straight back to the States and to hell with their contract. You are essential. Management were pretty taken aback, made snide remarks about the gossip going around about you and me. Prove it, you bastards, I said. Two separate flats in the same building does not an affair make.'

'No, it doesn't, does it?' I said feebly.

'So they have withdrawn your notice, temporarily. So please come back, Sophie. We need you. I need you.' His voice dropped. 'Can you come on Friday? That'll give you another couple of days with your mother. But then, I need you, we need you. Can you do that?'

'Friday? All right. I'll be back then. T-thank you for talking to the management. It was very upsetting, getting that letter. I actually need my job. I have several commitments. Expensive commitments.'

I could hear Joe thinking. 'Is that why you have a lodger?' he asked.

The lodger had at that moment crept into the kitchen to search for chocolate ice cream in the freezer. I grabbed at his jersey and pulled him against me. He squirmed and wriggled, grinning.

'The lodger is eating me out of house and home,' I said. 'He thinks he owns the place. And he is costing me a fortune. He beats me at gin rummy every evening. I should have taken up references.'

'I don't understand a word you are saying,' said Joe, distantly. 'The line is breaking up. Shall we see you Friday?'

'See you Friday.'

I put the phone down. Mark prised the lid off the ice cream carton and got out dishes for all of us. He was looking pleased with himself, grin like a split melon.

'Was that the boss?' he asked.

'The boss.'

189

'Cool, man.'

I threw the tea cloth at him. 'Learn some new words, buster,' I said. 'Start reading Shakespeare.'

CHAPTER TWENTY-FIVE

It was a new theatre, all chromium and stressed concrete and steel scaffolding, nothing like the elaborate Victorian Royale. As I walked in, I wondered how we were going to go evoke the sunlit court of Illyria, more or less Italian, on the east coast of the Adriatic, in this frozen, sterile wasteland.

Perhaps we could use the vague vacuum to somehow capture the essence of Shakespeare. He hadn't meant a play to be tied down to a vicinity or a place. He'd been a wandering actor, a minstrel strolling from town to town, performing anywhere.

I was shattered by the thought of his convoluted words being spoken in this place. It was so alien. He'd be tearing at his brown beard. (Or was it red?) It would be a marathon for the cast. Joe had an Everest to climb. He had to pull everyone up by their crampons.

I found my space, my colourless corner, tried to curl up in it on a grey plastic chair. Tested the light, turned it for the best beam on to the script. There was no draught but I was still cold. My metabolism was hitting zero. I wanted my son. Still, I would be phoning him this evening. We'd made a pact. I would talk to him first, then my mother and not wait to phone till he'd gone to bed.

'I want to know everything that's going on,' he'd said, very bossy.

'You're being nosey, you mean.'

'Champagne,' said Joe, his face lighting up as if I was an unexpected rainbow in the sky. 'Welcome back.' He was pouring me a glass of Brut champagne, not in a fancy flute but a plain dressing room tumbler. 'We've missed you, Sophie. Haven't seen you for weeks. Seems like years.'

He peered down into my face and the bubbles tickled my nose. 'Hello? Anybody in there?'

'This is the wrong theatre for Shakespeare. It has no ambiance,' I said, struggling down to earth. 'What are you going to do?'

'Then we'll have to make it right. Hello?'

'Hello you, too,' I said, soaring again somewhere into the ether. I was flying high. Wonderful him. It had to be him. I wanted to touch him, draw his face close. There was no way any of those things could happen. I took the tumbler but if I drank all of it, my prompting would go down the drain or up the flute.

'Drink it,' he said, his granite eyes twinkling. 'You'll be all right. Nothing is going to start until everyone is here. They are stranded on the Central Line. Signal failure somewhere. Sophie, you look so well and a bit tanned. Not stressed out any more. Dorset must agree with you.'

I nodded. 'It does. Such pure and wonderful air. Spectacular scenery, the dramatic cliffs, the sea, the Purbeck hills in the distance. There's space and time. I stand outside the cottage and drink in the fragrance of the sea.'

'Sounds idyllic. A cottage? With wonderful lodger?'

'Him too.' I wasn't saying anything but already I was smiling and it wasn't only the champagne. Joe noticed the smile.

'He sounded very young. A student?'

'You could say that. Yes, he's young but also grown up, quite mature.'

Joe hunkered down beside me. His face was older, more lined but so dear to me. And he didn't know it. He was grinning, a grin I now recognized with a clenching of my heart. I saw his face every day when I was with Mark.

'I'm glad you have found some happiness,' he said. 'But don't leave me out completely, Sophie. Lodgers grow up and move on.'

'I know that,' I said, nodding. I wondered if I dare touch his face. He was so close to me. Then the moment had gone and my thoughts were running away. He stood up as members of the cast arrived, talking, calling out to each other, waving to me. We parted like the Red Sea, moved on separately. It was back to work.

Fran was struck dumb when she saw me. Her scarlet-painted mouth pinched into a tight, strangled line. She strolled over, sucking in her flat stomach. 'I thought they had sacked you. Got rid of you.'

'No, apparently not,' I said with a secret smile which I knew would annoy her. 'I'm here, as you can see.'

'But they said they were going to sack you.'

'Clerical error. Never believe what you hear,' I said. 'Take your place, Fran. You'll miss your first entrance.'

His words soothed my heart, running on a lodge and a loop. Shakespeare knew how to do it. It was as if he had a vision that one day centuries ahead when he was long gone and dead, a prompt would be clinging to her job, hanging on to his words for dear life. I almost felt him beside me, peering over my shoulder. I could smell cinnamon and spices and old ale. A feather brushed my face. Or I thought it was a feather.

'Cut,' Joe shouted over his mike, about an hour later. 'Take five everyone. That was awful. Go look at your lines.'

He came over to me. He looked weary. 'Except you, Sophie. Faultless rendition, as always. Your voice is perfect for every part. You could do a one-woman show.'

'No, thank you,' I said. 'I wouldn't want the hassle.'

'Supper tonight with me? I want to hear about Dorset.'

'No time. You know we'll be here till three in the morning. That arrogant Yankee director will want everything perfect.'

He turned away but he was amused. I could tell from his shoulders. I amused him. Those shoulders, broad and muscular, taking on the burden of this make-believe world. But he had not been there when I needed him.

'How could they possibly sack you?' said Elinor, sipping warm water for her throat. 'I never signed any such letter.'

'Neither did I,' said Jessica. 'Where are all these people who are supposed to have complained? Byron says he never saw any letter. I can only think it's a few ladies in waiting and courtiers miffed because they don't have any lines at all.'

'Never mind,' I said. 'It's all over for the moment anyway. I've got my job till the end of this show.'

'It can't run forever,' said Elinor, being practical. 'I have the Greek's wife at Stratford next. *Comedy of Errors*, remember?'

'And I'm due to start filming in Italy next month,' said Jessica. We looked at her enquiringly. This was the first we'd heard of a film in the offing. 'It's only a small part,' she said quickly. 'Suddenly came up. But it's a start.'

'Fran will be after both of your parts if you have to leave before it closes,' I said. 'Though she could hardly play both at once. She might try. Nothing is beyond her ability to save the day.'

'She hasn't got the presence for Olivia. The role needs a touch of blue blood. She's so picky thin. Her blood must be part distilled water,' said Jessica.

'She needs more than a touch of acting,' said Elinor, going back on stage. 'And a touch of humility.' The five minutes were up. Joe was walking round the back of the stalls, thumping the back of the seats.

'The acoustics are different,' he said. 'The Royale soaked up the voice, all that upholstery and drapes. Here, the words bounce off the bare walls. You need to think carefully about your delivery.'

'I have enough trouble remembering the words without having to think about delivery as well,' grumbled Byron, waiting to go on. He closed his eyes in desperation. 'The stage is so big, like a football stadium.'

Fran swept passed me, knocking the script out of my hand with her bunched-up skirts. 'Don't think you'll get away with this,' she hissed.

'Late again, Fran,' I said mildly. 'Go shoot yourself in the foot.'

'You worry about your own ridiculous little job and I'll take care of mine,' she snarled.

'Rearrange the face then,' I said. 'You're supposed to look lovely and serene in this scene.'

She shot me a look of pure venom. Straight through the heart, if looks could kill. I glanced down at my front. No blood flowing from a deep knife wound.

'Smile,' shouted Joe on the mike. He'd seen her glaring. Fran composed a false smile and went to stand by Olivia. But she was seething. Everyone could see it. The air was taut and it wasn't with Shakespeare's plotting.

'Watch your back,' said Millie, from behind me. 'You are in one big trouble with that young minx.'

'I can take care of myself,' I said, keeping my eye on the lines. But I wasn't that sure.

'That I'll believe when the cows come home,' Millie said. 'They say there was a letter signed by everyone,' she went on. How does every nuance of gossip spread so fast in a theatre, like it was printed in the programme? Was nothing confidential? 'I don't believe a word. I certainly didn't sign it.'

'Thanks,' I whispered, with a smile, hoping she'd take the hint and go away. I couldn't prompt and chat at the same time.

They were rusty. Joe had to sharpen up the entire production. Some of the sets and moves didn't fit the new stage. Bill was hopping about like a demented kangaroo as Joe redesigned the set to fill in the gaps. I could hear his caustic comments more clearly than some of cast.

'Quiet in the wings,' Joe yelled. I didn't envy him. He had so much to do in so few days. The rain in the shipwreck scene would only work in a confined area.

But I was falling into the rhythm. This was where I belonged. Even if this was my last show, and it could be my last show. My last ever. If I never worked again, I'd had that one night of pure glory when I played Viola. Now I wanted a lifetime ahead of me with Mark. He was all that mattered. That young, tousle-haired youngster who was the spitting image of his father: face, voice, expressions, with an uncanny ability to draw, to see colours and shapes.

'Line.'

'Let thy fair wisdom,' I said. It was not like Olivia to go astray in mid speech. Something had thrown her. What was it? I tried to snatch a glance at her face but it was as glacial as usual. Then I spotted Fran in the wings, mirroring Olivia's actions, exaggerating her icy movements.

It was the delayed-timing trick which works on stage, but not in the wings.

The rehearsal was nearly over. We were all shredded, on our knees. I knew Joe was going to take us to pieces. Even me, perhaps. He could say what he liked. I wouldn't mind. I have a broad back. Well, not that broad.

He gathered us around, his face like granite, edged with despair. I stayed on the fringe, out of sight, where I should be as I was not remotely cast.

'I don't have to tell you. You know it. There is a lot of work to be done if we are to reopen on Wednesday. Well done, some of you. You still know your words, your moves. Full marks to those who adapted their moves. What have the rest of you been doing? Selling *The Big Issue*? Drinking? Going to lots of parties?'

There was a stunned, guilty silence. I knew that a couple of the courtiers had picked up some work as film-extras. On set by 6 a.m. I didn't envy them. All that hanging around, just before dawn, for a ballroom scene or a battlefield.

'So extra rehearsal this evening and no one goes home until we are back to the level of the Royale. I don't care if we are here till the small hours. It's your responsibility. One hour's break, then back here, with your heads strapped on.' He slapped his book shut. He was a man on the brink of bolting.

Then he called Fran over for a private word. He had spotted her cavorting in the wings. I couldn't hear what he said to her, but her face contorted with fury and she flounced off, making a tearful retreat. Maybe she wouldn't come back.

I went out into the gloomy, cloud-ridden street, searching for some bright light, somewhere to eat, some café that exuded warmth. Where I could sit and forget about the awful rehearsal.

It was a grubby little café, neon lights, formica topped tables and plastic orange chairs. I hated every inch of it but it sold plain food at reasonable prices. I could only afford reasonable. And I needed solid.

It was a plate of penne pasta. No café could go wrong cooking pasta, or could they? The cheese was non-existent. Two shreds of stale cheddar melted in an instant. I went up to the counter and helped myself to two postage stamp-sized wrapped portions of butter.

196

'Hey, you can't do that. You didn't order a roll.'

'Charge me,' I said.

I put the butter on top of the pasta, added salt and pepper, stirred it around, tried to bring some taste to life. I was stirring my life. Across the way was a park. Some children played with a ball, shouting with laughter, done up in bright anoraks and scarves, not caring about the cold.

Joe sat down, opposite me. He'd jumped the queue at the counter. The rich are bad at queueing. He looked so much older, worried, weary with the world. His luxurious New York home was a long way away. All that glitter and gloss waiting for him, to wrap him in comfort. Perhaps he was homesick.

'So,' he said, surveying my dish. 'Pasta à la nothing. What sort of meal is that? No cheese, no chives, no prawns, no sauce, no sort of taste to bring it alive. Pasta is dead stuff, you know. Dead wheat.'

'This is only a cheap street café. They haven't any skill beyond putting it on a plate. Pasta is a filling dish.'

'Is that what you want of life? A filler?'

'Of course, it isn't. But that's all there is time for now. Remember? Back in an hour. The director spoke. Humbler folk hurried away to eat.'

'The director needs some instant food, too.'

Joe had a fork. He'd picked it up from an empty table. He leaned towards me, his face an image from long ago. Those eyes were still the same. He might be worth several million dollars in the bank and real estate, but at this moment, all he wanted was some of my late, rapidly cooling lunch.

'We could share, dear,' I offered with a touch of Katherine Hepburn in *The African Queen*. I often wondered what they ate on that perilous trip down the river. There was no sign of food, only endless tin mugs of strong tea.

Joe got up and pilfered a plastic shaker of parmesan from behind the counter. The cheese flew like shards of chalk over the pasta, shreds of stringent taste that added a touch of Italy to West London.

'Was this lunch my idea?' he asked, forking.

'No, this lunch is my idea,' I said.

197

CHAPTER TWENTY-SIX

The letter was circulating the theatre and cast. Even the stage crew were reading it. My face was pink with the humiliation, the loss of dignity, the lack of privacy. I knew what it was all about. The damning, assassination letter with two-dozen signatures. The guillotine letter. Start knitting, folks, I'm being dragged along in a cart. I'd better wear two shirts like Charles I.

How they got hold of a copy was anyone's guess. Maybe Joe had demanded to see it. After all, he was the director. The boss man. He had a lot of influence. But it was not in his nature to pass it around like a prize specimen at a flower show.

I was starting to flag. There was a limit to my concentration and to my energy. Everyone was getting tired and tempers were honing sharp. Even Jessica, who was as cool as an iceberg most of the time, told Fran off twice for standing in front of her. Upstaging.

'Get your butt out of my space,' she hissed. 'Who do you think you are? Keira Knightley?'

'There is a resemblance,' Fran smirked.

'In your dreams, crab-face,' said Bill, loud enough for everyone to hear.

'Silence,' Joe shouted. 'Pick it up at the same line. We'll take a break at the end of this scene.'

At some point a catering courier arrived with a huge basket of sandwiches, beers and soft drinks. Joe had ordered them from a local delicatessen. We fell on the basket like starving refugees, tearing open the packets. I managed to get a whole round of granary with tuna, cress and tomato, and a carton of orange juice.

Joe came over to me to check a new move.

'Didn't you get any?' I said, offering half of my sandwich to Joe. He took it and bit into the moistness.

'No, the rampaging mob beat me to it.'

'Never mind. You had a filling lunch.'

'Filling about describes it. Sophie, I've seen the letter that was sent to the management about your unreliable work. Apparently Elinor demanded to see a copy and it looks as though practically everyone signed. A few names are missing.'

My heart did a peculiar jerk. 'Did Bill Naughton sign it?'

'No, nor had Elinor. But Hilda did and so did Millie. Very odd.'

'I don't believe it. Hilda and Millie? What do they know about prompting?' I was shocked. 'The skill, the concentration, the hard work.'

'Nothing. It seems weird, especially when they are your friends.'

'I thought they were my friends,' I said bitterly. 'Now I don't know who my friends are.'

'Better get started again or we'll be here all night. OK, folks. Back on stage. Act III. Where's Bill?' Joe slapped shut his laptop. The technology was being spiteful and spitting out crumbs.

'He's gone home, boss.'

'What? He's gone home? Has the whole world gone crazy?' Joe spluttered. 'He's the stage manager. I need him as much as I need the cast.'

'We can manage for a bit,' said the crew hopefully. 'Bill said it was very important. He's coming back.'

'I suppose I should be grateful for that,' said Joe, glaring impatiently. 'Anyone else feel like nipping home? Something important cropped up, fridge to defrost, answerphone to check? Anything more important than the show? To hell with our opening night on Wednesday.'

There was an embarrassed silence, a few coughs and foot fidgeting. I took the opportunity to finish my juice and try to make my bomb-proof concrete corner more comfortable. It needed the woman's touch. I made do with water and cough sweets. It was like sitting in an underground shelter, minus the buskers and the trains.

'Let's get on then. Act III music. Have we a prompt or has she gone off home, too?'

I didn't mind if he took it out on me. He knew I was there. He wanted to sharpen his tongue.

'Present and almost correct,' I said, almost Julia Roberts, meaning I'd nearly found the page.

The sandwiches and beer had done the trick and the rest of the rehearsal was not bad at all. Joe looked halfway pleased. He was nodding to himself as he made electronic notes.

The cast began to relax and thus their performances flowed, as Shakespeare meant the words to flow. Claud was perfecting the sadness and madness of impossible love. The scenes buzzed with vitality yet had a haunting quality. I even laughed at some of the jokes which I'd heard a hundred times before. They came over fresh and new.

'Well done,' said Joe at the end, pushing back his hair. 'A big improvement. Somehow we managed without the Stage Manager. We'll do new curtain calls tomorrow, making use of the bigger set. You can have the morning off. Have a sleep-in. See you at two o'clock sharp. Thank you all for working so hard.'

I heard the stage door open and the clump of Bill's crutches. He'd made good time, used a taxi both ways. The management were paying him expenses while he was on crutches. He was getting a taste for expensive transport.

'Stop. Stop, everyone. Wait a minute. Don't go yet,' he called out, coming on to the stage. He was waving a large envelope. Joe was about to say something but then thought twice about it. Bill's craggy face was thunderous. He looked as if he was about to explode.

'Listen to me. I've something to say,' he said loudly. Plenty of projection from our stage manager. There was a general slow down in hasty exits and the majority of the cast and crew began easing back, curious. It was rare to see Bill so angry.

He stood centre stage, took a deep breath. He'd never had a speaking part before.

'You've all seen the letter sent to management about our inefficient and useless prompt, haven't you?' There was a bit of murmuring and disagreement with his harsh words. I curled up, out of sight, shutting out the misery. I wanted to disappear, go home, hibernate.

'The letter was sent and signed by about eighty per cent of the company. But that letter smelt like rotten eggs. I knew there was something wrong with it but I couldn't work out what it was. Suddenly the answer was there. It came to me in Malvolio's scene when he reads the forged letter.'

Bill had everyone's attention now, including mine. I held my breath. What had he found out?

'Now, that letter was a clever forgery sent by Maria to Malvolio. This letter to the management is the same thing, only the modern equivalent of forgery. Get it? It's a load of photocopying.'

'What do you mean?' Voices rose, clamouring. 'Bill, come on, tell us.' 'Spit it out.'

'I wondered why my name wasn't on it,' Bill went on. 'Why not me? Then it dawned on me that my signature wasn't on it because the whole lot of signatures had originally been sent to me. So I rushed home to get the proof, to show you. And here it is.'

What was he talking about? It didn't make sense until he produced a large Get Well card. One of those enormous cards with room for everyone on the planet to sign. On the front was a drawing of a buxom blonde nurse saucily comforting a bandaged patient who had every limb in splints.

'This was sent to me when I was in hospital. Everyone signed it. I didn't sign it because it was sent to me. Got it? Elinor didn't sign it because she was taking it easy at home. Easy enough to photocopy the signatures off the card. Print a nasty letter on a sheet of A4, then rearrange the signatures below. Photocopy the whole and pop in the post. I bet if we compare the signatures on the card with those on the letter, we'll find they are identical in every little dot and flourish.'

I let out a big sigh. It had to be the explanation. No one had signed the letter. They were the names from the Get Well card sent to Bill. Photocopiers were brilliant these days, producing work as good as the original. No giveaway smudges or hazing.

I was trembling. My friends hadn't signed the letter. They didn't think I was inefficient and useless.

'Let's hear it for our Sophie,' Byron shouted.

They began clapping. They were climbing on to the stage, whacking Bill's back till he nearly fell over.

'There,' said Joe, lost for words for once. He patted me awkwardly as if I was a child. 'Now we know. Photocopied signatures.'

He leaped on to the stage and was shaking Bill's hand. They were comparing the card and the letter, nodding and agreeing. They were finding identical signatures, it seemed.

My legs were not working very well. They had turned to straw. I didn't think I could make the ten yards to centre stage. Somehow I made the journey, like it was to the Earth's core. I reached up and kissed Bill's cheek.

'Thank you,' I said, blinking back hot tears.

'I'm not just a pretty face,' he grinned. He put his arm round my shoulder and gave it a rough shake. 'No crying on stage,' he said. 'It's not allowed.'

Then I saw he was looking over my shoulder and Millie was easing forward, her face wreathed in smiles. He let go of me and was looking at her as if she was the only person there.

'What a clever old clod of earth you are,' she said. 'I shall have to watch you. You could turn out to be brilliant.'

'Hang around, sister,' he said, winking. 'I may surprise you.'

I had to smile. I had turned Bill down so many times, sometimes cruelly. But now he had found someone who liked him. Millie was all smiles.

Joe was taking me somewhere away from the crowds, his hand under my elbow. I would have fallen down without his support. But people were still crowding around, congratulating me. It was like the first night all over again. This was theatre. This was my life blood. Will Shakespeare would have loved it. The drama of life. He would have written it as a play called, say, *What You Will*. (Joke) And it would have been a rip-roaring success at The Globe. The prompt corner would have been matting and straw. The script a hand-written manuscript. His hand.

'So who organized this vulgar Get Well card for Bill in hospital and got signatures from everyone, but not mine?' It was Elinor, who should have gone home by now but hadn't. She looked radiant, younger, wearing elegantly chic Parisian black and skyscraper heels. She had a new admirer, some high-up executive in late-night television. It was never too late. He was coming by to give her a lift home.

'Yes, who organized the card?'

It wasn't hard to guess.

But Miss Goody Two-Shoes had scurried off into London's dark streets, down into the sewers where she belonged. We never saw her again for this production. Joe promoted the second lady-in-waiting to first lady-in-waiting and Hilda agreed to alter the grand dresses.

'It's the least I can do,' she said to me.

'Are you all right?' said Joe. 'Did I say something about having supper? Was that today? I've lost track.'

'I don't remember,' I said. 'I couldn't eat anything anyway. It's too late. I want to go home and go to sleep.'

I was nearly asleep. I might fall off the stage.

'That's a perfect idea,' said Joe, drawing me close. 'Would there be room for a frazzled, exhausted, grumpy old director who can't face his lonely king-sized bed?'

'I don't know,' I said, wondering if my hearing had gone. 'Does this grumpy director snore?'

'How should I know? I don't keep myself awake.' He was laughing at me and there was a tenderness in his eyes which I had never seen before. He touched my hair. It was still short and bouncy, as he liked it.

'I don't believe in sleeping with producers or directors,' I said. What was I saying? All I wanted was to lay down with his dear face beside me. I only wanted him. 'I don't need that kind of career incentive.'

'Quite right, too. It doesn't work with me. I only sleep with women that I love.' Joe took my hand and held it against his lips. 'And since you call'd me master for so long,' he said, using Orsino's last Act V words. 'Here is my hand: you shall from this time be your master's mistress.'

Viola had no answer to make, nor had I. There was still a lot to tell Joe and I did not know how to tell him. Or when. It wouldn't be tonight.

But I took him home as I had once before on a frosty winter's night hung with mist, and we climbed the endless stairs to my rooftop flat. The bed was still a single but the rose-patterned duvet was warm and comforting and soft pillows embraced us.

We left the curtains open so that we could search the sky for stars, wondering if it would snow. If it did snow, then neither of us knew. Sleep took us to separate dreams but we were together even in those dreams.

'You've cold feet,' I said.

'Mmn.'

CHAPTER TWENTY-SEVEN

The show closed after a six-week run to full houses. All shows close in the end and *Twelfth Night* was no exception. It wasn't a *Mousetrap* or *Sound of Music*. The Bard couldn't run forever. But he would certainly be on the boards again and again. Long after the others were gathering dust on shelves in theatrical museums.

The last night of the show was one to remember. The audience roared their approval and the curtain calls went on and on. I sat in the prompt corner listening to the applause, hugging the script to me, all my acquired history there between the lines. Joe came round to me and put his hand briefly on my shoulder.

'It's all over,' he said. 'A wonderful show.'

'Magical,' I said. All over. Joe would be going home for good now. I couldn't bear to think of it. He'd already made a couple of trips back to discuss new shows. I'd raced down to Swanage for walks and talks and hugs.

We had a fantastic after-show party on stage, tears and laughter, relief and euphoria. No one wanted to leave. It went on into the small hours. But there was work to do the next day, dismantling scenery, packing props and wardrobe.

'I hate putting a show to bed,' said Hilda, folding and packing costumes into hampers. 'It's so sad. All that work and now it's finished.'

'Till the next one,' I said. 'There'll be another one, I'm sure.'

The West Enders went into voluntary hibernation. The company had no theatre and had to wait until the Royale was rebuilt. We dispersed like migrating birds to softer climes.

Elinor had another contract to fulfil. Jessica went off to Italy to film. Byron successfully auditioned for a small part in a soap. Bill and Millie got engaged and we all needed a holiday after their party. Joe flew back to the States. I didn't go to Heathrow to see him off. I didn't want to see him go, walking through passport control.

The management apologized profusely about my abrupt dismissal, said it was a complete misunderstanding and they had been misinformed as to my contribution to the show. They had not realized I was the unknown who had saved the opening night from being cancelled.

It was quite a fulsome apology but not earth-chewingly grovelling. They did not feel they were to blame for the mistake. However, they did give me a glowing reference and a handshake, not quite golden, silver or bronze, but a shade of metal that bolstered my bank account for a few months, settled the urgent bills.

I was packing up the contents of my flat, only a few days after closing, when Elinor phoned me. I was trying to cut down on the self-breeding mountain of books and CDs and ancient 78 rpm records. Soon I would be settled in Dorset and there was barely room for me in the cottage, let alone all my clobber.

'Sophie dear, are you all right, after that ridiculous fuss?' It was Elinor.

'Sure,' I said, putting a pile of books aside for the charity shop, then changing my mind. How could I throw any away? They were like extended family. 'Life has to go on. I'm OK, really. How are you?'

'Madly rehearsing, as usual. Nice to have a part where I don't have to try and look young. I can relax my wrinkles and let them drop.'

I laughed. 'You mean, both of them?'

'You don't have to flatter me, my dear. Now, Sophie, you know I have a very nice man friend who owns the television company that produces this late-night chat show called *After Dark*. You may have seen it? No? Apparently they have been let down at the very last moment. Someone has cancelled. Very inconsiderate. And they are one guest short. So I suggested you.'

'Me?' I didn't really understand what Elinor was talking about. I'd never seen the show. 'Why me?'

'All you have got to do is chat about what it's like being a prompt at the Royale, throw in a few famous names, preferably mine. Add some funny anecdotes, you've dozens of them, I'm sure. Piece of cake. About ten minutes at the most. They'll pay, of course.' Elinor was breathless by the end of all that. 'Quite generously. And expenses.'

'But I'm not a chat show person. I don't know how to chat. Sorry, ask someone else, Elinor. You must know dozens of other, far more suitable people.'

'Anybody can do a chat show. You sit on a sofa, cross your legs and talk naturally. Easy as pie. Say you'll do it, Sophie. They are desperate.'

I nearly laughed. So desperate at this moment that they would take anyone, even a total nonentity like me. A couple of parrots could talk themselves into the job without even trying. 'So when is it?' I asked, casually, still packing, barely listening.

'Tonight, dear. Be at the studios by nine o'clock. The show goes on at eleven. Got a pen? Here's the address. Write this down.'

I panicked. 'Tonight? You mean, this tonight? I can't do tonight.'

'Yes, of course, you can. Are you doing anything else?'

'No, I'm not, but I can't. I can't go on television. I've nothing to wear, nothing suitable. I haven't got a wardrobe full of posh clothes.'

'Take a selection,' said Elinor, airly. 'They'll choose something. They can do wonders with a scarf. Are you writing this down? Good. Thank you, Sophie. Break a leg, darling.'

That's how it started. I was a last minute fill-in guest when *After Dark* were desperate. I was a face and a voice. I could recite *Mary, Mary Quite Contrary* and make it sound like a sonnet if I liked. They wouldn't care what I said so long as I filled in a spare space on that sofa.

I phoned Hilda in a panic, wondering if I could borrow something out of the West Enders wardrobe. The costumes were carefully stored in a warehouse while the Royale was being rebuilt. Hilda had the key.

'Of course you can,' she said. 'What about that red fringe dress you wore to the press night? You looked stunning in that.'

'A bit bright, isn't it?'

'You're worse then Elinor. You'd wear black day in and day out like every day was a funeral. I'll pick out a few dresses for you to take along.'

'Thank you so much. Or else I'll have to scour the charity shops for something to wear.'

'Never. We'll find you something for the show. For heaven's sake, we can't have you going on television in a charity dress. What would Joe think?'

'He won't know. He's back in the States. Directing a new show.'

'Are you sure?' There was something in Hilda's voice but I couldn't make out what it was. My mind was spinning with what to talk about, stories to tell, how to get the ordeal over without making a fool of myself. This was a madness.

What had Hilda said about Joe? I couldn't remember. The rest of the day raced into oblivion, filled with washing hair, face pack, doing my nails. Who'd notice my nails? Glittery nail varnish perhaps? A morale booster.

Those devil nerves were starting to attack me. What had Joe said? You need those nerves to give you an edge of danger, something like that. I was only going to sit on a sofa for ten minutes, for heaven's sake. Not exactly rocket science. And it was late at night. About three people and their dog would be watching. The dog wouldn't mind what I was saying as long as he had a biscuit.

Hilda met me outside the television studio. She had a couple of bulging carrier bags. 'The dresses are all non-crease. Just shake them out. I popped in a couple of pairs of sandals,' she said. 'Your hair looks great. Sock it to them, girl. Show them what you are made of.'

'Thank you so much.' My voice was already trembling. I was feeling sick. I was made of pink marshmallow. 'I'm sure the dresses will be wonderful.'

'Don't forget to mention the West Enders! You know what they say about publicity. Any publicity is good.'

If I got that far. I was going to pass out in the dressing room, collapse on the way to the set, fall off the sofa. It was written in the stars. There was no Joe to support me. There was only me. I was on my own.

A young make-up girl fussed over my face, redoing what I had already done so carefully, fluffing, powdering, glossing and crimping. She zipped me into the red dress, put sandals on my feet. My limbs weren't working on their own. She chatted away but I didn't take in a single word.

A groovy, spike-haired male assistant pinned on a body mike as if I was a shop dummy, gave me directions about not looking at the cameras but I didn't understand a word he said. He was speaking some foreign language, Albanian perhaps.

He pointed me in the direction of the set which was at the end of a bare, empty corridor. I was Alice in Wonderland going down a long tunnel, not knowing where I was going, wading through mud, waiting to die. Over a doorway was a red flashing sign saying 'Transmitting'. A girl with a clipboard held me back at a curtained doorway, then suddenly said 'Now,' and pushed me through. It was like walking on broken glass. My toes curled in the sandals.

The lights were bright, hot. For a second I was totally blinded by the light. I aimed for the sofa, a long leather affair stretching for miles. It was all I could see though it looked solid enough. What on earth would Mark think of his Mum now? Mark. Suddenly I thought of him, smiled at everyone, the invisible millions out there, radiantly, but the smile was secretly for Mark.

'Hello,' I said, holding out my hand, on autopilot. 'I'm Sophie Gresham, recently the occupant of West Enders draughty prompt corner.'

'Hello, Sophie. Welcome to *After Dark*. Come and sit down. It's lovely to have you here. I don't think we've ever had a prompt before.'

'Not many people know that we exist,' I said. 'Yet every show has one. We're one of the invisible little people.'

I didn't remember what else I said, loads of idiotic gibberish, off the top of my head, skimming through the surface of my life. The ten minutes were over in a flash, speed of light. The host was seeing me off the set, thanking me. He looked pleased but it could have been a polite act.

Someone guided me back along the corridor. I was completely lost.

Then I collapsed in the dressing room. They were wiping the sweat off me and fanning me with paper, and giving me sparkling water to drink. It tasted like champagne. I drank and drank. Soon I would be drowning.

'What did I say?' I gulped, asking the assistant as he took off the mike. 'Was it total rubbish?'

'No way, Sophie. It was funny. It was hilarious, in fact. Everyone loved it. Viewers are phoning in, droves of them. You did good, girl.'

The host rushed into the dressing room. 'Fabulous,' he shouted. 'Sophie, you were great, so funny. You're a natural. Come back again, any time. Prompt in a corner? You shouldn't be hidden in any corner. And those voices, all those different voices! Cate Blanchett, Renee Zellweger, Goldie Hawn, Nicole . . . coming out so naturally. You were absolutely spectacular. I loved it.'

He planted a big kiss somewhere on me, not quite sure where, fairly decent, I think. I was overwhelmed.

They sent me home in a taxi, with bundles of clothes and shoes and bottles of water. I was still in the red dress. I never wanted to take it off.

The phone was ringing. It never stopped ringing. I think Elinor had sent round-robin emails to everyone in the cast and crew. They'd all stayed up to watch *After Dark*.

Then Mark phoned. 'Wow,' he shrieked hysterically. 'My Mum's on the telly. In a late, late show. Everyone at school will be so jealous. Gran let me stay up to see it. Some lady we don't know phoned to tell us you were on. You don't mind, do you?'

'No. But it's very late,' I said, loving his young, excited voice. 'You should really be in bed.'

'In bed, when my Mum's on telly? You're joking. Fab dress. Do you get it to keep? You looked like a lampshade.'

'No, it was borrowed. Now you go to bed and I'll talk to you tomorrow. Goodnight, sweetheart.'

'Goodnight, telly star Mum. Shine on.'

Shine on. I slept with those words echoing through my head, my son's voice. I would be seeing him this weekend and nothing was ever going to part me from him again.

I awoke to the phone still ringing. Was it never going to stop?

'So how is one very funny lady?' It was Joe. He sounded as if he was in the next room. 'I caught the show. You're a dark horse, hiding all that talent. Well done. You were great.'

I tried to wake up, to clear my head. The red dress was flung over a chair. Then I remembered everything. It came back to me in a shock wave.

'How could you see it? You're in New York.'

He coughed. 'Satellite dish,' he said. 'They work wonders.'

'I was as nervous as hell.'

'The edge of danger. Remember what I told you? Go back to sleep now, angel. I just wanted you to know.'

The rest of the day went by in highly charged confusion. And not only because of Joe's call. I got another call from a business-like personal assistant. I was summoned immediately to some posh office, somewhere in the West End, to meet the production company. I wore a plain, straight navy slip dress Hilda had put into the carrier bag, hid my basic street anorak in another when I got there.

The office was acres of chromium and silver and a carpet as thick as a bouncy castle. I was surrounded by men in Armani suits, white shirts but no ties. A spectacularly skinny girl poured coffee and handed it round. It was my breakfast. Elinor's executive friend was there, silver-haired and gracious, not saying much, smiling encouragement. I gathered he owned the company.

The team of producers all began talking at once. They were offering me a regular spot on *After Dark*. My own spot on that sofa. It would be called Prompt Cornered.

'I don't want to do television,' I said.

'Surely everybody wants to do television?' They were amazed.

One of the men came over and hunkered down in front of me. He could see I was stunned. I hardly caught his name, Jones or something. He had very bright blue eyes, probably tinted contacts.

'You'd interview stars from the shows. Anyone you like. Clear

211

field, but then you'd tell it like it was when you prompted them, if you did, if you didn't then make it up. No one will check. Be yourself. All the backstage stories. Just like it is,' he said. 'About wardrobe mishaps, make-up melting, scenery falling down—'

'I don't want to work in London any more,' I said, wondering who was saying this. 'I want to live in Dorset with my son.'

'So we'd pay to put you up at a hotel in London, five star. The show would only be three nights a week, Friday, Saturday, Sunday. Email contact during the week. A weekend show only, Sophie. First-class travel, generous clothes allowance. Send a car for you if it's the wrong kind of rain on the line. Dorset isn't the Outer Hebrides. It's only a couple of hours away.'

'I've got a small flat in London,' I said, mentally rescuing dumped books and putting them back on shelves. 'Which I rent.'

'Even better. We'll pay the rent. A lot less hassle for Administration.'

'But I'm not on the Internet.'

'We'll lend you a laptop.'

'With a proper contract?' I asked, surfacing carefully, but still stepping on shards of glass. My brain was beginning to function with a strong instinct for survival.

'Three months initially, with an option. See how it goes. Well, what do you say, Sophie? It'll be fun, brilliant. So different. A real person talking sense about the theatre. The viewers loved you. They haven't stopped phoning in.'

What could I say? Every journey begins with a single step. I put out a foot. My left one, I think it was. Then I went shopping and bought some flowers for Hilda.

CHAPTER TWENTY-EIGHT

Mark was ecstatic. He shadow boxed round me in the kitchen, pulling no punches. I swear he'd grown another inch since I'd last been home.

'This'll be brilliant,' he said. 'You'll be at home all week.' Punch, punch. 'Then buzz off to London on a Friday and be home again on Monday morning. You'll be here practically all the time. Wow, awesome.' Punch, near miss.

'But not at the weekends,' I reminded him.

'Oh, that's OK. I'm always busy. I'll watch you on telly.'

'You'll do no such thing. *After Dark* is on far too late. You'll be in bed.'

I could see his brain ticking over, manipulating the situation. 'If we had a video, I could record the programme, then I wouldn't need to stay up so late. I could watch it several times and give you pointers,' he suggested loftily. 'You know, tips from the viewer's point of view.'

It was my umpteenth coffee that morning. I tried not to laugh. 'Thanks a lot. I guess I'm going to need all the help I can get,' I said.

'And Miss Ferguson at school is going to ask you if you are free to do drama coaching a few afternoons a week. She's going to write you a proper letter. I said you probably would.'

'So what are you now? My agent? Thanks very much. I need an agent like I need an industrial licence.'

'There's lot of schools round here, especially posh boarding schools. You could turn it into a proper job. Of course, you'd have to get a car.'

'And where would we park it? At the end of the lane, under a hedge?'

'The farm is trying to sell off its stables and outhouses. You could buy one of them and turn it into a garage. I expect they'd give you a special price.'

'A video, a car, a garage,' said my mother, bustling about, but at less speed. She was taking it carefully, moved with a sort of watchfulness. 'You're spending Sophie's money faster than she's earning it, young man.'

I was having other ideas about buying. Living in my mother's two-up two-down down cottage was decidedly cramped since my mother had come home from hospital. I was camping out in the sitting room, sleeping on a sofa bed which was well past its comfort date. The empty cottage next door began to look more and more like a smaller version of the Ritz in my eyes. I'd even tried the door but it was locked. The hinges were loose. There was some sort of wild honeysuckle entwined all round the door with bluey-green leaves waving in the breeze.

I'd spent time on the garden, planting and pruning, and banishing weeds to the next-door pasture. I planted canons of flowers for next spring, in a mosaic of clumps. Rows on flower patrol are not that much fun.

Then I discovered that both cottages once belonged to the farm at the end of the lane, before my mother bought this one. So I did some reconnoitring, first talking to the farmer's wife about buying a possible garage. They were eager to sell. Dairy farms were not doing too well, more forms to fill than cows to milk.

'So what's happening to the second cottage up the lane,' I said, bringing it into the conversation. 'Are you thinking of selling that as well?'

'I doubt if we could,' she said, shaking her head. 'It's in terrible condition, falling apart. And we can't afford to get it fixed up. No one would buy it as it is now unless it's a builder. The only thing that's good about it is the view. All our spare cash has to go back into the farm.'

'Do you think I could have a look round it?' I said. 'Would you mind if I explored?'

'Sure. Drop the keys back any time. But be very careful of the floorboards. They might be rotten and we're not insured. Take a torch.'

So that's how I came to be clambering around a derelict cottage when an unexpected visitor arrived to see me. It did need a horrendous lot of work. It needed new floorboards, new stairs, new kitchen, a proper plumbed bathroom. The rooms were lumbered down with shadows and sadness. The kitchen consisted of a deep earthenware sink, green with algae, peeling lino, unhinged cupboards and a gas stove dating back to before WWII. The broken loo was located outside in an outhouse. Huge spiders liked it a lot and had set up a colony. It was festooned with cobwebs and awash with signs of poverty and hardship.

As the farmer's missus had said, the only good thing was the view.

'Oh dear, oh dear,' I said to myself. My dreams began to disintegrate along with my savings. There was no way I could afford to buy this place and bring it into the twenty-first century. It needed a fortune spent on it, a fortune I didn't have.

I went outside and closed the door with regret. I had to be sensible. The view from the front step was spectacular. The icy-white cliffs, the gorse, the endless rolling blue sea of the bay that stretched to the horizon, dotted with sails like tiny swans. I breathed in the wonderful air, scented with salt and sea thrift and honeysuckle, determined wafts of sweetness. There was time here to be oneself, to flatten out the creases of a bad day. We'd got to manage somehow together, all of us next door. We'd make it work.

I closed my eyes to a sudden shaft of dazzling sunlight, brighter than the rest.

'Don't move,' he said. 'You look like a Viola, coming out of the sea, bemused and confused.'

I heard the click of a camera. Joe looked at me over the viewing sight. He was wrapped in his leather flying jacket, a woollen scarf up to his ears, dark cords tucked into sturdy walking boots. He grinned at me over the camera, floppy hair blowing in all directions.

I could not believe what I was seeing. He was here. Somebody pinch me.

'Joe?' I breathed. 'What are you doing here?'

'They told me to come clothed for the deepest Dorset countryside. Inches-deep mud and country lanes, they said. Haven't seen any cows yet.'

'The farm at the end of the lane is dairy. We often meet the cows on their way to the pasture, covered in mud and sludge.'

What a stupid thing to say. I hadn't seen him for more than ages, heart bleeding in all directions, and here I was talking about muddy cows. Get your brain together, girl. Be amusing. Ask him in. Don't let him go.

'How did you find me?' I asked. 'I never told anyone.'

'A little bird told me. Or was it a simple deduction? Management sent you a dismissal letter, therefore they must have some other address. You weren't at your flat then. I did check. So here I am. My car is at the end of the lane.'

'Oh yes,' I breathed. 'They held a next of kin address.'

'How are you?' He didn't know what to say either. We were starting again at A for asymmetric information. But his eyes were bright with interest.

'I'm OK,' I said. 'And you? Aren't you supposed to be in New York? Directing some new show? That's what they told me.'

'Yes, I am supposed to be but I'm not. I'm here, as you see. Some unfinished business to attend to.'

'Who told you that I was here now?' We'd get this sorted out first, at least.

'Hilda. All those evening calls you made. She was curious, in the nicest way, of course. You used her mobile and she noted the number, as you do. She was the kind friend who called and told your mother about the first *After Dark* show. And you know how middle-aged women like to talk. Quite a long chat, apparently.'

'I did wonder.' And I couldn't move. I was glued to the doorstep. Joe was here, in the real, flesh and blood, breathing. Was I going to do anything about it or was I going to let this man slip through my fingers again?

'We live next door,' I said. Pathetic. A chat show host who didn't

216

have a decent line of communication to say when she needed it. 'The other cottage.'

'So I thought.' He nodded towards the second cottage, sizing it up. 'This one is practically a ruin. Nice view of the sea though, and a very good sized garden. It has several possibilities.'

'Possibilities that are beyond me even with what *After Dark* pay me. Would you like a cup of coffee? I'm still a domestic goddess.'

He moved towards me and lifted me down from the step. 'I haven't come all this way for a cup of Fairtrade coffee, however well you make it. I've come for you, Sophie darling. And I'm not leaving without you.'

He bent his head and kissed me. It was a kiss that went on and on, eclipsing time. I could no longer think straight. Joe had come for me. He had travelled thousands of miles across the Atlantic and finished up along a muddy lane, windswept and cold, and was kissing me like we were never going to stop.

I clung to him as his arms folded even tighter round me. The keys to the cottage dropped to the ground with a faint tinkle. Joe, Joe, my darling man, was here, holding me and kissing me. I hoped this was going to last forever.

I wanted it to last forever.

'Excuse me, mister,' said a small tight, accusing voice. 'But that's my mother you are kissing.'

'Mark,' I said, surfacing. 'It's all right.'

Mark was standing about ten yards away, the usual wrecked schoolboy look, shirt hanging out, tie at half-mast, dragging a bulging sports bag at his feet. But there was no denying the look. The same eyes, the same floppy hair, the same arrogant stance. They stared at each other as if a curtain had opened.

'It's not all right,' said Mark.

I felt Joe stiffen in my arms. He was searching the boy's face, looking at a picture image of himself. His eyes were dark and as unreadable as the deepest night sky. It was a shock but he was taking it on board, trying to work it out.

'This is Mark,' I said, my voice full of pride. 'This is my son. He beats me at gin rummy, criticizes my show, forgets where he's left his bike, loses his gear, bosses me about like someone else I know.

217

My son, who's growing up fast.'

'You had a baby?' Joe was incredulous. 'When did you have a baby?'

'Yes, it happens, you know, it's how you produce children. Mother Nature helps along. Now he's this grubby schoolboy, wanting his tea. I've made his favourite chocolate muffins. You can have one too, if you'd like to come in.'

'You didn't tell me.' It was almost an accusation.

I looked straight at Joe with a dozen years of pain in my eyes. 'How could I? Why should I? You had gone. A cold, snowy morning, remember? And I didn't know where. You were a penniless actor, out of work. I barely knew your name. Don't you remember anything?'

'Yes, I do. You gave me your lunch.'

'I gave you more than a lunch.'

Joe turned to Mark. 'How old are you, young man?' he asked.

'Eleven,' said Mark. 'How old are you?'

'I'm thirty-six but with a mental age of about five sometimes.'

Joe tried to say something that would help, but there were no excuses he could use. It was too late for apologies. I didn't want apologies.

'When I cut your hair in the wings and saw the true shape of your face, I remembered you from that snowy night,' said Joe slowly. 'I'd always known that I knew you from somewhere but couldn't place the time or where. The years have been so full of people and work. But I said nothing, thinking it was probably something you wanted to forget, since you so obviously disliked me.'

Joe let his arms drop from me and I felt the cold, like a door being left open. He went towards Mark, hesitating, still absorbing the look of him. Joe was so tall, he towered over Mark. But my son drew himself up and looked at the man with a steely eye. He had the same strength, the same granite eyes.

'Mark. I know this must be a strange moment for you, for both of us, for all of us. But I'm Joe Harrison. I think I'm your father.'

My Mark, my wonderful Mark, bless every solid inch of him, was not thrown at all. He looked his father straight in the eye, unflinching. 'So where have you been all this time?' he said.

*

Joe bought the cottage next door, employed an architect who knocked down a few interior walls, but it took an army of builders to transform it into a comfortable house, a home where we three could live with space, without falling over each other. He gave me the medieval picture, velvet in all shades of gold, and we hung it in the windowed conservatory, built on the side of the house where it caught all the sun.

The taste fairy had made a last minute appearance at my christening and I found beautiful material in old rose, honeyed cream, periwinkle blue that went with old pieces of furniture I found at auctions with the patina of polished dreams. Mark changed his bedroom decor every few weeks. I said he could do what he liked as long as he kept it clean. He was currently into black and white with splashes of scarlet.

Joe built a long pine studio in the garden where he could work. His new business for designing sets and costumes for shows all over the world grew and flourished. This is where Mark often works with him, because Mark can also paint, draw and design. As they both soon found out once the hostilities ceased.

We discovered one of Mark's secrets. He had designed and made some of the scenery for the school play. 'Those trees are mine,' he'd whispered. He'd brought them home after the performance and planted them in the garden where they stood like sentinels till a Force 7 southeasterly blew them down.

Prompt Cornered goes from strength to strength but three evenings a week in London is enough for me. Joe sometimes comes with me and Mark spends the nights with his Gran where he still has a bedroom.

'Perhaps Mark could teach me to play poker,' she said. 'But I've no intention of losing my pension. I'd rather win off him. Cheeky monkey.'

Drama coaching at various local schools is absorbing afternoons. The kids are beginning to find the magic of Shakespeare and other great writers. No one shouts at me now, 'Prompt! Line!', but I'd be their stand-by prompt if I was asked.

My unashamed passion for words is not diminished by *Prompt Cornered*. The viewers like sound-bites from the classics and I can't stop them surfacing. They email me, asking for the source of my quotes.

It was a surprise when I found that Fran Powell was booked to be my guest one evening on *Prompt Cornered*. She had a nerve. Apparently she had asked to be a guest several times. I was worried because I didn't trust her an inch. She had an ulterior motive up her sleeve, I was sure. Nothing much had happened in her career since her removal from *Twelfth Night*, though I'd seen pictures of her in the tabloids, leaving clubs and first nights, tottering on pavements in four-inch heels.

'Say you don't want her,' said Joe.

'It might be all right. She might be desperate for publicity. She's done very little since that *Celebrity* spot. It seems to have ruined her chances.'

'Don't be so trusting. Say no.'

It wasn't that easy. The production executives thought Fran might be an up-and-coming star worth cultivating. They were taken in by her glamorous blonde looks and smooth-talking approach. She could be convincing.

I was back to being a bag of nerves. Joe insisted on coming with me but stayed standing in the wings.

'Don't let her get the better of you,' he said. 'Don't mention that infamous letter. Remember it's your show and don't let her monopolize it.'

'But she might.'

'Ignore her and anything she says. Be ready to move on.'

I was wearing my trademark slim trousers and tunic in some slinky silvery-grey material, casually thrown scarf. They always found me gorgeous scarves, Sophie's scarves, they said now. I'd lost weight. No more sitting about in the prompt corner, eating chocolate, and all that cycling up and down hills. I was getting my puff back. And I had a new bike with gears. Hilda helped me find the slinky clothes and her mother watched the show. They often discussed the show together with my mother. They had become my fan club.

Fran came on tightly wrapped in swathes of gossamer chiffon, cleavage thrust forward, skirt so short it was nearly banned. Her brittle blonde hair was a confection of sugar. She sat on the sofa, folding her legs into an openly enticing invitation. I could see the host sweating with apprehension.

'Hello, Fran Powell,' I said, trying to sound warm and pleasant. 'Welcome to *Prompt Cornered*. We used to know each other quite a time ago.'

'Yes, before I became a celebrity. I was a hard-working, struggling actress then, the understudy for *Twelfth Night*. You may remember I took over the leading part of Viola at the Royale, without any notice, on the opening night. Joe Harrison, that famous New York director, cut my hair in the wings and guided me through the whole show. He said I was marvellous. I think you were the prompt, though I didn't need a line from you. I was word perfect.'

I could only stare at her. Words deserted me. She had the nerve of a polecat. I swallowed an astonished gasp. What should I do? Contradict her in front of a million people? Pitch a fight? I let it go.

'Tell me what you have been doing lately,' I asked smoothly, very Glenn Close. The camera man winked at me. He was hoping for a bunny-in-a-boiler scene.

She rattled off a series of non-starters, sit-coms already forgotten, walk-ons that actually got cut. Her face was an advertisement for Botox. I noticed a ladder near her nylon-clad bony knees and actually felt sorry for her.

'Of course, I keep getting offers from New York,' she prattled on. 'Joe Harrison is constantly offering me parts on Broadway but I don't like the flying. He keeps phoning. Sad, isn't it? To let all these wonderful opportunities go by. But he says I'll be a star very soon. And he should know, shouldn't he?'

Joe was standing off the set, glowering, watching a monitor.

'How disappointing for you. Flying is not that bad. Planes are safer than cars, they say. Would you like a drink, Fran? Coffee or tea?'

It was part of the ritual. My assistant, a nice girl called Ginny, brought on a properly laid tray (my mother's long-distance influence) and poured out the drinks while we talked. Ginny had ambition. She always made the most of the ritual, almost Japanese in style.

Now, I was never quite sure what happened. I never moved. I never could. I was always too frozen with fright, even after all these soporific nights on the sofa. Ginny swore she did nothing wrong and I believed her.

But suddenly the tray went flying. The whole tray catapulted through the air. Coffee, tea, milk, the lot, fell into Fran's lap. Now, it must have hurt, no protection from gossamer skirt across her legs. Coffee splashed up over her chiffon-draped bosom. She screamed.

She not only screamed. She foul mouthed **** and **** and a lot more of *******. They bleeped her out and a couple of hefties heaved her off the set, to hose her down. She was opaque with rage, phoning her lawyer, threatening me with law suits.

I was left on the sofa to fill in for another five empty minutes while Ginny mopped up. Which I did, no trouble at all, thanks to the Bard. As Elinor would say, easy as pie, piece of cake, very clipped Bette Davis.

'Poison Powell Fran,' said the team at the de-briefing. 'We won't ask her again. We'll go through the video with a fine-tooth comb. Our lawyers will soon sort her out. We know her type. We saw what happened. It wasn't your fault at all. You were completely blameless, Sophie. You kept your cool.'

'I was watching,' said Joe, grimly. 'She deliberately tipped the tray in your direction when the camera was focused on you. But you know what aluminium trays are like. They are so light. It did a weird bounce on the arm of the sofa and whooshed back onto her.'

'Thank goodness you were there,' I said, sipping water, glad of Joe's assurance and support. 'But I feel sorry for her. Her career is going nowhere.'

'And nowhere even faster when news travels round that she's a trouble-maker and a liar. Lots of people remember that you played Viola for the opening night. One day you'll spot her serving in a café or managing a launderette.'

'I've told management our good news. They don't seem to mind at all. If I'm going to look a little larger around the stomach area for a few months, then it'll be all the more like a late, late night, very sexy and cosy programme, they said. And I can take a couple of months break whenever I need to.'

'How about Viola for a name if it's a girl?'

'I fancy Olivia,' I said. I put my dreams in his pocket where I knew they would be safe. 'How about Toby for a boy?'

'Or William?'

Telling Mark was not quite so easy, but when we did tell him, he looked at both of us, sort of grown-up, way out and lofty, but grinning and kicking a stone about with his foot. He wriggled inside his sweater, obviously taking in the news.

'Wicked,' he said, nodding. I was glad he'd learned a new word. There was hope.

I could sense his brain ticking off the possibilities.

'Can we have a puppy, too?' Mark asked, cashing in on the euphoria.